Anthony Price was born in Hertfordshire in 1928, was educated at King's School, Canterbury, and studied history at Merton College, Oxford. Apart from some temporary peace-time soldiering he has been a journalist all his life, beginning as a reviewer on the *Oxford Mail*, then Deputy Editor and finally Editor of the *Oxford Times*.

He won the Crime Writers' Association's Silver Dagger for his first novel *The Labyrinth Makers* and their Gold Dagger for *Other Paths to Glory*. All his novels reflect his intense interest in history and archaeology, and in particular in military history.

By the same author

ANTHONY PRICE

The Labyrinth Makers

GRAFTON BOOKS

A Division of the Collins Publishing Group

LONDON GLASGOW
TORONTO SYDNEY AUCKLAND

Grafton Books
A Division of the Collins Publishing Group
8 Grafton Street, London W1X 3LA

Published by Grafton Books 1988

First published in Great Britain by
Victor Gollancz 1970

The quotation from *Puck of Pook's Hill* on page 89 is
reproduced by kind permission of Mrs George Bambridge and
Macmillan & Company Ltd.

ISBN 0-586-20073-8

Printed and bound in Great Britain by
Collins, Glasgow

Set in Times

To Ann

1

Every 14 August for twenty-three years Mrs Steerforth put the same In Memoriam notice in the Daily Telegraph:

STEERFORTH, John Adair Steerforth, Flt Lieut, DFC, RAFVR. Lost at sea, September 1945. On this, his birthday, not forgotten – Mother.

It was not Mrs Steerforth's fault that the notice was inaccurate. She had spent a whole week composing it, adding words and then subtracting them, until in the end she decided that brevity was the soul of dignity.

The words 'not forgotten' were her only concession to sentiment, and they were the direct result of the inaccuracy. It was the thought of the cold and restless sea that made her heart ache; she was resigned to her son's death, but not to his lack of a known grave.

So for Mrs Steerforth the draining of the lake brought a sort of happiness: she was able to bury her son at last.

By the time Audley became involved with them, the lake, the aircraft and the man had parted company.

The lake no longer existed and the aircraft was spread out over the floor of a hangar at Farnborough. The man had been collected and taken away in a large cardboard box and later reassembled with unnecessary care in a much larger wooden one.

Audley never actually saw any of them, except in photographs. There would have been no point in his doing so, even had it been possible. The reports were clear and adequate; he wouldn't have found anything more of value, for there had been nothing of value to find.

Yet he saw that lost lake many times in his mind's eye. Not as it had become, a marshy puddle in a muddy wasteland. And not, perhaps, as it had been on the day it closed over Steerforth. The overhanging trees grew taller in his vision, the enveloping weed was thicker and the water more rank. He saw it as the remote and secret place it was, a drowner of small adventurous boys which had lost its reason for existing when the mansion on the hillside above it had burned a century earlier.

Then Steerforth had given it back a new reason for being there, a secret of its very own.

But it was not the moment of impact he saw. He could never even decide whether it was skill or chance that slipped the plane so exactly between the random beeches and set it down so precisely. Chance more likely, for in that torrential downpour a frantic pilot could have seen little. And luck could be so cruel, certainly.

It was the long decay afterwards which he saw, and the slow journey to nowhere.

He saw Steerforth changing into a horror, and a gorgeous windfall for millions of tiny, hungry eaters; and then into a mere framework, Icarus turned Yorick. And in that framework generations of pond life in turn lived and died, untroubled except for the small upheavals of bones and buckles, buttons and fastenings, each settling into its natural resting place.

And he saw the night when that well-ordered world ended.

The lake did not die in one spectacular cataract, but slowly and without fuss. In the darkness no one saw the streams rise further down the valley; and no one heard the slither and splash as matted balls of weed slid down the fuselage and engine cowlings, scouring the mud to reveal the faded khaki drab beneath.

Yet by dawn the Dakota had ceased for ever to be part of the ecology of the pond. It had regained its shape as an intruder, squatting in a shallow pool surrounded by mud flats.

No going back now; John Steerforth, loving son, not-so-loving husband, sometime hero, sometime villain, had surfaced at long last. A man who had left the footprints of trouble behind him – and time had just not quite succeeded in obliterating them.

A few more years, and his reappearance wouldn't have mattered: a natural statute of limitations would have neutralized him for ever. But now he was waiting for the unwitting causes of his resurrection.

Audley saw them lumping up the track beside the muddy scar of the natural gas pipeline – the track which their machines had gouged across the lower edge of the lake with such disastrous results. Sour-stomached after a weekend's drinking, the sons and natural sons of a long line of canal-cutting, railway-laying, tunnel-digging Irishmen.

First they saw the flooded pipe-trench, some stolidly, some gleefully, only the foreman aghast. And then one of them looked up the valley . . .

Audley's vision always faded at that precise point, where the official records began. First the navvies, then the police. After the police, in a welter of garbled air disaster messages, an ambulance which would have been too late almost a quarter of a century earlier.

Then, in the exhaust of the ambulance, the first journalist had arrived, exulting in a fine off-beat story which had broken in time for the midday editions.

And last of all, an RAF crash crew, baffled at finding a plane they hadn't lost.

It was the RAF who eventually stirred the dusty files and set them on the move towards Audley. But it was the journalists who first introduced him to Steerforth. In *The*

Times the introduction was brief and formal: Wartime RAF/wreck is/discovered; with more panache, however, the *Daily Mirror* splashed ONE OF OUR AIRCRAFT IS FOUND above a superb photograph.

Both introductions were incomplete, for the first facts were vague. It was as yet simply an echo of a supposedly wartime tragedy, with the names withheld. But it was the picture and not the text that stirred Audley's imagination in any case. It reminded him of another he had seen years before of the barnacle-covered bones of a Lancaster bomber which had appeared briefly on a North Sea sandbank during an exceptionally low tide. The Dakota in the lake shared the same atmosphere of loneliness and loss, which not even the selfconscious airmen in gumboots posed beside it could altogether dissolve.

But where Audley had looked and read, and then had turned to another page, there were others who had read between the lines – painstaking, unimaginative men chosen for their retentive memories, whose job it was never to forget names and faces. Steerforth and his Dakota had been on their lists as long as any of them could remember, unremarked until tracked down at long last. Even then it was not their business to ask questions; to take the appropriate action had always been the limit of their satisfaction.

Yet that in the end was enough to make Steerforth's resurrection certain and to set Audley's phone ringing before dawn just one week later.

As a child Audley had feared and hated the telephone bell. At the first ring he was off like a jack-rabbit in search of cover, desperate to avoid being sent to answer it. When cornered he was always too nervous to listen properly, but stood sweating and tongue-tied until the exasperated caller rang off. 'Is the boy deaf or just plain stupid?' he remembered his father ask rhetorically.

Long since he had taken the measure of the beast, but

10

his hatred remained. He would not have it beside his bed, and even the Department now accepted that no one should phone him at home except in the direst emergency.

That knowledge, and the looseness of his pyjama cord, filled his half-awake mind as he shuffled unhappily through the house, fumbling, blinking and grunting as he switched on each light in turn. Only in the direst emergency . . .

It was one of Fred's middlemen. Disarmingly apologetic, deferential, precise – and leaving not a millimetre for argument.

He replaced the receiver and settled his glasses firmly on his nose. To be hauled out of his warm soft bed at such an hour was bad enough. To be then summoned to London at the same hour was worse: it suggested that someone had been caught with his trousers down, or his pyjama trousers even.

But to be required in addition to dress for a funeral – that was utterly ridiculous!

Funerals meant going outside, into the field, among strangers. And he was not a field man, never had been and never wanted to be. The back room among the files and the reports was his field. It was far more interesting there, more rewarding and infinitely more comfortable. And it was the only place he was any good.

He sat at his desk, staring into the night outside. No one he knew had died recently. He focused on the darkness and his mind wandered away into it. Two hours to dawn maybe; the dying time now, when those who had fought hardest in their hospital beds suddenly gave up the struggle. This hour, this blackness, suddenly reminded him of long-forgotten boarding school ends-of-term. The boys with the furthest to go got up now, all excitement, to catch the earliest trains. He had caught a much later train, with no particular joy.

Methodically he switched on the tea machine, show-ered, drank the tea. The Israelis were certainly not up to anything. Shapiro could be relied on there at least. And the Russian ships were in the wrong place for the Arabs to try anything important.

Uncalled for and long forgotten end-of-term memories intruded. He remembered the boy in the next bed for the first time in over twenty years. Which was interesting: it meant that the right key unlocked a whole set of memories, and then one could recall and clarify the past, flexing the memory like the muscles.

Whose funeral? Half-dressed, trailing a faint smell of mothballs and fumbling with his ancient black tie, Audley decided he was hungry. But there was no time and his funereal suit reminded him that he had to watch his weight now. Where once the trousers had needed braces, now they were self-supporting.

He opened the safe and removed the files on which he had been working. Ever since May '67 they had expected marvels from him. And that had been no miracle, but mere exasperation and lurking sympathy for the Israelis. They had ignored it, anyway, just as they had ignored the Lebanese report and the Libyan one before it.

Audley sighed. It was not Fred's fault, he thought. Fred was good. Perhaps it was his own fault, a defect in presentation. The difficult thing is not the answer, he reflected, but the working.

The light grew as he drove. No rain today, but a cold, unseasonable wind, just right for a funeral to cull the weaker mourners. The countryside was only just waking up, but the towers of London were already ablaze with light, and there was more traffic than he expected. Every year it started earlier and ended later, and one day the start and the end would be indistinguishable. I must retire early, he thought. To Cambridge.

* * *

With malicious pleasure he parked in one of the habitual early birds' places, near the entrance. Here there were fewer lighted windows, surprisingly – except for a row high up, with one blank window in the middle. So that's my room, Audley thought.

Inside the sergeant's eyebrows raised fractionally as he passed. But it gave him no pleasure. Only by order, routine and unchanging habit could the hostile world be kept at bay. Even the presence of Mrs Harlin in her usual place – Mrs Harlin certainly represented all those virtues – could not turn 6 A.M. into 10.

But it was simple common sense not to take his irritation and disquiet out on Mrs Harlin. She was the source of certain simple comforts, and in any case secretarial staff were taboo. In his limited experience Audley had observed that those who took advantage of secretaries, either mentally or physically, usually lived to regret it.

He could not bring himself to wish her a good morning, however, but only the tortured semblance of a smile. And she rewarded him by editing her welcome to a stately and sympathetic nod.

'Dr Audley – Sir Frederick wishes me to tell you that there is a file on your desk. If you would let him have your observations on it in the conference room at 7 o'clock he would be most grateful. The regular records staff is not available yet, so if you require anything else perhaps you could ask me?'

Audley blinked and nodded.

'And I am just about to prepare a pot of tea for Sir Frederick. May I bring you a cup?'

'That would be very kind, Mrs Harlin.'

The world was upside down, and he, the last man right way up, had to go along with it. Even his own familiar room seemed in the circumstances unfamiliar, with darkness outside, but without the atmosphere of a day's work done.

His only comfort lay in the file itself, which was not too thick and freshly photo-copied. Sixty minutes allowed, and he no longer felt any disquiet, only that old examination thrill. He extracted a red biro from his breast pocket and a fresh notebook from his stationery drawer.

When Mrs Harlin slipped in unobtrusively with his tea ten minutes later he was already prepared for her.

'There's some more material I'd like, Mrs Harlin. To start with, *The Times* and the *Mirror* for last Tuesday, Wednesday and Thursday. Then from Records – here, I've made a list.'

Mrs Harlin was poker-faced. 'I'm truly sorry, Dr Audley, but Sir Frederick requested that you concentrate on that one file for the moment. He said that everything else would be available in due course.'

Candidates would not be permitted to consult textbooks. And Fred had foreseen that he would start cutting the corners straight away. Which was in itself informative, though aggravating.

By 6.45 he had completed the initial reconnaissance of the material. He closed the file and turned to the five photographs he had spread over his desk.

Five faces . . . five men. Four had baled out and lived. One had stayed aboard and had taken twenty-four years to die.

He lined up the survivors. Tierney the second pilot and Morrison the radio operator, the men with such good memories; Maclean the navigator and Jones the passenger, who had mildly contradicted each other. If they were all still alive it would be interesting to discover how much Tierney and Morrison had decided to forget, and how much Maclean and Jones had managed to remember.

He stared at them for a time, then turned them face downwards and drew the fifth face towards him.

John Adair Steerforth.

Photographs could lie just as persuasively as people, but this was surely Lucifer's face: handsome, proud and dissatisfied. Perhaps there was a trace of weakness about the chin, but the mouth was firm and the slightly aquiline nose aristocratic. Women would have loved him very easily – hard luck on them that he was dry bones. Or maybe good luck?

At least the funeral was explicable now. But his own role and his involvement was still inexplicable. On the face of it there was not the slightest link with the Middle East here.

On the face of it. He opened the file again. A document like this was no simple collection of facts. It had a story of its own to tell. The newness here was deceptive: the material and language was dated. But it had been cut since, possibly twice, and edited – once clumsily, and then more skilfully. Audley recognized the pattern. He gathered up the scattered papers and his notebook. Now was the time for some of the answers.

Fred welcomed him with a graceful apology.

'Butler and Roskill I believe you know, Dr Audley. And this is Mr Stocker, who represents the JIC.'

Butler and Roskill were both European Section men as far as Audley remembered. He had once briefed Roskill on the Dassault company's dealings with the Israeli air force, and the young man had impressed him. Butler looked exceedingly tough, with his short haircut and bullet head.

But Stocker was the one to watch, particularly as Audley had never quite understood the exact role, or at least the ultimate power, of the JIC.

Fred gathered them with a glance.

'You've all read the Steerforth File now. What do you make of it?'

Butler would be first.

'A collection of non-information,' said Butler in a voice that was Sandhurst superimposed on Lancashire. 'A lot of clumsy people looking for something, and we never came close to finding out what it was.'

'I don't think they were all that clumsy,' said Roskill mildly. 'I think they were in a hurry.'

'Well, *we* were clumsy. The interrogations weren't handled firmly – there was no co-ordination. We should have leaned harder on the ground crew. And on the Belgian.'

Audley wondered what a firm Butler interrogation would be like.

'The RAF Court of Inquiry was just whitewash. The trawler captain's evidence proved nothing.' Butler was getting into his stride now. 'And the survivors' evidence was conflicting.'

'Baling out isn't a clear event,' protested Roskill. 'I once baled out of a Provost. I don't believe I gave a very clear account of it, though.'

Butler shook his head.

'The conflict was between the two who were vague and the two who rehearsed from the same script. It was all too pat – first the radio, then the engine. It smells – to me it smells.'

Good for Butler, thought Audley. He was worrying the right bits of evidence, sniffing instinctively at the weaknesses. A firm Butler interrogation might be a lot more subtle than the man's personality suggested.

'On this evidence,' concluded Butler, 'there's no proof that the Dakota ever came down at all. It could have been a put-up job from start to finish.'

Good for Butler again.

'But it did crash,' said Roskill. 'We've got it.'

'Roskill has the advantage of you there, Butler,' said Fred. 'You've been out of England – and you're not such an avid newspaper reader as Dr Audley. The Dakota came down in an artificial lake in Lincolnshire, not in the sea at all. And last week that lake was accidentally drained – it was an accident, wasn't it, Roskill?'

Roskill nodded. 'Carelessness, anyway.'

'And Steerforth?' Butler asked.

'Steerforth was still in the cockpit,' replied Fred shortly. 'Now, gentlemen, as you will have read, our interest in this began by pure chance, when it was learnt that the Russians were interested in the missing aircraft. First there was the known agent, Stein. Then there was the military attaché. And there was also the Belgian, Bloch, who claimed he had nothing to do with the others.

'We couldn't touch the attaché, of course, and as Butler has pointed out, we didn't get anything out of anyone. We came to a dead end. Officially Steerforth was a dead hero, who chose to crash at sea rather than hazard life on land. Unofficially he was a smuggler who'd picked up something so hot he didn't dare crash with it. You will note the references by the crew to the unauthorized boxes in the cargo space. Steerforth's property, apparently.

'But at least the other side didn't get anything either, so the matter was more or less shelved. Until the Dutch got in touch with us in 1956, that is.'

He pushed three slim files across the table.

'Ever since the war they've been busily reclaiming more bits of the Zuyder Zee, and in every bit they find wartime aircraft wrecks – German, British, American. They're very good about them. Very correct and dignified, with no sightseers or souvenir hunters allowed.

'But one day they came to ask what was so special about Dakota wrecks. Every time they came across a Dakota they'd had all sorts of Russians sniffing around. Just Dakotas. British Dakotas. It didn't take much checking to decide which Dakota interested them.'

Butler cleared his throat.

'But we've got Steerforth's Dakota now.'

'Indeed we have. We've got the Dakota, and Steerforth, and the mysterious boxes. But there was nothing in the Dakota, and nothing in the boxes either.'

'Not exactly nothing.' Roskill unwound himself. He was a nonchalantly clumsy man who gave the impression that he hadn't finished growing, and that upright chairs tortured him.

'Builder's rubble, that's what the boxes contained. Or perhaps I should say bomber's rubble, because the experts are more or less agreed it's Berlin stuff, vintage '45. Otherwise the Dakota was clean.' He grimaced. 'If you don't count a ton of mud.'

'Had the boxes been tampered with?' asked Butler.

'The wood was pretty rotten, of course. But no – the lids were untouched. I'd say they were as consigned.'

'Identification positive?'

'Steerforth or the plane?'

'Both.'

'Oh, yes. No trouble there. Numbers for the plane, perfectly readable. Identity tags and teeth for Steerforth – and an old arm break. Absolutely no doubt.'

'Cause of death?'

'We can't be precise there. Drowning while unconscious is my guess. There was no evidence of physical damage.'

Butler looked round the table.

'And nobody spotted it for twenty-four years?'

Roskill shrugged. 'It was out of the search area. Overhanging trees, thick weed. God only knows how he put it down there. And the weather was poor for a week or more afterwards, the worst sort of search weather. It's not so surprising – it's well off the beaten track.'

Roskill added three more slim, identical files to those on the table.

'It's all in there. Plus my estimation of the probable course of the aircraft – he must have made a much wider

turn than was assumed after the crew and the passenger
baled out. That's what put the search off the scent, apart
from the low cloud they had to contend with. He would
have crossed the coast again a good ten miles south of the
direct route – if he hadn't put down in the lake. Which
was a damn good piece of flying, as I've said.'

'Why did the plane crash?'

'It's in my report,' said Roskill, with the smallest
suggestion of asperity.

Butler persisted. 'How well does it tally with what the
crew said?'

Roskill shook his head. 'It's going to be very hard to
say. It was the port engine they complained about, and it
took a clout from a treetop coming in. That and twenty
years under water – it doesn't make the detective work
easy.'

He looked round the table. 'To be honest, we may
never know. There can be a million reasons. If it's plain
human error, like fuel mismanagement, we'll certainly
never know now. They'd been losing height – we know
that from the survivors; I've known cases where a pilot
had an engine malfunction and simply shut down the
wrong engine. Not even a DC-3 would stay up then, and
at that height it would have been fatal. Or maybe he
simply misread his altimeter. I tell you, there are a million
ways it might have happened.'

'All right, then,' said Fred, heading off any further
technical argument. 'How does this fresh information
change your interpretation of the original conclusions, Dr
Audley?'

Audley looked up from his notebook to meet Fred's
mildly questioning gaze, which in turn caused the other
three men to look at him. He had been reflecting just a
moment before, with satisfaction, that so far he had not
said a word since arriving.

But then he really had nothing yet to say – nothing, at

least, which he could say in front of strangers. He certainly couldn't say 'What am I doing here, for God's sake?' at this stage in the proceedings.

'Dr Audley?'

It would be an interesting academic exercise to discuss the nature of an unknown object which was able to retain its value over so many years. No secret terror weapon, no list of traitors now in their graves or their dotage could last so long. Newer and far more terrible weapons had made the technology of the 1940s antediluvian. And a whole generation of younger and differently motivated traitors had superseded the honest simpletons and rogues of Steerforth's day.

And no single Dakota could carry enough mere loot to hold the Russians' interest down the years. Or in the first place, when they were bulging with German valuables.

'I assume,' he said tentatively, carrying on his thoughts aloud, 'that the Russians *are* still interested. That's why we are here now, at this hour, without our breakfasts?'

Fred smiled.

'They are indeed, Dr Audley. In fact I'm afraid they were down at the crash site pouring beer down navvies and interviewing talkative aircraftsmen before we were. But I meant have you anything to add to the Steerforth File in the light of his reappearance?'

Audley started to adjust his spectacles, and then stopped awkwardly. He had been trying to control that gesture for years, without real success.

'I mean, are the Russians still interested, after having learnt that those boxes contained rubble? Did they learn that? It's an important distinction.'

'Assuming that they did – what then?'

'I should have to know rather more about Steerforth. There is a possible sequence of events, but I wouldn't like to advance it yet.'

'Why not?' This was Stocker at last. 'You have a

reputation for drawing remarkably accurate deductions out of minimal information. I'd very much like to hear what you make of this.'

Audley felt a flush of annoyance spreading under his cheeks. It galled him that he had a reputation for understanding without reason. Intuition had its place, and was valuable. But only in the last leap from the ninth known fact to the inaccessible tenth, and never at the very beginning. And even at the last it was not to be trusted.

He knew he ought to control his feelings, and hold the only real card he possessed. But he couldn't.

'I'll tell you one thing I do know' – he tapped the Steerforth File with his index finger – 'that Major Butler was more right than he knew when he said that this was non-information. I'd like to see the original file, for a start.'

'The original?'

Audley sighed. Maybe he did have that flair. It would be easier to admit an inspired hunch than to explain that he could look between the lines of this material to see the gaps in the narrative, the sudden thinness of the material, the changes of style, the tiny inconsistencies of editing. All of which suggested the removal of something too intriguing to be left to the common gaze.

He looked to Fred for support.

'Quite right too,' said Fred. 'You shall see it. Stocker only wanted to know – '

' – I only wanted to see Audley pull a rabbit out of his hat.' Stocker smiled, and was transformed by his smile from a faceless JIC man into a human being. Audley felt that he had been small-minded and pompous.

'And you did pull a rabbit out. Only it was not the one I expected. I'm sorry to have played fast and loose with you. Sir Frederick warned me. But the missing bits don't concern Steerforth, I assure you. You'll still have to find

21

out about him for yourself. Which I believe Sir Frederick is arranging for you.

'On which note I will bid you good morning. It has been a pleasure to see you at work, even if only briefly. But I shall be seeing you again soon.'

Audley could only blush, and shake the hand thrust out to him. Then Stocker was gone, and the atmosphere lightened perceptibly. Audley observed that both Butler and Roskill were grinning.

'I really cannot understand,' said Fred, 'why the JIC always produces threat reactions in you people – even in you, David.'

There was no point in suggesting that Fred himself had formalized the conference in Stocker's presence by dropping all the Christian names he usually affected. He probably intended to foster the JIC mystique, not reduce it.

'It has a perfectly reasonable co-ordinating function, which you all know perfectly well. But no matter. Have you any more immediate questions?'

Roskill stirred. 'One thing – only I don't quite know how to put it. This Russian interest, after all these years – couldn't it be just a case of bureaucratic obsession?'

'And we could be making a fuss about nothing? Or something that has become nothing? It could be, Hugh, it could be. But if it isn't – then it could be rather interesting. Weighing the possibilities, I think we have to go ahead, at least for the time being.

'Have you got any more questions, David?'

'I have – yes. But not about Steerforth. First, if it is decided that I must attend his funeral – I must assume it is his funeral – I must be allowed to have my breakfast first. I cannot go to a funeral on an empty stomach. Second – '

Fred held up his hand.

'David, I do apologize. You shall breakfast with me in

a few moments. Mrs Harlin has the matter in hand. And then you will be going to the funeral – you've got the transport laid on, Hugh?'

'8.45 from here, Sir Frederick. It's a good two hours to Asham. We'll pick up the other car in Wantage.'

'Very good. And you're concentrating on locating the original cast, Jack?'

Butler nodded. 'Mostly routine, but it may take a little time. They may be all dead, except the Joneses.'

'I hope not for all our sakes. In the meantime, gentlemen, I have some explaining to do, I believe, for Dr Audley's benefit. I'll excuse you that.'

The departure of Roskill and Butler cued in Mrs Harlin, with breakfast. And breakfast conceived on a scale which shattered Audley. The condemned man's meal, or at least one designed to give an elderly vicar strength to go out to evangelize the Hottentots.

Before they had even sat down Fred moved to forestall argument.

'I know you're not a field man, David. But I don't see this quite as a field assignment. More an intellectual exercise in human archaeology.'

'But I deal with words, Fred, not people. I'm no good at interrogating. I don't know how to start.'

Fred snorted.

'Absolute nonsense. You interrogate our people all the time. Extremely closely, too, if what I hear is true.'

'I know them. That makes it different. Get me the reports on this as they come in. I'll do the job just as well that way – probably better. But why me, anyway? I'm a Middle East man.'

Fred lowered his knife and fork.

'And a damned unpopular Middle Eastern man, too.'

Audley stopped eating too. Here was the truth at last.

'Did it ever occur to you, David, that you might annoy

someone with that recent forecast of yours – before the Lebanese business?'

Audley bridled. 'It was true.'

Fred regarded him sadly. 'But undiplomatically packed. It didn't leave anyone much room to manoeuvre in.'

He cut off Audley's protest. 'Damn it, David, it wasn't a report – it was a lecture. And an arrogant lecture, too. You're a first-rate forecaster who's stopped forecasting.'

'I've never twisted the facts.' Audley could sense that he was digging his heels into shifting ground. 'That forecast was accurate.'

'If anything too accurate. If you were a gambler I'd say your cards were marked. And you're too far in with the Israelis.'

'I've used Israeli sources. I don't always believe what I get from them though.'

'You lunch with Colonel Shapiro every Wednesday.'

'Most Wednesdays. He's an old friend. But so are Amin Fawzi and Mohammed Howeidi. I meet a great many people.'

Fred sighed, and started eating again.

'I don't give a damn, of course. As far as I'm concerned you can have your own old boys' network. You can poke your nose anywhere, as it suits you. But that last report was the final straw.'

Good God, thought Audley: he was being taken out of circulation. Banished to the Steerforth File, where he could not cause any annoyance except to four ageing members of the Royal Air Force Volunteer Reserve.

Yet Fred was smiling, and that didn't fit.

'For a devious character you are sometimes surprisingly transparent, David. If you think that you are going to be put out to grass, you are mistaken. You ought to appreciate your value more clearly than that. What you need is a dose of reality. You've been leading a sheltered life for too long.

24

'In any case, you surely don't think the JIC would send one of their troubleshooters here at such a godforsaken hour just to watch you being cut down to size?'

Audley remembered the edited Steerforth File and felt a pricking of humiliation. He had gone off at half-cock.

'And you can thank your rugger-playing past for this, too. Or rather your impact on Dai Llewelyn – you remember him?'

Audley frowned. There had been quite a number of Welshmen in the old days. Mentally he lined them up, and Dai Llewelyn immediately sprang out of the line-up – an exceptionally tough and ruthless wing forward for the Visigoths. A far better player than Audley had ever been, older and craftier.

'He remembers you rather well. He says you were a black-hearted, bloody-minded wing forward, and not bad for a mere Englishman.'

'He was the black-hearted and bloody-minded one. If I've got the right Llewelyn, he was a rough player.'

Fred nodded. 'He's still a rough player – for the Arab faction in the Foreign Office. But he seems to have a certain regard for you. He said your talents ought not to be wasted – provided you didn't play against his team. He has a marked weakness for sporting metaphors.'

Audley remembered Llewelyn well now. Almost a stage Welshman, all rugger and Dylan Thomas, until you crossed him. Then you had to look out.

It was on the tip of his tongue to protest that he hadn't been playing against anyone. But it wasn't quite true, and the thought of Llewelyn marking him again was somehow a shade frightening. He sensed that it would do no good any more to protest that he was a Middle Eastern specialist.

Fred shrugged off his objection.

'David, you're like a good many thousands of ordinary British working men: you are going to have to learn new skills. Or rather, you must learn to adapt your old skill in a new field. And I think you'll find the new field gives you greater scope. You've got the languages for it. You'll just have to catch up on the facts.'

Fred reached over and rang the buzzer.

'You wanted to know what had been taken out of the Steerforth File . . . Mrs Harlin, would you get me the Panin papers?'

Audley jumped at the Harlin presence at his shoulder. She moved as stealthily as a cat. Then the name registered.

'Nikolai Andrievich Panin. Does that name ring any bells?'

The tone implied that he was not expected to know very much, if anything, about Nikolai Andrievich Panin.

'Didn't he have something to do with the Tashkent Agreement?' he said tentatively.

Even that was too much. Fred raised his eyebrows and pushed himself back from the table.

'How in the name of God did you know that?'

'I just know he's a sort of troubleshooter – someone like Stocker, I suppose, except that he usually deals with internal affairs,' said Audley, trying to gloss over what appeared to be a gaffe. 'Once he was an archaeologist, or something like that. A professor, anyway.'

He hadn't said anything in the least funny, but Fred was laughing nevertheless.

'Like Stocker? I must tell Stocker that. He'd be flattered. And he'd also be impressed, because you seem to know quite a lot for a Middle Eastern man. It was his idea that we should give you Panin, too. If you can do half as well with him as you have with Rabin and Mohiedin, there'll be no complaints.

'But you wish to know his connection with Steerforth. It's quite simple: he's only been in England once, and that was to look for Steerforth twenty-five years ago. He

26

was the fly-by-night attaché who turned up at the Newton Chester airfield.

'When he became more important he was edited out of the Steerforth File, which is an open one.'

Mrs Harlin entered noiselessly, carrying a red folder as though John the Baptist's head rested on it.

'Actually,' continued Fred, 'we know very little about the man. But we do know that every year he spends a month in the spring excavating a site in ancient Colchis. Keeping his hand in, as it were. It's the only sacrosanct date in his calendar.'

'Or it was sacrosanct.' Fred stared at Audley. 'This year he packed in after only four days and flew back to Moscow the day before yesterday. And for once we know why.

'It seems he thinks Steerforth is still interesting, even with a load of rubble.'

2

A cold wind came off the shoulder of the Downs, over the low wall of the churchyard, and straight through Audley's old black overcoat.

But he preferred the chill of the open air to the mockery of the service in the little church; there had been too many double meanings in the beautiful old words.

'For man walketh in a vague shadow, and disquieteth himself in vain; he heapeth up riches, and cannot tell who shall gather them . . .'

It all applied too exactly to Steerforth. And whatever the priest said there was not going to be any resting in peace for him. Resurrection was the true order of the day.

But now at last the wretched business was coming to a close and his work could begin: the official intrusion into private grief.

He scrutinized the mourning faces again. They were a disappointing lot. A few journalists; the RAF contingent from Brize Norton, with Roskill uniformed and anonymous among them; and a scattering of morbid onlookers. Only Jones represented the Steerforth File, and Jones could hardly avoid his wife's husband's funeral.

He had hoped for a better catch. But it seemed that not one of Steerforth's crew had come to see his captain's bones committed to the earth at last. Perhaps they didn't read the papers; perhaps they were all dead and buried too.

The rest of the mourners were Roskill's concern, anyway. His own lay just ahead: the family group already labelled in his memory, but only glimpsed for a moment in the flesh as they had followed the coffin out of the church. At least his point of contact was obvious, and he weaved his way through the crowd to catch him as he shepherded his family towards the lych-gate.

'Mr Jones?'

The man turned slowly. He had a rather heavy, outdoor face. The years had filled it out and lined it, but the dark, alert eyes were still those of the young airman in the file. What the file had not suggested was the uncompromising air of self-possession.

'My name is Audley, Mr Jones. I'm from the Ministry of Defence. Would it be possible for me to have a few words with you later?'

The eyes and the face hardened. But if there was a hint of resignation there was certainly neither fear nor surprise.

Jones gestured courteously for Audley to proceed through the gate in front of him, a measured, easy gesture. It might have been two old friends meeting on a sad occasion which did not admit an exchange of words, and it effectively sealed off Audley from the other mourners.

'Of course. I suppose you people never really give up. I've been half expecting you.'

Audley was nonplussed. This formidable man was already outrunning the script. No cock-and-bull cover stories would be any use on him, even if Audley had felt able to construct them. Nor would he repay pressure.

'If it's inconvenient just now, as I'm sure it is, I could see you this afternoon. But I'd rather not put our meeting off until tomorrow.'

Jones considered the family group by the line of cars in the lane, as though gauging their mood.

'No. Better now while they're busy with their thoughts. But I'd rather you didn't bother my wife. And my daughter – I should say my step-daughter – is obviously

29

of no interest to you. If I talk to you now, will you guarantee to leave them alone?'

They were getting perilously close to the cars.

Audley felt that nothing but honesty would serve here. 'You know that I can't guarantee anything like that. But I'll do my best.'

'Fair enough. You can be a Ministry of Defence man charged with deep condolence from the Minister himself. That will please the old girl at least. And then you can come and have a drink with us.'

Jones's tone implied that he did not consider the occasion one for condolences, which was not really surprising under the circumstances. 'The old girl' could only mean Steerforth's mother, for Jones was not the sort of man who could refer to his wife in such terms.

Margaret Jones, the Margaret Steerforth of twenty-five years before, was still an attractive woman – one of those women who fined down with age. Her beauty had not faded, but had mellowed to serenity which not even the present strain had disrupted.

'My dear,' Jones took his wife's hand in an easy, affectionate way – he did everything with the same air of confidence, 'this is Mr Audley, from London. He is representing the Minister of Defence.'

Audley muttered a few conventional words awkwardly. He still thought of her as Steerforth's wife, and had to force himself to address her correctly. She looked at him as though she could sense the cause of his confusion, but was far too well-bred to let it disturb her.

'It's good of you to come, Mr Audley,' she said evenly. 'The Air Force authorities have been very considerate. As you can imagine, this has all been rather a shock to us, the past coming back so suddenly after all these years.'

Jones took the pause which followed – Audley could think of no appropriate reply – to introduce the older woman who hovered at Margaret Jones's shoulder.

30

Audley took in the blue-rinsed white hair and well-corseted figure. Not quite *grande dame*, but trying hard to be, he thought, and mercifully not too sharp-looking.

'I heard, Martin. As Margaret said, the authorities have been most considerate. And you are connected with the Royal Air Force, Mr Ordway?'

It seemed simpler to say that he was. Mrs Steerforth dabbed her eye with a handkerchief.

'It took me back many years to see those young officers carrying the – carrying my son. So young, they were. Always so young. Just like Johnnie and his crew. You were too young to take part in the war, Mr Ordway?'

She looked at him. Then her eyes unfocused, dismissing him.

'He was such a fine boy, Mr Ordway. And such a good pilot – they all said so. I miss him still. We all miss him.'

She spoke as though Jones, right beside her, did not exist. Yet clearly she wasn't trying to be offensive: hers was simply the narrowed viewpoint of the elderly, the self-comforting assumption that her feelings would be shared by all sensible people. An assumption in this case probably fed by an obsessive love.

Jones seemed resigned to her disregard, but her words hung embarrassingly between them and she pressed on to make things worse, focusing on Audley again.

'And this is my granddaughter,' she said with emphasis, ' – my son's daughter.'

The baby girl of this morning's file was a tall, thin ash blonde, and there was no doubt about her parentage. She had not only her father's fairness and bone structure, but also the same haughty stare. Only it was coloured now by indifference, not discontent: Steerforth's daughter evidently found her father's funeral something of a bore.

The Jones boys, both in their late teens, were less thoroughbred and more sympathetic. Where their step-sister looked bored they were obviously intrigued with this forgotten chapter from their mother's past.

'My dear,' said Jones, 'I've invited Mr Audley back to the farm for a drink. I can show him the way and Charles can drive you back. It was rather a squash coming, anyway.'

The elder Jones boy hastened to protest his ability with the family car and his mother seemed almost pleased by the prospect. It occurred to Audley that she saw him as a target for her mother-in-law's proud memories rather than a welcome guest.

But the opportunity was too perfect to miss, whatever ulterior motives prompted it, and he accepted with the merest pretence of reluctance.

As he led the way to the car he caught a glimpse of Roskill talking earnestly with a young man holding a notebook. Prising out the list of mourners. He caught Roskill's eye briefly, and had no time to avoid being snapped by a photographer who seemed to spring up from nowhere.

'Have you had much trouble with the Press?' he asked.

'Not more than I expected. None with the locals – I was NFU chairman last year and I'm well in with them. We had a few chaps from London – they must be damn short of news. But I was civilized with them and they were reasonable enough. There's no story to be had here anyway.'

They reached the car, and for a moment their eyes met over the roof.

'He was a good pilot, you know,' said Jones conversationally. 'But I wouldn't have described him as a fine boy in a hundred years. He was a selfish bastard.'

Obviously, reflected Audley as they drove off, there was little to be gained from a gentle approach either. Jones had accepted him with too little surprise to be trapped into revealing any long-held secrets he still wished to hold.

'You didn't say that twenty-five years ago.'

'I don't remember what I said twenty-five years ago. But I had squadron loyalties then. And I hadn't met his widow then, never mind married her.

'I know I didn't believe that he was dead, certainly – and I didn't say that either. Turn left here.'

They branched off the secondary road on to an even narrower one which steadily climbed the shoulder of the Downs. Already the plain was flattening out below them.

'Why didn't you think he was dead?'

'Don't you think you had better explain what you want? And you can show me your credentials first, just in case. I do remember that there were some rather odd characters asking questions in the old days. I take it you are some form of military intelligence.'

Audley smiled to himself as he passed over his identification. Some form indeed!

Jones passed back the wallet. 'You don't look the type. But I assume that is to be expected. Not that you aren't big enough.'

'Why didn't you think he was dead?' Audley repeated.

Jones was silent for a moment.

'It's not going to be easy remembering anything fresh,' he said slowly. 'But you'd better get one or two things clear from the start.

'I had nothing to hide then, nothing personal, and I've got nothing to hide now. I flew with Steerforth that one time only – as a passenger. You've read the record, I'm sure. I'd been stuck in Berlin with food-poisoning. It just happened to be his plane I flew back in. He was always wangling the Berlin flights.

'And I hardly knew him. I only went to see his widow because the other chaps were crocked up. I fell for her then, and I married her as soon as it was legal, when Faith was just a tot.'

Jones paused again.

'They are two of the four people I love best. I'll tell you now that I'm not going to have them pushed around by anyone. And I'm not going to be pushed either. Not just to set your records straight. I don't care what he did.'

Audley pulled the car on to the shoulder of the road, on to a patch of smooth, wind-driven turf. He turned the engine off and sat back, wondering how Roskill or Butler would handle this man.

'You're ahead of me, Mr Jones. A long way ahead of me.'

'That's where it's always best to be.'

The wind whipped the downland grass beside the car. It was peaceful, but not in the least still, very much like his own Sussex Downs. He watched the birds wheeling and diving over the fields. Down below a toylike tractor was busy.

If Jones had not believed in Steerforth's death he must have had long years of uncertainty, waiting for the knock on the door. But would that have sharpened his wits so much over the years? Sharpened them so much that he was able to identify Audley straight off?

Jumping to conclusions was what he himself was supposed to be so good at. It was disconcerting to be on the receiving end.

'Why did you expect me, or somebody like me?'

'I didn't. But you didn't surprise me. I'll never forget all those questions at the time. They left a mark on me when I'd been softened up. When I baled out of that Dak I was sure I was going to get killed – I can remember quite clearly thinking how unfair it was to be killed after the war was over. I've always associated Steerforth with trouble ever since, and when he turned up again I was just waiting for it.'

'You said you hardly knew him. But I'd have to know someone pretty well to call him a tricky bastard.'

Jones opened the car door. 'Let's get some air,' he said. 'It's easier to be frank in the open.'

Audley followed him over the springy turf on the hillside until he stopped by a wire fence. Audley experienced the familiar downland sensation which both excited and frightened him.

Down below him the neat patchwork of fields, the squat churches and neat houses with smoking chimneys – that was the rich, fat, peaceful land of England. Up here on the Downs was a different ambience, more ancient and hostile. The downlands could be creepy on a hot, still day. And in the evenings there always seemed to be things moving outside the circle of a man's vision.

All right then, he thought, as Jones carefully took a pipe from his pocket, tapped it on a fence post, and sucked it thoughtfully, let us see how frank we can be.

'Let's start then from your theory that he wasn't dead. Why wasn't he dead?'

'It was too damn convenient, for one thing. The customs men coming down on the squadron like that, and Steerforth conveniently missing.'

'He'd been smuggling?'

'Christ, man – don't let's play games. You know he'd been smuggling. Half the squadron was up to some little game or other. It was an open secret. The only rule was not to overdo things, but Steerforth wasn't the man for rules.

'What I thought afterwards was that he'd made his killing, just one step ahead of you chaps. And now he'd planned a neat way of getting out, with no one looking for him. It was nicely calculated – the squadron got its scapegoat, unofficially of course. And no one bothered to dig very deep. Officially he was just another dead hero.'

'Who left his wife and family just like that?'

'Maybe I've done him an injustice. It seems now that I probably did. But I know he didn't give a damn for his wife and family. You can take that for a fact, whatever the old girl says. He'd had babies and nappies right up to the neck – believe me, I know.'

Jones frowned. 'And that business about baling out – I thought a lot about that, and it never quite made sense. He really was a good pilot, you know. I saw the plane he brought back from the Arnhem drop, and if he could fly that he could fly anything. There were any god's amount of airfields he could have put down on in eastern England when we came back from Berlin that last time. But no – as soon as we made a landfall – out we had to go.'

'His second pilot explained all that at the inquiry.'

'His second pilot? What was his name?'

'Tierney.'

'Tierney.' Jones thought for a moment. 'Tierney. A ferrety-looking chap, with a little moustache? He was Steerforth's shadow. If Steerforth was up to something, he'd have been part of it.'

'But you baled out.'

Jones gestured impatiently. 'When the captain says bale out no one argues the toss. And I'm telling you what I thought later, not what I thought at the time. I can remember a bit now – it started to rain like hell. A thunderstorm. Tierney and the wireless operator yelled for me to jump. The Dak was lurching around as if it had been hit. I was bloody scared. I thought I was going to die.'

'I see. He disappeared too conveniently and you needn't have baled out at all. But if you thought this later on why didn't you say so?'

'I only started to think it when everyone began asking us questions. It wasn't just the inquiry – that was routine. It was later on.

'First there were two chaps who said they were Poles. They wanted to know where the plane had gone, if it had been found and so forth. And then they wanted to know what it was carrying – they said that friends had got some of their stuff out of Poland and Steerforth had agreed to carry it out. At a price, of course.'

'And what did you tell them?'

'There wasn't anything to tell. There were some boxes in the cargo bay, but I thought they were down in the drink with the Dakota – that was common knowledge. They seemed pretty upset by it all, as though it was my fault, so I told them to shove off.

'Afterwards it dawned on me that they must have thought I was one of his crew. Which meant I'd probably have been in on the deal. And that made me think. The way they hung around our pub, that made me think, too. So when I went down there again I took a Pole who was in the squadron with me – Jan somebody – with me – '

' – Wojek. Jan Wojek.'

'That's right. How did you – but, of course, you'd have him in your records like me!' Jones shook his head resignedly. 'All these years, and we're all still in your files, Jan and I. And Tierney and Steerforth, and all the others . . . Once filed, never forgotten. Though I suppose you've got it all taped in computers now. It's frightening.'

'You took Wojek down with you to the pub.'

'All right. We went down to the pub, and I told Jan to tell these two to bugger off – which he did in no uncertain manner.'

He paused, and then slipped his fist into his palm.

'By God, I remember it now! Because I was surprised at Jan getting so angry with them. He came back to me breathing fire.

'He said they were no more Poles than he was a Scotsman. Bloody Russians, he said they were – and Jan hated Russians as much as Germans. He reckoned his elder brother was at that place – Katyn? – where they killed all those Polish officers. We hadn't heard about it

37

officially, but there was a grapevine among the Polish aircrew.'

So that was how it had all started, thought Audley. The first report had come from Wojek simply because he hated Russians on principle. It had happened before, often. National hatreds were poor sources of useful information, but excellent watchdogs.

But Jones was almost enjoying his memories now, warming to the task.

'Then there was another foreigner. A little chap, not at all like the other two – one of them was very sharp. In fact I can remember him – the Russian – quite well now. I only saw him properly twice, maybe three times in the pub. But he was one of those people you can't really forget: he had a broken nose – it gave him a sheep-like look from a distance. Not from close up, though.'

Audley's stomach muscles tightened. Jones had described Nikolai Andrievich Panin with remarkable accuracy.

'Have you got him in your files too?'

Audley started guiltily. Jones was too quick by half. And I, thought Audley, am not very good at this job.

'Of course. But we'll talk about him again some other time. Tell me about the little foreigner.'

'He was nothing. A Frenchman, I think. And scared out of his wits. I never even gave him a chance to explain what he wanted. He just muttered something about Steerforth's cargo and I told him to go to hell. I can't remember anything more about him – except that I think he was quite relieved to clear off.'

That fitted too. The Belgian had been an ex-policeman with a dubious wartime record. He had readily admitted that he had been hired, and paid, anonymously to trace Steerforth's plane. There had been no mention of any missing property. But he had soon sensed something bigger and possibly more dangerous, and he had wanted no part of it, he said.

A little man, but a big complication, thought Audley. He gave an extra dimension to the Steerforth mystery, which admitted only one explanation. But it was an explanation as yet without any facts to support it.

'Then there were your people,' said Jones. 'But you'll know all about that, I've no doubt.'

'There are two points I'm still unclear on,' said Audley slowly. 'You hardly knew Steerforth, yet you knew he was a selfish bastard?'

Jones nodded.

'I married his widow. My knowledge of Steerforth is second-hand, but I'd say it's better than first-hand really.

'When I decided to ask Margaret to marry me I wanted to make sure I didn't have a ghost lying in bed between us. Maybe some men could just forget that there was a past. I couldn't, because I just wasn't sure he was dead. So I had to exorcize him, alive or dead. To do that I had to make her tell me about him.'

'Wasn't that rather cruel?'

'If she'd loved him it would have been. But they didn't even like each other any more. Only she didn't know that until she'd heard herself say it – to me. Then I knew I wouldn't have to share her with him.'

Audley cast a sidelong glance at Jones. Half a loaf would never have been good enough for him. The file had assessed him as an innocent bystander whose involvement with Steerforth had been accidental. Only his subsequent marriage with the man's widow made him suspect. But now that too could be discounted. Not only was there no likelihood that he was withholding anything on Steerforth, but it was unlikely also that Steerforth would have confided in a wife who bored him.

Nevertheless Jones's own assessment of that last flight

tallied usefully with Butler's and his own: it had the smell of a put-up job.

The silence of the hillside was broken by the sound of a car climbing the gradient. As it reached the level stretch below them it began to accelerate, then slowed down and pulled into the verge beyond Audley's. Roskill got out and looked expectantly up at Audley.

Again he had the feeling that the action was outrunning the script. For Roskill to disturb him like this only trouble was sufficient reason.

He stumped down to the road with undignified haste.

'I'm sorry to break in on you, Dr Audley,' Roskill apologized, 'but when I phoned in to the office to say I was coming home there was an urgent message for you. I'm to tell you that the professor – no names, just the professor – has been positively identified in East Berlin. And rumour puts him on a flight to London on Tuesday.'

Audley blinked unhappily, and Roskill completely misconstrued his reaction.

'I'm sorry it sounds so bloody mysterious, but that's exactly what the Harlin said, and I'm afraid it comes from that JIC character, not Fred.'

Audley tried to think. A moment before the task ahead had seemed reasonably clear, no matter how unfamiliar his own role in it was: a simple and leisurely reconstruction of the events of the last week in Steerforth's career, with the willing or unwilling help of the survivors of his crew. Panin had only been a potential complication.

But now Panin was a reality, and Panin appeared to be on the move. And unlike Audley, Panin knew exactly what he was doing.

He grasped the nettle. 'Hugh, I'm going back to London at once. You run Jones home and then get tracing the crew as fast as you can. Tell Butler to drop everything and get after the Belgian.'

He turned towards Jones, who had stepped on to the road a discreet distance away.

'Trouble?' There was a suggestion of amused sympathy in Jones's eyes.

'What makes you think that, Mr Jones?'

'The same reason I wasn't too surprised to see you. If you've got Steerforth, you've got trouble: you can't just bury men like Steerforth.'

'You may have him too, Mr Jones.'

'I've got a shotgun too. Just leave me your telephone number, and I'll let you know if I shoot something interesting.'

3

Audley stared from his study window out across the South Downs and tried to make sense of Nikolai Andrievich Panin.

Usually he found it relaxing to watch the evening spread over that landscape, dissolving the familiar landmarks one by one. But Panin refused to let him relax on this evening.

The Russian had to be the key to Steerforth. It was his involvement alone which had kept the dead pilot alive in the files over the last decade; it was his interest which had aroused the department and had even provided Fred with an honourable way of sacking Audley: Panin was big enough to make the sack look like promotion.

Big enough, but wholly enigmatic. For no one seemed to know what made Panin tick and what kept him wound up. He hadn't been tagged as a coming man until after he had arrived, and then it was too late. They had simply never caught up with him.

Audley looked down at the thin file in front of him and the pathetic handful of notes he had made during the afternoon. Kremlinology was at best a foggy enterprise, more divination than detection, full of Delphic hypotheses about men whose passion for secrecy appeared at times to be pathological.

But Panin had raised this passion to an art form.

There wasn't an ounce of meat on the bones of the man's career. He had allegedly been at Moscow university before the war, and certainly returned to it afterwards, emerging as an acknowledged expert in the arts and customs of the ancient Scythians, for what that was worth. In between he had been a staff officer in Khalturin's crack division of Chuikov's army, and that in theory brought him to Berlin in 1945. But between the time he had been identified across the public bar of the Bull Inn, Newton Chester, and his appearance at the famous Twentieth Congress of the Communist Party, when Khrushchev had denounced Stalin, nobody seemed to have set eyes on him. He had been as quiet as Steerforth.

So someone had been keeping Panin on ice among his Scythian burial mounds, in preparation for the better days between the Twentieth and Twenty-Second congresses. Yet he wasn't one of Khrushchev's 'golden boys', like Polyansky: he was everybody's man and nobody's man.

Moreover he seemed to Audley to have the remarkable talent of knowing unerringly when to be somewhere else.

He had been as far away from the Khrushchev faction in '64 as he had been from the doomed followers of Malenkov and Molotov in '57. Even the single relationship which tied him in with the intelligence agencies was equivocal, through the last hypothetical co-ordinator of the KGB and the GRU, Mironov.

But Mironov was a Brezhnev appointment, and he had no links with Brezhnev. And when Mironov flew so mysteriously into a Yugoslav hillside four days after the fall of Khrushchev, Panin was visiting a dig in the far-off Altai mountains.

Intelligent anticipation or inside intelligence? The file didn't say, and the bare facts wouldn't tell – and the facts about Panin always seemed to be weeks or months out of date when they finally filtered through.

Even Audley's own Middle Eastern knowledge was made useless by Panin's shrewd uninvolvement with unprofitable causes. If he had been in the ranks of the Shelepin-Semichastny followers during Khrushchev's defeat, he had been conspicuously absent from them when Kosygin clipped their wings during the June War-Glasboro period.

But a Kosygin man would surely not be on such friendly terms with Grechko, the bully of the East Germans and the Czechs . . . except that any friend of Grechko ought not to be a friend of Moskalenko . . .

It was no use, no bloody use at all. The names and the convolutions of power swam before Audley's eyes. In the Middle East the protagonists were like old friends, whose reactions were at least partially predictable. But here he was among blank-faced technocrats and strangers, of whom Panin was the strangest of all. It would take months of study before any of them would start to talk to him through their comings and goings, absences and appearances, and in the oracular reports of their words and deeds.

He had to find a short cut to the man's character, or at the very least, to his motivation in 1945.

Suddenly he realized that his line of thought had been interrupted. Mrs Clark's geese, the guards of his privacy, had been disturbed; they were shrieking their displeasure at a car which was nosing its way up the track towards the house. He could see its headlights flashing intermittently between the overgrown hedgerows.

Courting couples occasionally tried the lane, which didn't look as if it was going anywhere when it left the main road. But nowadays the geese always intercepted them and drove them back. Yet this driver was not deterred; the headlights halted for two or three seconds near the glow of Mrs Clark's cottage, but then moved forward again. It could only be coming to him now, thought Audley savagely, and it couldn't be a friend, since no friend of his would ever come calling casually.

The car finally emerged from the lane on to the broad expanse of cobbles, swinging round to stop precisely in front of the porch. It was a white Mini, a tiny toy of a car – nobody he knew drove such an object. But the driver seemed in no hurry to get out, and Audley dared to hope that the engine would start up again. Then the door opened and a tall, tweedy woman in glasses and headscarf climbed out.

Audley was halfway down the stairs to the front door before the bell clanged. If it was charity he would buy it off as quickly as possible, and if white elephants were required for some village occasion he would promise a whole herd of them.

He hardly ever used the main door, and was embarrassed to find that Mrs Clark, ever burglar-conscious, had shot both the huge iron bolts. And when he swung the heavy door open there was an agonized protest of ancient hinges which made him smile: it was altogether too like the opening sequence of a Hammer film, with himself as the ghoulish butler. The coming plea for Oxfam or jumble would be an anticlimax.

But his caller made no plea. She stood waiting in the pool of light, obviously expecting him to speak first.

'Can I help you?' he volunteered at last.

Now she was surprised, and it dawned on Audley that she knew him and had assumed that he knew her. For a long moment he groped for her face in his memory, without success. Somebody's wife? Somebody's sister? Somebody's –

'Dr Audley, don't you remember that we met this morning. Faith Jones – Faith Steerforth?'

He made the identification as she spoke. Somebody's daughter! It was unpardonable, but her unexpected glasses and the shadows thrown by the harsh overhead light had deceived him.

For another long moment he stared at her, at a complete loss for words.

'Aren't you at least going to ask me in?'

The 'at least' was like a gauntlet thrown down before him. It assumed hostility and carried the fight into the enemy's territory. But how could she have become hostile to him so quickly?

'Miss Steerforth – Miss Jones,' he apologized. 'Forgive me. Please come in.'

He motioned her through the hall, down the passage and into the sitting room. She looked around her with unashamed curiosity, as though valuing the place.

'You've got a lovely house, Dr Audley. And lovely furniture. I didn't know policemen were so well paid,' she said aggressively.

That flecked him on the raw. He thought of the long struggle to preserve these things that he loved so much, and of the things that had gone to save the rest.

'This house, or what's left of it, has been in my family for a long time, Miss Steerforth. Or is it Miss Jones?' He tried to keep the anger out of his voice, and achieved a sneer instead.

'I call myself Jones, Dr Audley. But you can call me Steerforth if you prefer. That's the name on my birth certificate.'

She took off her glasses and regarded him with the same disconcerting haughtiness he had felt outside the churchyard at Asham, doubly disconcerting now because the to-hell-with-you look which characterized the surviving pictures of her father was even more pronounced. Except now it was tinged with hostility rather than boredom. Only something her mother or step-father had told her could have roused her like this. And only the card he had given to Jones could have enabled her to track him down. But that didn't ring true of Jones – it was puzzling.

He realized suddenly that he was out-staring her out of sheer surprise and curiosity. There was uncertainty just beneath the arrogance, and it would be prudent to give that uncertainty time to grow.

'I was just about to have a drink, Miss – Jones.' He

46

moved to the door without giving her a chance to refuse. 'I'll get you one too.'

It was only when he had reached the kitchen that he remembered he didn't have a casual female drink in the house any more. He could hardly offer her a choice of beer or brandy, which left only too-good claret or execrable Spanish Burgundy. He searched for the Burgundy abstractedly. Why the hell had she come to disturb him? And why did she think he was a policeman? Not that those answers were of any importance, since she could know nothing about the father she had never met.

He fumed as he pulled the cork. He had lost his confidence with young women; since his break-up with Liz he had been like the pilot who hadn't dared to go up again immediately after the crash. The sooner this nuisance of a girl was packed off, the better.

But the nuisance looked so woebegone and vulnerable when he returned to her that his determination weakened. She had put on her glasses again, but it seemed that her supply of courage had run out: the strange old house and the strange policeman had begun to overawe her.

He set a glass on the table beside her. 'Now, Miss Jones, what's the trouble?' Confident neutrality was the note to strike. 'But I must tell you straight away that I'm not a policeman. I think you've been misinformed there.'

She looked down at her feet.

'I think – I think maybe I've made a fool of myself,' she said slowly.

Audley relaxed. It wasn't going to be so embarrassing after all. So long as she didn't start to weep, anyway; anger was preferable to tears any day.

'I've driven all the way from Asham making up things to say to you. But now I'm here they all seem rather stupid and melodramatic. I don't know what to say now.'

Audley gestured towards the wine. 'Drink your drink – it isn't very good, I'm afraid. Then let's hear some of the things you made up and I'll tell you if they fit.'

'They don't fit – I can see that now. But my father – my step-father, that is – said you were a sort of high-up policeman.'

'Your step-father told you that?' It still didn't sound like Jones.

Faith Jones shook her head in embarrassment.

'No, he didn't. That's what makes it worse. I overheard him talking to Mummy. Not deliberately – I'm not an eavesdropper. I was in our spare room, and you can hear every word that's said in the dining room underneath. And I wouldn't have listened, except that I heard my father's name – my real father's name.' She paused. 'It was rather a shock. I just couldn't stop listening.'

'Why was it a shock? You must have heard them talk about him before. You must have asked them about him.'

'They've told me lots about him. Grandmother talks about him all the time, even now. But – '

And it came tumbling out. The brave pilot, hero of the Arnhem drop, with a medal to prove it. Jones had been a little more guarded, or more honest, and had admitted that he hadn't really known her father. But even he had stretched a point and pretended that he believed Steerforth had stayed with the Dakota to save other people's lives. And the little girl had thought herself lucky to have two gallant pilot fathers instead of one, and had never missed the one already in heaven.

And then she had grown up and strayed into the wrong room, and overheard a conversation with a very different flavour.

'It was Mummy who started it. She always sees through people. She said: "That man asked you about Johnnie, didn't he?" And Daddy didn't want to answer at first, but she insisted. She said she had a right to know.

'And then finally he said: "The bastard was up to

something big," or something like that. And he said he'd always suspected that he'd been up to no good, but it must have been even more important than he thought, because you were here asking questions.

'And Mummy asked who you were, and he said you were obviously a special sort of high-up policeman. He said you put on a good act pretending that you were doing a boring job you didn't enjoy. But underneath he thought you were hard as nails – he said you were a mailed fist in a velvet glove.'

God bless my soul! thought Audley. Jones had seen clear through him, and then had drawn the wrong conclusion because it was the logical one. How many others had made the same mistake, he wondered, from Fred downwards? It was amusing – it was even rather satisfying. But it was ridiculously wide of the mark, and this young woman had presumably seen more clearly, with less reason and more intuition.

He leaned forward and filled her glass again.

'No mailed fist. Just an ordinary hand in the glove, Miss Jones. What happened then?'

'Then it was awful, because Mummy said: "So it's all happening again." And Daddy wanted to know what was happening again. Then she started to cry – and she never cries, or almost never.'

Her voice faltered, and Audley was terrified for a moment that she was going to follow her mother's lead. But she bore up, and continued.

'She said that after he'd disappeared two of his crew had kept coming round asking about him as though he were alive. And then they'd asked her if he'd left any messages or instructions. They wouldn't leave her alone.

'Daddy was nice to her then, and said she ought to have told him. And she said he was the only one who didn't pester her with questions.'

That was one good thing, thought Audley. It put Jones

in the clear beyond all doubt. If he hadn't put the key
questions in so many years he certainly hadn't been
looking for any answers.

'And what happened then?'

'Daddy said she didn't have to worry. He said he'd
make damn sure no one pestered her again. If they did
he'd get in touch with you – he'd put your address in the
book.'

'So you went and looked me up.'

Faith Jones nodded.

'But why come and see me now?'

The corners of her mouth turned downwards appeal-
ingly. For a moment he could see the little girl with the
two brave fathers who had suddenly and cruelly discovered that one might have feet of clay.

'I realize it was silly now. I was so mixed up – but I
wanted to come and tell you, or ask you, not to bother
them any more. Because they really didn't know anything
about – about whatever it was he did.

'And, Dr Audley, I want to know what he did that was
so awful. I mean, I ought to be told, oughtn't I?'

She looked at him as if she was screwing up her courage
to say something awkward.

'When I was at college no one was ever interested
in the war. We were all CND – I went on the marches.
But though I've never admitted it I've always been
terribly proud of my real father. When I was browsing
through Blackwell's in Oxford years ago I saw a book all
about his aeroplane. I bought it and I read it. It wasn't
very interesting, but I read it. I – I know a lot about
Dakotas.

'And now I've learnt that he wasn't very nice at all –
because if my step-father says he was a bastard, I'm sure
he was. Daddy doesn't often make mistakes about
people.'

Audley forbore to point out that Daddy – her switching
between fathers was confusing – had not been so right

about the mailed fist. But she'd made her point, and he would have to produce some sort of answer out of common decency. Except that Steerforth was in some degree a classified subject.

She was looking at him, half expectantly, half fearfully. And she was, despite her glasses, rather an attractive girl in a scraggy, angular way. Not his type, in as far as he had a type. Not at all like the unlamented Liz . . .

'Have you had anything to eat?' he asked, with sudden inspiration.

She shook her head.

'Good. Then we'll both have something. My Mrs Clark has left me an immense piece of cold ham. Come to the kitchen and carve it for me – and bring your glass with you.'

She followed him obediently, and the incongruity of the situation struck him. Steerforth had not even been a name to him twenty-four hours ago. He had encountered him at dawn and buried him before midday. And now he was having supper with the man's daughter.

What made it more odd was that he really knew nothing about this girl, who was in some sense part of his work. He had been much better informed about other girls who had been permitted to slice ham and cucumber on his kitchen table, and who had certainly not been connected with important matters. And that had been due more to personal inclination than professional precaution. Not that it had helped much, he reflected. Perhaps his passion for information had ended by inhibiting other varieties of passion.

At least such considerations did not complicate this relationship. Audley stopped with his hand halfway into the cutlery drawer as an idea welled up in his mind. He observed her out of the corner of his eye. That Steerforth face of hers was not so apparent now, but it was there all the same, undeniably there. To use her was against the rules, but in certain circumstances that face might have its uses.

Jones wouldn't like it, but Jones didn't have to know: this was between father, real father, and daughter. And if Stocker and the others didn't like it either, they would still be mightily impressed with his unexpected expertise with young women. So to hell with all of them!

The only drawback was that he would have to tell her at least some of his hypothesis. But then it was only a hypothesis, as yet little more than a hunch without real evidence and totally without any key information.

He dismissed the possibility that she was not what she seemed. The time factor, the logic of her presence and his own instinct ruled it out. But he interrogated her gently throughout their kitchen table supper nevertheless – three glasses of wine had just sufficiently loosened her tongue and restored her confidence.

At least she was satisfactorily ordinary – the very blueprint of an educated middle-class female. High school, Young Farmers' Club forsaken as she moved leftwards to Bristol University and CND. Then gently rightwards again as she worked for a diploma in education, and so to teaching at a custom-built comprehensive.

Except that she taught physics and chemistry – he was careful not to show unemancipated surprise – and had no steady male admirers.

'Shouldn't you be teaching now?'

But of course they had a huge half-term at state schools, and she had compassionate leave into the bargain.

'What were you doing at Blackwell's?'

'Blackwell's?'

'You bought a book on Dakotas there.'

'I went to a commem. ball there – at Oxford, I mean.'

The ball had not been a success – 'I don't mind men making passes. But he took it for granted.'

Audley nodded sagely. 'Wouldn't have happened at

Cambridge. I mean, it wouldn't have been taken for granted.'

She smiled at that, and Audley judged the ice to be sufficiently melted. It was time to get her interested.

'Miss Jones, you want to know about your father – you want to know what he did, in fact. And the answer is that we really don't know. All I can do is to tell you what we think he did. Perhaps you'll be able to help us a little in return. Would you be willing to do that?'

She looked at him uncertainly. 'I don't see how I can help you. I don't remember him – I only know what Grandmother told me.'

'No matter. Anyway, I take it she told you what was supposed to have happened – lost at sea, and all that?'

She nodded. That story would have lost nothing in Grandmother's retelling.

'Well, there were certain people who were very interested in the whereabouts of your father's plane at the time. Presumably because of what it was thought to be carrying.'

'The crew – ' she began. 'The two who pestered my mother – '

'Forget about the crew for the moment. These people weren't crew members. One of them was a Belgian and the others were Russians.'

'Russians?'

'Your father was flying regularly to Berlin, twice a week often. That was when we were just setting up the four-power allied control commission there. His squadron was on a freight run. But there was also a great deal of what you might call private enterprise on that run too. You could get just about anything in Germany in those days if you had cigarettes to trade with, and there were a lot of valuable things about with temporary owners. Your father was very well-placed to transport the merchandise.'

'You mean he was in the – what did they call it? – the

53

black market?' She spoke coldly, almost contemptuously.

Audley sipped his coffee. 'You shouldn't think too badly of him for it, actually. It's a rather modern idea, not letting the winners plunder the losers blind. There were a lot of chaps doing it.'

'My step-father didn't do it.'

Jones was evidently on a pedestal.

'No, I don't believe he did. But your father was in it up to the neck, and one day he seems to have picked up something extra special. Something hot.'

'But you don't know what it was?'

'We don't – not yet. And I don't think he really did either. Or at least he didn't understand its true value.'

Faith Steerforth broke in: 'But whatever it was – you must have it now. If it was on the plane.'

'There was nothing on the plane. That's the whole problem. Nothing but seven boxes of broken bricks.'

'Somebody had taken it?'

'We don't think so.'

'Then he never had anything. Or maybe someone switched those boxes before he was given them.'

She was quick enough, certainly.

'It's possible. But we don't think it's likely. The Russians must have been satisfied about the Berlin end before they came over here. They're very thorough when they want to be – so thorough that they never forgot about the plane. In fact they already know there wasn't anything in it. But they are still interested!'

She shivered.

'That's what's so beastly. It's what frightened Mummy – people being interested again all these years afterwards. It must have been something terribly valuable.'

'Not valuable in terms of money, Miss Steerforth. The Russians don't have to worry about money.'

She stared at him. 'But he didn't have it, whatever it was. So what's all the bother about now?'

Audley was about to answer when the grandfather clock struck in the distance – eight, nine, ten.

'It's very late, Miss Steerforth. Isn't anyone expecting you?'

She glanced at her watch, but shook her head.

'I'll go to a hotel somewhere. But you must tell me why there's this trouble first. I promise I'll go then.'

Audley thought for a moment. There were no such things as conventions these days, after all.

'You can stay here if you like. There's a spare bed – and I'm a Cambridge man, I assure you.'

She looked at him in surprise. Patently – and rather humiliatingly – she had not considered him in that light at all. He was still some sort of policeman, and consequently sexless.

Then she smiled. 'That's very kind of you, Dr Audley,' she said. 'But please stop calling me "Miss Steerforth". I know it must be confusing for you, so just call me "Faith". *He* chose the name, anyway.'

'Steer – your father did?'

'Yes. It's silly really. Grandmother told me that long before I was even born he said he'd like to have three daughters, to look after him in his old age. And he'd call them Faith, Hope and Charity. It's silly, because he said he was naming them after three old aeroplanes.'

For the first time Steerforth came alive to Audley. No longer bones in a lake, but a man who had lived and made ordinary, everyday plans – plans for three daughters, anyway.

'Malta,' he said. 'That was where his old planes came from. At one time in the war they had just three to defend it, and they called them Faith, Hope and Charity.'

She looked at him. 'I'd like to stay if I may, Dr Audley.'

He couldn't help smiling at her. It was actually rather pleasant to have some female company again after so long.

'Very well, then – Faith. I'll tell you what all the fuss is about. It's really quite simple in outline: somehow your father picked up something valuable, and then everyone thought it was lost at sea with him. Only now we know he wasn't lost at sea and he wasn't carrying the thing when he crashed. Yet the Russians are still interested. Now doesn't that suggest anything to you?'

He waited for her to speak, but she wouldn't be drawn.

'Well to me – Faith – it suggests that whatever he'd got hold of was already here. If the Russians are so sure it's the only possibility left. And once you accept that, actually, the other awkward bits in the puzzle fit much better.'

'Other bits?'

'There were those seven boxes of bricks, which shouldn't have been on board. All four survivors saw them. Your step-father and the navigator couldn't describe them very clearly. But the other two were very helpful.'

'The two who – '

'Those two, yes. Warrant Officer Tierney and Flight Sergt Morrison. They should have conveniently forgotten the boxes if they were valuable, but instead they remembered. And by remembering they put everyone off the scent. Which is exactly what they intended. Because what's lost at sea doesn't have to be accounted for, does it?'

'But that would mean – ' she squared up to the implication ' – that he meant to crash!'

'That's exactly what it means, yes.'

'You can't mean he crashed in that lake deliberately.'

'I don't mean that. *That* was a real crash – and it wasn't meant to happen. What was meant to happen was the story Tierney and Morrison actually told.'

'But my step-father wouldn't have stood for anything like that. He would have spoken up – I know he would!'

'He was just a passenger. He did as he was told, and he didn't really know what was happening. In fact it was just the same as the boxes: two vague stories, and two detailed ones – much too detailed.'

She regarded him thoughtfully. 'All right, I take your point,' she said slowly. 'But I don't see how you make it fit what's happening now.'

'Where doesn't it fit?'

'Well, if the real boxes were already in,' she paused. 'And if my father was dead . . . then Tierney and the other one got everything long ago. You're twenty years too late, and so are the Russians – you're just wasting your time.'

'Maybe I am – but the Russians aren't.'

Not Panin. Of all people, not Panin. That had to be an article of faith.

'So they're infallible, are they?'

'Not infallible, but not stupid. Besides, there is an alternative, you know. In fact you as good as suggested it yourself.'

She frowned at him. 'When did I?'

'You told me that Tierney and Morrison pestered your mother. The Belgian and the Russians were only interested in the plane. But those two were desperate to find your father. Even our people noticed that at the time.'

'They were his friends.'

'So they hounded his widow? No, Faith. He hid it and he didn't tell them where. And then he disappeared – and there wasn't a thing they could do about it.'

There was no point in adding that what had probably hit the surviving conspirators hardest was the growing suspicion that they had been double-crossed by Steerforth, just as the Belgian had been double-crossed.

Faith Steerforth looked past him, into the darkness outside.

'Then it's still where he put it,' she said softly, half to herself.

'It's the only explanation that makes sense of what's happening now, Faith,' said Audley. 'The Russians must have come to the same conclusion, too. And they think it can be found.'

4

Audley set his cup of vile coffee down on the plastic tabletop and glowered into it. Meetings with Jake Shapiro, with the exception of their standing Wednesday lunch, were always in places of Jake's choosing and always in uniformly horrible places.

And the vision of Faith Jones poking around the old house in his absence didn't appeal to him either, even though her behaviour as an unsolicited guest had been unexceptionable: she had neither messed up the bathroom nor talked at him during breakfast.

But there was no other course of action open to him. He had to meet Roskill this morning, and he had to keep the girl to hand now that he had decided to make use of her. It was no good consulting the resident Kremlinologists; he had recognized Tom Latimer's hand in the Panin file, and if Latimer was still undecided about the man then no one else would be of use. And that left only his own sources.

The kitchen swing-doors banged at the back of the narrow coffee bar as Jake barged through them. He slapped the waiter on the back, whispered in his ear, lifted a cup of coffee out of his hands and swept on past him without stopping. He slid the cup along the tabletop and eased himself along the bench opposite Audley.

'David, my not-so-long-lost friend! It's good to see you again so soon – but not on a Saturday. I thought it was always the day when you stayed home and cut those rolling lawns of yours – and for me it is the Sabbath! So you have me worried on two counts!'

Jake's humour had been degenerating for nearly twenty

years from its original abysmal Cambridge level, and Audley's only defence was to sink unwillingly to that level.

'I thought you'd like to know that there's a jobbing machine shop down in Gosport which makes spare parts for all those grounded Mirage IIICs of yours, Jake.'

Jake slapped his thigh in delight.

'Just what we've been looking for! Now we shall not have to buy them from the South Africans – the way they've been getting through their spares must be baffling the French. Or if not baffling them, amusing them. But seriously old friend, what is this business of Saturday working? It's not good, you know. And besides, I have a date with my El-Al stewardess this morning, so spit it out.'

Now for the moment of truth. If Jake had heard a whisper that he'd been shifted from the Middle East he wouldn't give much, even for old times' sake. Jake was an honest horsetrader, but only when the trading prospects were reasonable.

'Nikolai Panin, Jake. What can you tell me about Nikolai Panin?'

The grin faded from Jake's face – too quickly for a genuine grin. He brushed his moustache thoughtfully.

'Panin's not a Middle Eastern man.'

'No, he isn't. I'm just doing a little job for a friend, and I need to catch up on him.'

Jake raised his eyebrows.

'Little job? Don't let them snow you, old friend. Panin's a hot number these days – are you in trouble?'

As ever, Jake was quick to sense changes in the wind. Much too quick.

'My only trouble is I'm too good by half. Don't worry about me. Just tell me about Panin.'

Jake pursed his lips, and then nodded.

'You might be the right man for Panin at that! You're both secretive sods.'

'Both?'

The Israeli gave a short laugh. 'Don't tell me you don't know, David. If you asked me to I could pretty soon number off the Central Committee, left, right and centre. The ones that matter, anyway. But not Comrade Panin – nobody knows who pulls *his* strings. And if we did we'd know quite a lot more about some other people!'

He drank his coffee thirstily.

'You know about Tashkent?' he continued. 'That's what really put him on the map in a big way. Up to that time he'd always been an internal man, as far as I know.'

'What does he really do?'

'What does he do? Bugger me, David, if I really knew exactly who does what in that goddamned Byzantine set-up do you think I'd be sweating out my time on this little island, trying to screw tanks out of you?'

'Is he KGB?'

'That's another million dollar question. If you ask me they're all KGB, right down to the children and the nursemaids. Particularly the nursemaids. But your Panin, I just don't know. He's a fixer, a smoother-out.'

'Tell me something he's fixed.'

'Well, since you ask me, I think he had a hand – or maybe I should say a foot – in kicking out Khrushchev. But I couldn't prove it. Then again, he's always kept well in with the military. Very proud of his war record, too. He was a fighter, not a commissar. Joined up with the 62nd Army on the Volga, came through Stalingrad, slogged it all the way to Berlin. Came out as a staff major with the 8th Guards – one of Khalturin's little lambs. I wouldn't have liked to have been a German squaddie in a house they'd decided to take.'

'For a gullible lad sent straight from the kibbutz to buy our tanks, Jake, you're quite well posted on him.'

Shapiro grinned. 'I do my homework, unlike some who are more celebrated for it. Besides, I've met the famous Panin.'

'You've met him? Where?'

'Embassy party at Delhi, just after Tashkent – I was doing a little research on whose tanks had lasted longer in the Rann of Kutch. And there he was – and he talked to me in excellent English, too.'

'What was he like?'

'Like? He's got the face of a rather sad clown – nose broken in the war and set badly. Or maybe not set at all. But he knew me, because he immediately started to talk about the Masada dig, which I'd just visited. He was too bloody clued-up by half. And I didn't know him from Adam. So I went straight off and tried to find out about him, and came straight up against a brick wall, more or less.

'In fact I've been studying him off and on ever since – as I've no doubt lots of Western layabouts have been. And with precious little success, because you've now got the sum total of my studies. In return for which I expect to get the sum total of yours in due course, my dear David.'

Nothing was more certain than that Jake would render a bill of some sort.

'And that really is the sum total?'

'I might be able to come up with a few more names. But it wouldn't signify, because he covers too much territory. That's the trouble – you can't pin him down. In any case, David, you'd best tell me more exactly what it is you want.'

Basically the Israelis knew no more than the British: they both knew simply what was common knowledge. But Audley had expected that. What they did have, however, was by far the best record of events in Berlin in 1945; it was a mere by-product of their long hunt for the missing Nazi butchers, but it was rumoured to be astonishingly complete. That, though he didn't know it, was going to be Jake's special contribution.

'Well,' began Audley judiciously, 'there are several periods of Panin's career I'd like to fill in, but I think you'll only be able to help me with the early one, which is really the least important. I may not even need it, but if you could pass the word to one or two of your Berlin old-timers, they might know something.'

Jake's face hardened. Different nations had different raw places, tender spots, where no leeway was ever allowed. For the Indians and Pakistanis it was Kashmir. For Frenchmen it was 1940. For Jake, and for many other Israelis, it was still the missing Nazis of 1945. He should have remembered that.

'I give you my word, Jake, that as far as I know this has nothing to do with war criminals. Absolutely nothing. And you know how I feel about that.'

The Israeli relaxed. In as far as he trusted any Anglo-Saxon he trusted Audley. Which was not far, perhaps, but far enough.

He nodded. 'Okay, David. I'll drop a word to Joe Bamm – you can always get him at our Berlin place. He's forgotten more about the old days than most other people ever knew. In return, if you turn up any little thing about one of *them*, don't you sit on it.'

He looked at his watch. 'Is that all, then? Because if it is my Delilah awaits me.' He paused, unsmiling again. 'But just you watch it, David, my old friend. You're not dealing with simple Jewish farm boys and stupid Arab peasants any more. You're dealing with real chess players now. If I were you I'd wear belt and braces. They haven't changed one bit, the Russians, whatever your starry-eyed liberals say.'

Audley had one more self-appointed contact to establish before going to the office, but there was no time unfortunately to make it a face to face one. The hated telephone had to be used this time.

'Dr Freisler? Theodore – David Audley here.'

Theodore Freisler was outwardly the archetypal German of the twentieth century world wars, hard-faced and bullet-headed. But within the Teutonic disguise lived an old nineteenth century liberal, whose spiritual home was on the barricades of 1848. His books on German political history were highly regarded in the new Germany, though even in translation Audley found them unreadable. The mind which produced them, however, was at once gentle and formidable: Theodore was a wholly civilized man, the living answer to Jake's unshakeable suspicion of everything German.

'Theodore – I'm glad to have caught you. I'm always expecting to find you've gone back to Germany.'

Theodore had quite unaccountably settled in Britain, in an uncomfortable flat near the British Museum, during a historical conference in 1956. And although he was always revisiting Germany and talking of returning to the Rhineland he had showed no sign of actually doing so. Audley had wondered idly whether he was producing some terrible successor to *Das Kapital*, to set the next age of the world by the ears.

'One day, David, one day. But until that day I shall make my personal war reparation by letting your chancellor have most of my royalties. That is justice, eh?'

'You'll have to work a lot harder to shift our balance of payments, Theodore. But you may be able to help me just now.'

Their friendship had started years before when Theodore, no Nazi-lover, had volunteered the information which had set the Israeli propaganda on the German experts in Egypt in its proper perspective. Since then he had been Audley's private ear in West Germany on Arab-Israeli policies.

64

'I am at your service, Dr Audley.' The formality marked the transition from banter to business.

'Theodore, I've got a riddle for you: what is it that was of great value to the Russians in 1945, was attractive enough for a private individual to steal, and is still of interest to the Russians today?'

There was a short silence at the other end of the line.

'Is this a riddle with an answer?'

'If it is I haven't got it.'

'Do you have any clues?'

'It came out of Berlin in the summer of '45, possibly in seven wooden boxes, each about the size of that coffee table of yours, Theodore. Roughly, anyway.'

'You don't want much, do you? In 1945 there were a great many things of value to be had in Berlin, and the Russians took most of them. But of value *now* – '

'You can't think of anything?'

'Give me time, Dr Audley, give me time! But it is time that makes a nonsense of your riddle. There was much plunder to be had then, but that would not interest them now. Not even Bormann's bones would interest them now! That is perhaps the one thing that you can say for them: their sense of material values is not so warped as ours in the West.'

'But you're interested?'

'Interested in your riddle? Yes, of course. It is the lapse of time which makes it interesting. But can you give the date of the theft more precisely?'

'Not the theft, Theodore. But it left Berlin end of August, beginning of September.'

Theodore grunted. 'I will ask my friends, then. But it is a long time ago, and I cannot promise success. Also, some riddles do not have answers. And if there is an answer, is it a dangerous one? I don't wish to embarrass my friends.'

'To be honest, Theodore, I don't know. But just give

me a hint and I can get someone else to do the dirty work.'

Theodore chuckled. 'Ach, so! I do the searching, others take the risks and the good Dr Audley sits in his ivory tower putting all our work together – that is the way of it! But I think I shall move circumspectly, since you do not know what it is I am to find.'

Audley had to take it in good part, for it was true enough.

'If you're too busy – '

'Too busy? I'm always too busy, David. But not too busy for a friend – never too busy for a friend. And besides, it interests me, your riddle. Something old, but still valuable to them, eh? And "them", I presume, is the Komitet Gosudarstvenoi Bezopasnosti?'

'That's by no means certain, Theodore.'

Nothing was certain, that was the trouble. All he had was an elaborate house of cards built on only partially inter-locking theories. But as he drove back to the office Audley felt fairly satisfied. He had set things moving for which he did not have to account to Stocker: Jake would dig further out of sheer curiosity, and anything Theodore turned up could be cross-checked in the Israeli Berlin files as well as the London ones. If only he had one good hard fact to convince himself that it was all worthwhile . . .

Without that one hard fact, however, there was really nothing he could do. Butler was hard at work in Belgium; half an hour with Roskill should be long enough to work out Monday's schedule. There was no point in rushing things, and he could look forward to a blessedly peaceful weekend. Even the presence of the Steerforth-Jones girl seemed acceptable now. It made a change to have a girl about the house again, even though she hardly qualified as a girl-friend. She might even cook Sunday lunch!

Even the department was reassuringly empty, with Mrs

Harlin's chair unoccupied, a certain sign of the absence of external crises. On such a quiet Saturday as this Lord George Germain had lost the American colonies – and well lost them, too, in the interest of his long weekends.

He tiptoed past Fred's door and slipped into his own room noiselessly.

Stocker, the man from the JIC, was sitting in the armchair opposite the door.

'Good morning, Audley. I hope you don't mind me lying in wait for you like this in your room, but I wanted to get to you first. Have you made any progress?'

Audley composed his face. 'Here and there,' he said guardedly. 'It's rather early days yet for anything concrete – if there is anything.'

Stocker gave him a thin, satisfied smile.

'Well, I can give you something nice and hard: Nikolai Panin's coming to see you.'

Audley carefully set his brief-case alongside the desk, unclipped it and drew out the Steerforth File. It never did to let anyone throw you. Or to show it when they did. Friend or enemy, the same rule applied.

But if Panin was coming to England, then the thing – whatever it was – must truly be in England and could be found. Until now he had never quite believed in his own theory: it had been a mere intellectual exercise in probabilities. Now it was all true because it had to be.

'You don't seem very surprised.' Stocker sounded disappointed.

The devil tempted Audley, but only momentarily. There were times to take undue credit, but assumed coolness was usually more highly regarded than omniscience.

'On the contrary,' he replied mildly. 'I'd rather discounted the possibility. But then we've got twenty years of lost ground to make up. He didn't say what he wanted of me by any chance?'

Stocker sat back, seemingly reassured by Audley's fallibility.

'Actually he doesn't know yet that he'll be meeting you, so you have one small advantage at least. To be precise we've simply been informed that a certain Prof. N. A. Panin, a distinguished member of the Central Committee, would like to visit England informally, in a semi-official capacity. Apparently he wants to discuss "a matter of mutual interest" with what they term "an official of appropriate seniority".'

'That hardly describes me. It might describe you.'

Stocker laughed shortly. 'It had the Foreign Office a little baffled, I think. Indeed, they were all too ready to agree that it was more our concern than theirs, Their Mr Llewelyn actually suggested that this might be very much up your street – I believe he's a friend of yours?'

God help the Israelis, thought Audley. And Allah protect the poor Arabs too.

'Anyway, I'm going to lay down a welcome mat for our distinguished visitor, Audley. And then you are going to take over from me. You are going to show the professor all the sights of interest.'

They had it all worked out: mark the mysterious Professor Panin with the inconvenient Audley. No matter that Audley isn't trained for this sort of thing. What he doesn't know he can't give away.

Or did they really think he could do what no one else had yet done?

'And just what am I expected to do with him?'

'Be nice to him. Find out what he wants and why he wants it. Get to it first. Then give it to him.'

'Give it to him?'

Stocker coughed apologetically. 'The official view is that whatever it is, it's unlikely to be more valuable than his gratitude. If it was valuable to us he'd never come openly asking for help, which is what he appears to be doing. It's thought that one good turn may lead to another.'

'And what do you think?'

'My dear Audley, I've always found gratitude a some-what intangible thing. But on the whole I go along with the official view. We don't want to offend him if we can help it. We'd like to know a lot more about him, but we don't want him to put one over on us, if you see what I mean.'

Audley didn't – and did to the uttermost degree. Everyone was in the dark.

'But I've got freedom of action?'

'Within all reasonable limits.'

'And I can have Roskill and Butler as long as I need them?'

Stocker smiled. 'But of course – and anyone else you need. Roskill and Butler have got German and Russian – but then you're quite a linguist too, aren't you?'

Audley couldn't make out whether he was being superior or matter-of-fact. Fred was always matter-of-fact because he never needed to be superior.

'I read them. I've got no ear for languages.'

'No matter. I'm told the professor speaks perfect English. Anyway, you've got until Tuesday to wrap it up. He comes in on the scheduled Aeroflot flight at 11.30. And for the record – just what have you got on Steerforth?'

Audley looked at him bleakly. 'He took something and hid it. If Panin thinks it can be found we must agree with him, I suppose.'

Stocker got up. 'In that case I suggest you find it first, Audley. Then all your troubles will be over. If you need any help just ask for it – I'll see you're not held up.'

When he had gone Audley sat staring despondently at the file. In the past he had stood as an adviser on the fringes of operations which had seemed to him ingeniously simple or hopelessly devious. Or brilliantly complex. Or plain stupid. Whatever Panin was about, it wouldn't be stupid. And this time he was in the barrel.

5

'There's the place,' said Roskill, pointing down the street. 'Two small boys with their noses against the window.'

Audley followed him through the dense Saturday crowd, many of whom seemed bent on playing chicken with the motorists. The pavements were hardly less dangerous than the road, with mothers bulldozing their way ahead with prams and pushchairs from which children peered through ramparts of cornflakes and soap powder. Roskill adroitly slipped into the wake of one of the most aggressive pram-pushers and Audley skipped after him.

The crowds parted left and right before the woman's advance, which continued providentially to a supermarket just beyond their destination. There she slewed the pram inwards with superb timing and Audley and Roskill were able to join the two small boys unharmed.

'I dunno wot it is,' said one boy to the other. 'They got the red, white an' blue wrong way round too.'

'Which one?' asked Roskill.

The boys looked round in surprise. Then the smaller pointed to one of the numerous model aeroplanes on display.

Roskill peered down. 'Bristol Blenheim Mk IV,' he said. 'Those are Free French markings – the French who were on our side in the war.'

He straightened up. 'Morrison's had this shop for twelve years,' he said, indicating the legend above the shop window, The Modeller's Shop. The large off-white letters needed repainting, as did the shop itself. 'Not exactly a gold mine, apparently.'

Audley took a deep breath and pushed open the door.

Ahead and just above him an enormous yellow-nosed Stuka was just beginning its dive; on every side colourfully illustrated boxes advertised the progress of half a century's war in the air. To most of them he could not put a name with certainty: bright, barbaric little biplanes and triplanes and more familiar modern British aircraft in respectable green and brown camouflage. And – yes – an Israeli Mirage swooping down on a hapless Egyptian MiG. No mistaking those two!

'Can I help you, sir?'

The thick mousey hair of twenty-five years ago had thinned and retreated. The nose had reddened and sharpened and spidery gold spectacles sat on it now. The whole face had aged prematurely and less gracefully than Jones's, a sagging and unhealthy version of the filed photograph.

'Are you two gentlemen together?'

Odd how obscene the innocent statement sounded these days – a commentary on the times!

'We are, Mr Morrison.'

'Yes, sir. What can I do for you? We've got one of the finest ranges of models in Southern England. Planes, ships, cars, armoured vehicles, British and foreign. Working models too.'

'Planes we're interested in, Mr Morrison.'

Morrison was obviously trying to place them both, and having no success.

'You're in luck, sir, then. We've just got the latest Airfix range in – '

'Dakotas.'

'Dakotas? Yes, we've got Dakotas.' The little man turned, scanned the shelves behind him and selected a box. 'This is by far the best Dakota model, sir. The Airfix one. It's been on the market for several years, but it's very popular. With alternative American wartime transfers, or Silver City civilian ones.'

'We're after a Royal Air Force Dakota, Mr Morrison.'
Roskill was joining the game now – a cat and mouse game when played like this, but one which might be over quicker this way.

'Well, sir, in that case I should buy the Airfix model and then some RAF transfers separately.' Morrison shifted his glance from Audley to Roskill.

'And you've got 3112 Squadron transfers?' Audley spoke this time, and the man's gaze came back to him.

'I beg your pardon?'

'3112 Squadron,' said Roskill. 'F36547 – G for George. Pilot – Flight Lieutenant Steerforth, navigator – Flying Officer Maclean, second pilot – Warrant Officer Tierney. And radio operator – Sergeant Morrison.'

Morrison looked from one to the other uneasily.

'Who are you? What do you want?'

'We don't actually want a Dakota, Mr Morrison. We've got the Dakota. We've got Steerforth. And now we've got you.'

'Who *are* you?'

'In fact there's only one more thing we want, Mr Morrison, and you are going to tell us all about it. With no lies this time.'

Morrison took off his glasses and polished them furiously. Sweat glistened on the pouches under his eyes.

'Please tell me who you are,' he pleaded.

Audley hated himself. 'We are not your old comrades, Mr Morrison,' he said brutally. 'And we've no time to waste arguing. You brought it in to Newton Chester.'

Morrison's will crumbled like a piece of rotten wood.

'I – yes,' he mumbled.

Audley breathed out. Some men's defences could only be approached with all the precise formality and deliberation of an eighteenth century siege, with parallels and saps, gabions and fascines. Surrender was a mathematical certainty if the attacker had the force, the time and the

73

patience. But others could be knocked off balance and taken by a *coup de main* before they could recollect their wits. Morrison was a weak man who had fallen to a crude surprise attack. A text-book case.

'What was it?'

Morrison gestured unhappily. 'I don't know. I swear I don't know. He never told me.'

'*Steerforth* never told you.'

The wretched man shied away from the name as though it would shrivel his tongue.

'What did Steerforth tell you?'

'It's such a long time ago – I don't remember.'

'You're in trouble, Morrison. We know perfectly well that you haven't forgotten. You read about the Dakota in the papers a few days ago. You haven't forgotten.'

Morrison turned his head from side to side as though his collar was too tight.

'I think he said it was – incredible. But he wouldn't say what it was. He just said it was worth the risk. He said it was priceless.'

The words tumbled out now as though Morrison couldn't get rid of them fast enough.

'And it was in the boxes.'

Morrison nodded. 'I suppose so.'

'How many boxes? Seven?'

'I think so.'

'Were they heavy?'

'I don't know. He – Steerforth – and Tierney carried them aboard. I just kept a look-out.'

That was all he was worth. Just a look-out man.

The shop door-bell rang. Audley turned to find an entire family trooping in, breaking the spell utterly, destroying the illusion. Morrison sighed with relief.

'What time do you close, Mr Morrison?'

'Five-thirty.'

'We'll be back at 5.25. We can take our time then. I

know you can remember a great deal more if you try.'

He turned to go, but the man's courage had risen in the presence of others.

'I didn't catch your name, sir.'

Audley toyed with the idea of maintaining the element of uncertainty. But it would be embarrassing if Morrison then did the sensible thing and called the police. In any case, they had him now, and their official status would probably strengthen their hand rather than weaken it. He held his identification open for Morrison to see, just above the spotty face of the latest customer.

'Until 5.25, then, Mr Morrison. Don't go away.'

Outside the crowds seemed even thicker and more determined. The two small boys were still glued to the window, and one of them instantly buttonholed Roskill.

'Mister. Wot's that one?'

Roskill peered into the window again. 'Savoia-Marchetti SM 79,' he said shortly. 'Italian torpedo bomber.' Then he turned to Audley. 'There's a tea shop over the road. We can wait there.'

Audley nodded morosely. He had told Faith Jones he would be home by three, then by six. Now it would be more like seven. His quiet Saturday routine was totally dislocated. And Sunday would be equally ruined, since it was now clearly imperative to grill Tierney and the others as quickly as possible.

Roskill was a man who put his stomach first, an old campaigner: he consumed a schoolboy's tea with relish before attempting to make serious conversation, while Audley toyed with a sickly cake.

Finally he dusted off the crumbs, carefully wiped his fingers and grinned at Audley.

'That was bad luck, just when you'd got him on toast. But I've got a tape of it in case he gets forgetful' – he patted his coat pocket – 'or stubborn. Do you think he knows what it was?'

Audley shrugged. It was quite possible that Steerforth had kept the nature of the cargo to himself, or shared the secret only with Tierney.

'It isn't vital yet, anyway, Hugh. What we need is a line on the hiding place.'

'Always supposing it's still there.'

'It's there.' He had to keep on believing in that.

'But they won't have the answer.'

'They won't. But remember, they've never really thought of looking for it. If they're like Jones they'll have thought that Steerforth was alive, which meant there was no point in looking.'

'How are they going to give us a line on the stuff then?'

'It's the time factor, Hugh – they can narrow down the time factor for us. Remember the breakdown of Steerforth's movements in the file?'

'You mean between the flight in on Tuesday and the flight back to Berlin on Friday?'

Audley nodded. 'That's the crucial period, yes. They brought the boxes in on Tuesday evening. They got them off the plane somehow – we want to know how and where. There must have been a temporary hiding place then.'

'Steerforth was duty officer from 08.30 on Wednesday to the same time on Thursday, wasn't he?'

'Right. And he went to London all day Thursday with the navigator and Wojek the Pole. So he had just Tuesday and Thursday nights to shift the boxes, which didn't give him much scope, I'm hoping.'

'And you really think we stand a chance of tracking the stuff down?'

'Depends on how much we can make people remember, Hugh. And whether we're lucky – as he was.'

Roskill cocked an eyebrow. 'Steerforth was lucky?'

'If I've got it worked out right he had to have one real piece of luck. Look at it this way: he takes over a cargo in Berlin to deliver to that Belgian Butler's looking for at the moment. He takes a look at it and decides to keep it for himself.

'Now he's got two problems. First he's got to double-cross his employers so they won't come chasing him. He does that by pretending he can't bring the stuff out on the first trip and then by losing the aircraft, complete with a dummy cargo, on the second trip.

'But he's also got the practical problem of finding somewhere to put the genuine cargo in the meantime. And he has to come up with the answer to that sometime during the flight back on Tuesday. The first problem sounds harder, but it wasn't really. They just had to get their stories right. They'd had to bale out once before, so they knew the drill. It was the second problem that was awkward.

'It has to be some beautiful, simple, hiding place, because he hadn't time for anything elaborate. And that's where he was lucky, because it was so good that those boxes are almost certainly still where he put them.'

The traffic and the crowds had thinned appreciably when they left the tea shop. The pavement outside Morrison's Model Shop was empty.

But when they were halfway across the road Roskill paused in mid-stride, cursed and accelerated.

'I think the little bastard may have run out on us,' he exclaimed.

Audley hurried after him. The blind on the shop door was pulled down, to reveal its 'Closed' legend, and the door itself was locked.

Roskill looked up and down the street. 'These shops must have a back entrance,' he said. 'If you'll watch the front I'll try the back.'

Audley settled down self-consciously in front of the window. At his eye-level it was clean, but lower down small dirty hands and runny noses had left a tide mark. The models on show were meticulously made; he could even see tiny pilots in the cockpits. Did Morrison spend his free evenings crouched over a desk with glue and tweezers and fine paint brushes? Or did the manufacturers have a staff of middle-aged women who spent their lives endlessly assembling their products to catch the imaginations of small boys?

It seemed an age before the door rattled as Roskill unlocked it to let him in. He felt absurdly like a thief being admitted by his confederate – the more so because Roskill dropped the latch as soon as he was inside.

'Has he gone?'

Roskill shook his head and beckoned him.

'No, he hasn't gone anywhere.'

Audley followed him through the shop into an untidy stockroom. A dingy office ahead was littered with invoices and printed lists which had overflowed an old roll-top desk: Morrison was an untidy businessman. But Roskill pointed to an open door on the left, leading to what was obviously a cellar beneath the shop.

'He's down there. And he's dead.'

Audley squeezed past a packing case and stared down the worn wooden staircase. A single naked bulb hung from a flex at the foot of the stairs, and Morrison lay in a heap directly beneath it. One of his legs rested awkwardly on the stairway, the trouser leg rucked up to reveal a pathetic expanse of white flesh. There was a hole in the sole of his shoe. Halfway up the stairs his glasses lay, unbroken. He had been a small man in life. Now he seemed even smaller.

Audley felt a mixture of revulsion and relief. He had feared, or half-feared, a pointless suicide, for which he might have had to take some of the blame. This ridiculous accident would be less embarrassing, however inconvenient.

'He fell down these stairs?'

'Maybe.' Roskill looked at him coldly. 'And then again maybe not.'

The hair on the back of Audley's neck prickled: that 'maybe not' was like a death sentence.

'I took a very quick look at him. Just on the off-chance that he wasn't as dead as he looked,' said Roskill. 'He had a nosebleed before he . . . fell down the stairs.'

'Before?'

'He bled down his shirt. But you don't bleed down your shirt when you're falling downstairs. And you don't go to the cellar when your nose is bleeding – not when the washroom's out in the yard.'

'Are you saying that someone killed him?'

He stared down the staircase again, taking in the ancient, flaking whitewash on the walls and the dust-laden cobwebs hanging from rusty nails. It didn't make sense. Violence was rare because it almost always stirred up more trouble than it stifled. Nor was it the present Russian style, certainly not in England, where it was capable of launching a major scandal.

But reason and instinct wouldn't raise Morrison from the dead. And there was no sweeping him under the carpet either.

'All right, Hugh. We'll go by the book. I'll phone the police first. Then you phone the department. Tell the duty officer to warn Stocker. And when Butler phones in tell them to warn him too – if someone followed us down here they could be following him over there.'

It was like a nightmare; bad enough to be pitched into the field, out of his depth – but worse to be involved in incomprehensible violence.

'How much do you want the police to know?'

'We've got to know how he died. But either way we

79

shall have to get them to go easy on it – you better get Stocker on that. No doubt he'll know how to do it. And go through Morrison's pockets while I'm phoning – there might be something there.'

He turned back to the faded black telephone in the untidy little office. The important thing now was to keep the initiative, to emulate Fred, whose dealings with the Special Branch were always conducted in a manner which left no doubt as to who was calling the tune.

'. . . This is Dr D. L. Audley of the Ministry of Defence.' *L'Etat, c'est moi.* 'I am speaking from the Modeller's Shop in – ' he stumbled for want of the address. But there it was on an old-fashioned letterhead. 'There seems to have been a fatal accident, but I'm not altogether satisfied with the circumstances . . .'

That was the authentic Fred note: not so much an investigation as a consultation required. Just in time he remembered the final refinement: 'Kindly send a senior officer with your squad.'

When Roskill took over the phone he went back into the shop, which was clean and cheerful compared with the stockroom. Just behind the counter was a low stool, with a small, smooth-edged hole in the linoleum below it – the hole Morrison had worn over hundreds of uneventful days, sitting waiting to sell models to small boys.

Audley's brief flicker of self-satisfaction faded. No more pocket-warmed coins would cross this counter; the supermarket next door would inevitably take over.

He'd met Morrison for five minutes and bullied the life out of him. Whatever the cause of death was, the guilt was his, and he'd compounded his crime by feeling nothing but distaste and annoyance for the inconvenient thing in the cellar.

He looked down at the cutting Roskill had taken from the man's wallet: ONE OF OUR AIRCRAFT IS FOUND. No one deserved to have his minor crimes come looking for him after half a lifetime, least of all a crime which had gained him nothing but a bad conscience. It was a poor recompense for Normandy, Arnhem and the Rhine, the days of fear and danger.

There was a peremptory rap on the door, which caught him unprepared. He had expected to hear the familiar klaxon first.

'Dr Audley? You put through an emergency call?'

'I am Audley. I put through the call. Mr Morrison appears to have fallen down the stairs into the cellar – through there. He's dead.'

He led the party, which had shed a uniformed man at the door, through into the stockroom. Roskill, still busy on the phone, nodded to them without pausing in mid-sentence.

The leading member of the squad peered down the staircase for a moment, nodded to the other two men and turned back to Audley. He was a large man, taller even than Audley, with a mild, quizzical expression. He looked as if he had seen everything, heard everything, believed very little of it, and could no longer be surprised by anything.

'I'm Detective Inspector Roberts, sir. Could I see your identification please?'

Audley passed the folder over.

'And this gentleman?'

'Squadron Leader Roskill, my colleague.'

'Might I ask who he is telephoning?'

'The Ministry.'

'Are you here on official business, sir?'

'We are.'

'Might I know the nature of that business, sir?'

'Mr Morrison was helping us with some information concerning a matter we are investigating, inspector. A matter falling under the Official Secrets Act. He was only marginally concerned with it. We spoke to him briefly early in the afternoon and arranged to see him again at 5.25, just before he closed. We found the shop locked, and Squadron Leader Roskill went round to the service entrance. He found the body at the bottom of the stairs.'

Roberts nodded. 'You said in your message that you were not altogether satisfied with the circumstances here, sir. Could you tell me why?'

Audley repeated what Roskill had said.

'Inspector, there was no question of any proceedings against Mr Morrison. He was disturbed by our visit, but there was no reason why he should take his own life. If he wanted to, in any case, I don't think he would have used such a method. When I first saw him down there I thought it must have been an accident. I still think so.

'But if there is any question of foul play it is of the very greatest importance that this is established quickly.'

Roberts gave him an old-fashioned look.

'Can you think of any reason – any reason that you can tell me – why anyone might harm Mr Morrison, sir?'

'Honestly, inspector – no. This sort of thing just doesn't happen. Not now – not here.'

'A lot of strange things happen now – and here, Dr Audley.'

'Not this sort of thing, inspector. But if it has, we have to know, so I'd like you to make a special effort.'

Roskill joined them, thrusting out a hand to be shaken.

'I'm to blame, inspector. Sorry about that, but when you don't like the look of a thing you can't make it look right by thinking about it.'

The inspector smiled for the first time, and it occurred to Audley that his own confidence over being able to handle the police from a lofty height was misplaced. Everything he had said had been either pompous or stilted, while Roskill had set everything in perspective and at the right level in a couple of easy sentences.

'Dr Audley's right, of course – this sort of nastiness is

out of date now,' Roskill continued. 'But people don't fall downstairs when I want to talk to them either. They run away.'

He passed over a sheet of paper to the inspector.

'You'll want to do some checking on us. There are some names and telephone numbers to check on.

'And just to set your mind at rest I can detail our movements for you. There was a family in here when we left – I can describe the badge on the boys' blazers. And there were two lads outside all the time – from a local secondary school almost certainly. They may have seen something, and they'll remember me. I can give you a full statement.'

The inspector relaxed visibly, and it further dawned on Audley that he had equally stupidly overlooked the need to establish not their status, but their innocence. His own assumption of authority and their equivocal position had set an awkward question of protocol, which he had not had the sense to resolve simply because it had never occurred to him.

The shop doorbell rang.

'That'll be our surgeon,' said Roberts. 'Are you a medical doctor, sir?'

Audley shook his head.

'Well, you won't mind if we get on with things. And I won't detain you long. In fact Squadron Leader Roskill can give us all the necessary details, and you can endorse his statement later if you wish.'

Which was one way, thought Audley, of saying 'I don't quite know who or what you are, you self-important sod, but I'd much rather deal with your underling anyway.' And fair enough, too. Complicated trouble this early on a Saturday, with the evening still stretching ahead, would be enough to set any policeman's teeth on edge.

Roberts turned away without waiting for an answer,

under cover of showing the way for the police surgeon and the photographer who was with him.

Roskill caught Audley's eye.

'I got straight through to Stocker. He's going to smooth things down, and he said we'd better clear this end up and then pack it in until tomorrow. But if you like I'll hang on here and see if they find anything – I can give you the details in the morning.'

'Can they get Butler back?'

'He'll be back.' Roskill grinned. 'He won't get much sleep, but that'll only sharpen his claws. Oh – and they're sending a man up to Knaresborough to keep an eye on Tierney and another down to Asham to watch over Jones now. Just in case, Stocker said.'

There seemed to be manpower to spare, certainly. It had never been like this in the Middle East. But he didn't like the way Stocker was manipulating the action, and there was a suspicion now at the back of his mind that Roskill's primary role might well be to keep Stocker informed of the progress of events.

It was time to assert himself a little, anyway.

'Very well, Hugh. You stay on here. You can pick me up tomorrow and we'll take Tierney as planned. But I don't think he'll be so easy, so we'll do it in two stages. First, you and Butler can approach him officially. Then –'

He paused for effect.

'Then Miss Steerforth and I will have a go.'

The effect was gratifying enough: he had every bit of Roskill's attention for the first time since tea. But to leave him dangling now would be small-minded. If he was reporting back to Stocker it was only because he had been ordered to. And it was not Roskill's fault that the afternoon had ended so badly: leaving Morrison had been Audley's own mistake.

'If Tierney's the man he used to be he'll be tricky, Hugh. He'll know more and tell less. So I'd like you to push his good side, and if that doesn't work I'm going to tempt his bad one. We might get somewhere between us.'

6

As he drove homewards Audley felt a black depression settling on him.

The familiar countryside, springlike after the previous day's chill, made it all the worse; he should have been driving home to a quiet, secluded weekend. Instead he was driving from trouble towards trouble, with trouble on each side of him.

Faith Jones had had the best part of a day to pry and fret around his house, and there was no guarantee that she'd be willing to go north with them next day, for all the good that might do. There was no certainty even that she'd still be waiting for him.

But the girl was the least of his unhappiness. The last two hours had confirmed his fears that he was simply not up to this job – it was all a horrible error of judgement. The breaking of Morrison had been luck, not skill, and he knew in his heart that sending in Roskill and Butler first against Tierney next day was less part of a crafty plan than mere hopeful cowardice. Theodore Freisler had put his finger on the truth: he was afraid of the dirty work.

Worst of all was Morrison's death. It didn't seem real yet, but when the unreality wore off Audley suspected that he was going to be frightened.

But as he turned on to the cobbled forecourt, with the anger of Mrs Clark's geese ringing in his ears, he noticed with pleasure that someone had cut the grass – a bit of Mrs Clark's famous initiative. The grass was his invariable Saturday job, and it had nagged at his mind all day.

And Faith Jones's Mini was still there, in the old barn

where he had told her to put it that morning. He pulled in alongside it.

The stone-flagged kitchen was cool and calm after the uncomfortable afternoon and the sweaty drive home. And Faith Jones, in the blue-jeans-and-shirt uniform of youth, was pouring a beer, just as cool and calm.

'Your Mrs Clark told me that you always pour yourself a glass of beer when you come home late from the office. She says you can always keep on the right side of a man if you greet him like this, too. Even if he doesn't want it – it builds his self-respect, she says. Personally, I think it's a much older custom. I think Mrs Clark has got a racial memory going back to Anglo-Saxon times.'

She offered Audley the beer with a curtsey that somehow avoided being either serious or mocking.

He accepted it, nonplussed. 'I didn't know Mrs Clark was aware of my drinking customs. But it's very welcome, Miss Jones.'

'Don't go formal on me. You agreed to call me Faith last night, and you've been "Mr David" to me so much today that I can't possibly call you "Dr Audley" any more.' She smiled at him, and he took cover in his glass.

'And as for Mrs Clark not knowing about your drinking habits, there's precious little Mrs Clark doesn't know about you. And what Mrs Clark doesn't know by learning and experience she knows already by instinct I would guess. So since I've spent quite a lot of today with her I'm afraid I know rather a lot about you too now.'

Audley choked on his beer. The roles had been reversed now, with the proverbial vengeance.

'But don't worry,' Faith went on airily. 'She thinks quite highly of you. In not quite so many words she told me that you'd be a very good catch for any girl of sense. And she's been busy giving me angling hints all day.'

Audley floundered, trying desperately to find something to stop the conversation.

'She must think quite highly of you too, to confide in you after such a short acquaintance.'

'I took care to tell her that I was a farmer's daughter. But I think it was despair as much as anything. Once she'd made the mistake of taking me for your latest girlfriend she clutched at me like a straw. She thinks my predecessors have been too few – and all highly unsuitable!'

'You shouldn't have led her on, Miss – Faith.' Audley knew he was still floundering. 'You should have explained that we had a – a business relationship.'

He knew as soon as he had said it that he had made himself more ridiculous, and she made things worse by seeming to take him seriously.

'I don't think Mrs Clark would quite have understood such a relationship – any more than I do, really.' And then sudddenly she was serious. 'I couldn't very well tell her that you're out to prove that my father was a thief, and maybe worse.'

Audley put down his glass and stared out at the neat, well-cut lawn, with his back to her. Her banter was after all preferable to reality, but because it only concealed her misgivings the truth was better out.

'I've already proved that. I did it this afternoon. I bullied a little inoffensive shopkeeper who sold toy aeroplanes and who used to be your father's wireless operator. I made him admit it. And now he's dead.'

'He's – dead?'

'His name was Morrison. I think he died accidentally, falling downstairs. But one of my colleagues thinks he didn't.'

'Didn't fall downstairs?'

Audley turned round. 'Didn't die accidentally,' he said harshly.

Faith Jones was frowning at him.

'David – what are you?'

Audley opened another can of beer and offered it to her. She shook her head and he poured it for himself, carelessly, watching the froth well over the rim of the glass.

'What are you?' she repeated. 'What do you do? Are you really some sort of cloak-and-dagger person – the sort one reads about and never quite believes in?' She paused. 'But I suppose you wouldn't admit it if you were, so it's a silly question.'

Not silly, but unanswerable, thought Audley. At present he was a sheep in ill-fitting wolf's clothing, but she'd never believe that. Then his eye caught a slim blue and gold book lying with a browsing pile on the mantelpiece above the boiler.

'Do you believe in fairies, Faith?'

She looked at him blankly.

'*Puck of Pook's Hill* is on the shelf behind you. There's a bit in it at the beginning where Puck gets huffy at being called one. Give me the book and I'll show you.'

He riffled through the pages to find the passage he almost knew by heart. '. . . "What you call *them* are made-up things the People of the Hills have never heard of" . . .

'Except of course that we have heard of them. But I know just how Puck felt now. You can't generalize about – the People of the Hills.' He turned back a few pages. '"Giants, trolls, kelpies, brownies, goblins, imps; wood, tree, mound and water spirits; heath-people, hill-watchers, treasure-guards, good people, little people, pishogues, leprechauns, night riders . . ." I'm not a troll or a night rider, certainly. You might call me a hill-watcher.'

She shook her head in despair.

'Be serious, David.'

'But I am being serious. Your step-father wasn't really very close – I'm not a policeman. I'm more like a meteorologist, a Middle East weather man. At least, I was until yesterday. I tried to forecast what certain countries were going to do. Does that answer your question?'

Faith thought for a moment before answering.

'The Middle East – that's what all those Arabic papers and things in the sitting room are about.'

Audley nodded. He'd have to cancel *Al Ahram* and *Al Kuwat al Muslaha* and the rest now and wade through *Molodaya Gvardia* and *Ogonyek* just as painfully.

'But my father had nothing to do with the Middle East. He only flew in Europe.'

'That is true. I'm a little out of my territory.' And out of my depth, he nearly added. 'Which is why I just might need your help. After this afternoon I'm not sure I ought to involve you – or if you're willing to be involved. But you said last night that you'd give a lot to find out just what your father did.'

She looked at him in surprise.

'Do you mean there's really something I can do? I wouldn't have thought you – you People of the Hills – would ever use outsiders.'

'They don't – but I do. I've got all sorts of odd characters digging already. You'd be surprised.'

She started guiltily, hand to mouth. 'One of them wouldn't be called Esau, would he?'

'He certainly would.' Esau was Jake's private *nom de guerre* – it was an ancient joke between them that he grew his own hair shirt, to belie his name.

'I'm sorry. He phoned just about teatime. But he left a number – it's on the pad by the phone, and it's good until 7.30.'

Audley almost ran to his study. Jake wouldn't phone unless he had come up with something worthwhile.

The number was not one he recognized, and it turned out to be one of the fly-by-night Soho clubs where Jake seemed to spend much of his free time. But they were only too happy to summon Mr Esau.

'Esau?'

'My dear David! Your little girl-friend – whom you so shamefully neglect – she remembered to give you my message!'

'She isn't my girl-friend.'

'No, of course not. Your secretary-housekeeper with the county accent. How stupid of me to misplace her!'

'Come to the point, Esau.'

'The point? My friend, the point is that I value you so highly that instead of rushing to my morning assignation I put in a call to that other friend of mine.'

Jake's interest in Panin was evidently more than casual to have galvanized him so quickly. But of course Jake was ambitious.

'David, you know that *your* friend has returned to the scenes of his youthful conquest?'

'I do.' The Israeli Berlin end was good, evidently.

'I never doubted it, even though you carelessly omitted to tell me. But no matter. My friend mentioned it in his acknowledgement. He promises to give the matter some of his valuable time. But in the meantime he did give us a snippet. Have you ever heard of G Tower?'

'No, I haven't.'

'Neither have I. But it seems that your friend spent quite a lot of his time there back in the old days. G Tower – you'd better look it up. I'm sure you'll have lots of information on it, whatever it was.'

'I shall give it my earnest attention. And that was all?'

'All! At such short notice I think that's not at all bad. But, yes. It is all for the time being – except that there is a small matter that I'd like your advice on.'

The bill, or its first instalment, was about to be presented. With Jake there was always a bill.

'But I won't burden you with it now. My – secretary-housekeeper is waiting for me, as I've no doubt yours is, David. I'll have a word with you next week some time.'

'I shall be at your service.'

Even before he had replaced the phone Audley was weighing the advantages of getting through to the department to have G Tower located quickly against the disadvantages of handing his discovery to others. He rejected the disadvantages almost at once. There just wasn't enough time in the morning for him to do it before driving north. And he knew that secretiveness was another particular occupational vice which he had to watch. Some people tended to become submerged by the facts. He always had to fight the urge simply to keep them to himself.

He nerved himself to override protests. The information service was there to be used, but hardly for apparently esoteric intelligence on a Saturday evening.

But when he got through he was surprised at first by the helpful reception, until it dawned on him that the word really was out. Stocker must have been as good as his promise. So of course they would establish the identity of G Tower, and with the utmost despatch. And then they would phone him back.

And then they would pass on the details to whomsoever else it also concerned . . .

He returned to the kitchen to find Faith laying supper, as domesticated as any of her predecessors.

'Ham and salad again – Mrs Clark says you live on it through the spring and summer . . . Did your Esau deliver the goods?'

'He may have done. I shall know later this evening.'

She stopped work and faced up to him.

'If I'm going to help you, you know, David, you're going to have to take me into your confidence. If that poor man really was killed this afternoon I've a right to know what I'm letting myself in for. And I'd prefer to know what I'm doing.'

'That's reasonable enough. Providing, of course, that I can trust you.'

'You want me to tell you that I'd fight for Queen and Country no matter what?'

'Would you?'

'No, I wouldn't. Would *you*?'

Audley shook his head.

'The same question doesn't apply to me. I'm old-fashioned. But I didn't put the question properly. Can I trust you to trust me?'

Faith made a sour face. 'That's a hard one, isn't it! And a dirty one, too.'

'I don't see why it should be. You'd give me answers on much more difficult questions. You'd tell me that the Americans were wrong in Vietnam. You're sure that Porton is as wicked as Aldermaston. You think moon rockets ought to be beaten into ploughshares. But it doesn't matter, because I'm not putting the question to you – I have to put it to myself.'

He took the cutlery from her and continued the work.

'Who cut my lawn today?'

She shook her head in disbelief. 'What an odd person you are! I cut your lawn for you. When Mrs Clark came with your groceries this morning and found you gone she practically ordered me to do it. She even showed me how to start the mower. What's that got to do with trusting me?'

'Mrs Clark is a good judge of character. If she trusts you with the mower and the lawn, then perhaps I can trust you in other matters. Are you willing to find out exactly what your father did, for better or worse?'

'I want to. And I can't see the harm in that.'

'There could be more to it than that. I told you last night that your father took something. There's a Russian who knows what it was. And he wants it so badly that he's willing to ask us to help him find it. At least, that's what we think he's going to ask us.'

'Is he a good man or a bad man?'

'He's a very important man.'

Faith shivered. 'If good and bad aren't words that mean anything to you, then you'd better not trust me. Because I'd be an idiot to trust *you*.'

Audley caught himself on the very brink of accusing her of naïveté. Of course she was naïve – and so was he to expect anything else. Again, too, that unforgivable crime: if he was to use her he had to persuade her first.

'We just don't know about him, except that he has great power and influence in his own country. And that's why we've got to find out what it is and why it's so important to him. We'd like him for a friend, but we can't trust him. You must see that!'

'It always comes back to trusting people. You never trust them and they never trust you! It's just a game to you!'

'Trust them!' He felt the anger he couldn't stifle tighten his throat. 'Be like Dubcek? Or like Nagy and Maleter? And Jan Masaryk? Christ, woman, we don't have the *right* to trust them.'

He could see the pit ahead of him, but he was no longer able to avoid it. He didn't even want to avoid it now, anyway.

'Of course it's a game. And if everyone played it sensibly we'd be a damn sight better off. It's the people who try to turn the pie-faced noble sentiments and the crude doctrinaire slogans into practice who start the shooting. So you'd better pack up your cosy scruples and your moral dilemmas and take them back to school with you, Miss Jones. They'll look better on a blackboard.'

He paused for breath, and despised himself. There was a flush on her cheeks, the colour spreading as though he had hit her. Shopkeepers and schoolteachers were easy game. And tempting game, too, after the Stockers and Joneses, who could always keep him in his place.

'I'm sorry, Miss Jones. None of that was fair. And you could be right,' he said dully. 'But I do care about the game I play – or used to play. In fact, I think I've been landed with your father because I cared too much about it: I hated to see the Middle East turned into a Tom Tiddler's ground – mostly by your friends the Russians, but by us and the Americans too. I've no right to take it out on you, though.'

She turned, and he thought for a moment that she was simply going to leave the room. But instead she reached for a chair and settled astride it, resting her chin on the back.

'What do you want me to do, then?' she said.

He regarded her with surprise. She had not seemed the sort of person to submit to bullying.

'You mean that you're still willing to help me?'

'More than ever now, David. I don't pretend to understand you. Or maybe it's just that I don't understand what makes someone like you do this sort of thing. But I somehow don't think you'd commit yourself to what was wrong. And I'm sorry I said it was just a game. That was – well, it was far worse than what you said.'

No olive branch could be more fairly offered.

'Let's eat first,' he said, absurdly relieved that she was not going to pack her bags.

As they ate she chattered unselfconsciously about her day – a strange day among strangers in a strange house. It was curious they had all accepted her, the postman, the Co-op milkman and Mrs Clark. Did people take it for granted now that bachelors would have girls around the house from time to time, or was it that she was unselfconscious? Audley found it soothing except that his first false impression of her haughtiness outside Asham churchyard niggled at his sense of contentment. He wasn't usually so far wide of the mark.

There was a dreamlike quality about the meal. It wasn't just that she was so different from Liz – though without her glasses she was probably as pretty, if considerably less well endowed physically. It was rather that behind this normality, behind the milkman's attempt to sell her double cream and Mrs Clark's assumption of her role as Liz's long-delayed successor, was the cold reality.

They were not friends, or even chance acquaintances: they were links in a chain of events going back half a lifetime, joined by a man long dead – and now by a man newly dead. The tranquillity of small talk and washing-up on the draining board was false. Somewhere out there in the growing darkness skilled men were still taking the Dakota to bits. An hour away Morrison was on a slab and Roskill would be waiting for the police surgeon's report; across the Channel Butler was hunting the Belgian who had been scared out of his wits all those years ago. And beyond all of them was Panin.

They were the real world. This was a gentle illusion.

In the end it was the telephone bell which shattered that illusion. He caught Faith's eye on him as he sat willing it to stop, and was startled by the hint of understanding. He shook his head to dispel the idea. Dreams could not be shared so easily. She had more reason to be nervous about any step towards the truth, however much she desired to know it.

The calm, well-bred and rather bored voice on the phone finally snapped him out of his introspection. Dr Audley wished for particulars of G Tower . . .

'A bomb-proof anti-aircraft complex in Berlin, sir. They started building it in the winter of '41. In the Zoological Gardens – south of the Tiergarten, across the

Landwehr Canal. Just beside the zoo's aviaries – nice piece of Teutonic town planning.'

A flak tower. He remembered a monster towering above the ruins of Hamburg in 1948.

'Much bigger than that one, sir. More like a fortress than a flak tower. Every mod. con. – internal power generators, water supplies, the lot . . .

'Main battery on the roof – eight heavy guns and four light batteries. Under them the garrison quarters, with ammunition hoists. Then a military hospital, fully equipped, staff of sixty. Under that the cream of the Staatliche Museum collections, safe as the Bank of England. And then two floors of air raid shelters, with room for 15,000 – though they got twice as many in towards the end. Plus 2,000 dead and wounded. It was safe right up to the end – eight foot of reinforced concrete and steel shutters – but *not* very pleasant . . .'

Audley tried to envisage 30,000 panic-stricken civilians crammed into a concrete box with Russian shells and bombs smashing against its sides.

'But quite safe, as I said. It's even thought that Goebbels planned at one time to direct the defence from there – there was an emergency broadcasting station on the ground floor, and the main communications centre – L Tower, that was – was just nearby. But in the end he stayed at the other end of the Tiergarten . . .'

Audley was no longer listening. Instead his mind was racing back over the previous thirty-six hours, to the one assumption he had been at least reasonably sure of, but which was suddenly crumbling before his eyes.

'. . . also at Friedrichshain, smaller of course. G Tower was by far the biggest. About 130 feet high . . .'

It had been a preconception, of course. And even if it didn't fit the facts any more, it still rang true.

'And there were animals in the zoo right up to the end.' The boredom was replaced by incredulity. 'Bloody lions and hippos mixing it with the Russians, I shouldn't wonder.'

Abstractedly he thanked the man, who seemed quite taken with the Wagnerian last hours of the Thousand Year Reich as it affected the unfortunate beasts in Berlin zoo, and replaced the receiver.

He began to reach down towards his brief-case, but stopped midway. He knew perfectly well what was in the Panin file, which reposed there entirely against regulations. And it was no use pretending that there wasn't a possible link here between Panin and Steerforth, even if it wasn't the sort of link he had envisaged. Indeed, if it made sense in 1945 it made nonsense in 1969.

But it would have to be checked.

Theodore Freisler might well know the answer. But there was one man who would certainly know it. He took his address book from its drawer and looked at the grandfather clock, weighing the lateness of the time against the slightness of his acquaintance with Sir Kenneth Allen. Their meeting in Rome had been strictly social, but nonetheless daunting; Audley had felt intellectually laundered after half an hour's conversation, then weighed up and courteously dismissed as a middle-weight.

But the great man had been on occasion consulted by the department, and whatever he might think of Audley he would never turn him away. Moreover, if the bored voice was now passing on his G Tower information, then Stocker might come to the same conclusion, and he wouldn't hesitate to haul Sir Kenneth from his high table or senior common room. And if Stocker's was the second call – that rewarding possibility was enough to decide him.

When he returned to the kitchen a quarter of an hour later Faith was just finishing the last of the washing-up. She turned towards him with a look of muted expectation which faded as she saw his own puzzled expression.

'Didn't you get what you wanted?'

'What I wanted?' He sat down at the old kitchen table and stared at the scarred and scrubbed wooden surface. 'I didn't get what I expected, certainly. And I got rather more than I expected, too.'

He looked up at her.

'You know, Faith, I think I know what your father's cargo was.'

'. . . we met at Rome at the Egyptian studies symposium, Sir Kenneth.'

'Indeed, I remember you well, Dr Audley.' That beautiful voice was heavy with authority, but utterly free from arrogance. 'Your paper on Shirkuh was admirable. I entirely agree with you that Nur ed-Din and Saladin have taken too much attention from him. But what can I do for you?'

'I think you may be able to help us with a problem we have in the department.'

That made it official, but Sir Kenneth was not a man to be hoodwinked anyway.

'Indeed?'

'I believe you were on the Allied Art Treasure Committee in Berlin in 1945?'

'I was, Dr Audley. A relatively humble member, though.'

'Do you remember G Tower, Sir Kenneth?'

Faith was staring at him.

'The Schliemann Collection.'

She frowned.

'Troy, Faith – Troy! The topless towers and the windy plains – Troy!'

The frown faded. Her jaw dropped a fraction, and then tightened. She said nothing.

'You've heard of Heinrich Schliemann?'

'Of course I've heard of him,' she said sharply. 'He discovered Troy, everyone knows that.'

'More than Troy, Faith. Much more than Troy. He found the royal treasure – one of the greatest treasure troves of all time.

'He stole it from the Turks and he gave it to the Germans. And after the war the Russians found it, and they took it – and they lost it. No one's set eyes on it since the summer of 1945.'

Anger was not an emotion in which Sir Kenneth Allen indulged, but his displeasure was magisterial: '. . . in that matter, Dr Audley, the Russian High Command was something less than straightforward with us. I do not question their removal of the Schliemann Collection from G Tower, or their right to it as spoils of war. They had suffered great loss of their own treasures, great loss. They had the right to a measure of recompense.

'But to remove it – and there is no doubt that they did remove it – and then to allow it to be lost: that was an unpardonable act of carelessness.

'Some of my colleagues still believe that it was never lost, and that it rests in the Kremlin vaults. Mere wishful thinking! If it had survived it would have been restored to East Berlin, to the Staatliche Museum, long ago . . .'

Faith sat down opposite him, her shoulders drooping.

Then she braced herself. 'You said you think you know? But how sure are you – and how do you know, anyway?'

'Nikolai Andrievich Panin, Faith – that Russian I told you about. He's my clue. You see, I thought if I could find out just what he was doing in Berlin back in 1945, before he came looking for your father's Dakota, it might give us a line on what was supposed to be in the plane.'

Her eyes widened. 'It was the same man *then*?'

'That's really what all the fuss is about. He was just a nobody then, doing what he was told. But he's very far from being a nobody now.'

'And what was he doing – when he was a nobody?'

'He was a soldier. One of the very few who made it all the way from Stalingrad to Berlin. But before that he was an archaeologist, and there's only one thing that would interest him in G Tower.'

'G Tower?'

'That was where he was working after the Russians took the city. It was an anti-aircraft fort as big as a city block. A fort and a hospital and an air raid shelter. And a treasure house.'

'. . . Coins, tapestries and sculpture were recovered, but not the Schliemann Collection. All the Staatliche has now of Troy is a pathetic handful of minor objects.*

'And what makes the tragedy absolute, Dr Audley, is that but for England's stupidity the collection need never have gone to Berlin in the first place. Schliemann offered everything to the British Museum – as a gift. And Winter Jones turned him down . . . He turned him down because there was no room for it!'*

Fate had been cruel to the treasure of Troy. The Russians and the French had bid high for it. The Greeks, having overlooked it in one sack, claimed it by right of Homer. But all three nations had combined to help Schliemann resist Turkey's demand for the restoration of her property, each in the hope of receiving it as a reward.

And the British turned it down as an inconvenience!

'The irony of it, Dr Audley, is that it would have been safe in every museum except the one which acquired it . . .'*

So the Germans got it, only to lose it to the Russians, who in turn lost it (in Sir Kenneth's considered view) to some grubby black marketeer who melted it down for its simple gold value.

King Priam's gold. Hecuba's crown, and rings for

101

Helen's fingers. The drinking cup of Paris and the weapons of Hector.

'*Of course it didn't really come from Homer's Troy: it was a thousand years older than that. But that is beside the point, Dr Audley. It was beautiful and it was beyond price . . .*'

Someone else had said that already: little Morrison, that very afternoon – echoing Steerforth.

Audley looked across the table at Steerforth's daughter, the offspring of a man who might well have pulled off one of the great art thefts of history. She presented a picture of dejection, and he sympathized with her: it was hardly a distinction for a respectable chemistry mistress.

'Cheer up, Faith! I could be wrong.'

She regarded him unhopefully.

'You don't think you are wrong, though, do you?'

'I could be. In a way I shall be surprised if it is the Schliemann treasure Panin's after. Up to now I'd discounted the possibility of mere loot – it shouldn't interest the Russians as much as this. And it certainly shouldn't interest a man like our Russian. He's got far bigger matters to attend to than a heap of golden trinkets stolen from a museum.'

She shook her head at him. 'You really don't understand what you've been saying, David, do you? It's just a heap of golden trinkets to you! I suppose you've never read about what Schliemann discovered.'

She didn't wait for him to answer.

'I know you know about Schliemann. Everyone knows it – it's a good capitalist legend. Inside every banker there's a romantic archaeologist! And one in the eye for all the experts who said Troy was a fable!'

She thought for a moment, before speaking.

'When I was a little girl I read a book which described your heap of trinkets. I can't remember all the details now, but I do remember one bit about the jewellery.

'There was a golden diadem, David, one of a pair. All gold wire and little rings and leaves and tiny ornaments. There were over 16,000 pieces in it. And that was just one item in the hoard. Just one item! And there were *thousands* of golden objects. Earrings and rings and bracelets and buttons and cups and ornaments.'

She paused. 'Nowadays people don't take Schliemann very seriously – he dug up the wrong Troy, and everything he dug up he thought was part of Homer, when it wasn't at all.

'I expect the real Trojan war was just a squalid little squabble over trade and taxes – not at all like Homer's war either. Nothing like the legend at all. But the legend was glorious and heroic and the treasure he found fitted it perfectly, so in one way he wasn't wrong at all. And if your Russian archaeologist is half a real man – if he's got any heart at all – he'd never rest while there was a chance of giving it all back to the world . . .'

She shrugged helplessly. 'And that's what my father stole – and it's not just loot, David. It's not just stealing from someone: it's stealing from the whole world. It's – it's a crime against humanity.'

Her sudden anger astonished him almost as much as her unaccountable knowledge. Scientists, even female ones, were in his experience neither so vehement nor so well-informed on classical art.

And now she was pacing up and down the kitchen.

'My gallant father! The bastard!'

He felt bound to check her, to defend the unfortunate man, whatever he'd done.

'Hold on there, Faith. We still don't know that he took it. And if he did, we don't know that he realized what he was taking. It was just loot to him – stolen gold for the taking. And he wasn't the only one who reckoned there was something owing to him for services rendered!'

She turned on him.

'Didn't know? Didn't know! Oh, David – he knew! He knew all too bloody well! He knew because I know – doesn't it surprise you that I know so much about Troy?'

Again she didn't wait to be asked, but stormed furiously on: 'I know because I inherited a big, beautiful book from him all about Heinrich Schliemann and his wonderful discovery of Troy. And I loved that book because it was his – I've read it a dozen times. When I was little I even wanted to be an archaeologist because of it – that's a laugh now, isn't it!

'I found all his books in the attic when I was little. Mostly he had rotten taste – pulpy thrillers with a bit of pornography that I didn't understand, printed abroad. And a set of unread Dickens.

'But there was this one beautiful book that I adored. To me *that* was his real book. And it was, wasn't it! He must have bought it to find out just exactly what he'd got his dirty hands on.'

She stopped, and looked at him in anguish.

'Clever David!' she said bitterly. 'You guessed right, didn't you? And now you've got the one extra little bit of evidence you need from the villain's daughter. But you did try to soften the blow, you really did. And that was kind of you.'

He pitied her. She must have known subconsciously the moment he had mentioned Troy, and then had blundered on until her conscious mind had picked up its own warning signals. It was a cruel way to come to the truth.

And what made it worse was that he still couldn't blame Steerforth in his heart. It *had* been just loot to him. But to her it would always be the unforgivable crime because it had betrayed childhood love and admiration, however she tried to rationalize it.

'Never mind,' he said. 'We'll set the record straight: we'll get it back.'

7

The geese woke Audley from an uneasy, confused dream.

Yet he knew as he woke that it had not been a dream really, for he had never been completely asleep. It had come from the no-man's-land between thought and sleep, a mere jumble of the day's undigested experiences.

He remembered that he had been reading Ceram's *Gods, Graves and Scholars*, which had been the only thing on his shelves which mentioned Schliemann and Troy in any detail. And Ceram's words had fed his tired mind with images – images of the original panic-stricken burial of the treasure, which had been so hasty that the keys were still in the mouldered locks of the boxes; images of the Schliemanns working feverishly and secretly to hack their prize out of the deep trench in the mound at Hissarlik, with the wreckage of six later Troys and three thousand years poised above them.

And images of Steerforth working no less feverishly to hide that prize . . .

And then he had thought irrelevantly of the animals in Berlin zoo, caged not far from the treasure, with the Russian shells bursting about them. Had the Berliners eaten their elephants in the end, like the Parisians in 1870?

It was the beginning of a half-nightmare, which switched back to the trench at Hissarlik. But as he looked down into it, it became the wooden staircase in Morrison's shop. No treasure for Morrison . . .

Then his mind registered the shrieking of Mrs Clark's geese.

At first he thought it was morning, until he saw the

moonlight streaming in through his open windows. The damned birds had woken him once before in the night, protesting at some prowling cat or fox, and there was no stopping them once they had started. All one could do was to shut out as much of the noise as possible.

He reached out for the light switch, only to discover that it no longer seemed to work. He fumbled for his spectacles and shuffled towards the window, cursing under his breath.

He stopped dead a yard from the window, shocked totally awake: someone was crossing a moonlit patch of lawn just beyond the cobbles.

He blinked and drew to one side of the window, covering the lower part of his face with the dark sleeve of his pyjamas – white faces showed up even in darkened windows. The figure, moving delicately across the grass, disappeared into the shadow beside the barn. Ten seconds passed like an age, and then two more shadows crossed the moonlit patch from the driveway entrance to the safety of the barn's shadow.

The geese still cackled angrily and Audley felt his heart thump against his chest. Three was too many for him. He had no gun in the house – he had never needed or desired a gun. Faith was asleep just down the passage. If mere burglary was the intention – God! He hadn't even put the Panin file in the safe. But if it was burglary he might frighten them off by switching on the lights.

But the light hadn't worked, he remembered with a pang of panic. And if it wasn't burglary . . . he saw Morrison again, in unnaturally sharp focus, at the bottom of the stairs. *This sort of thing just doesn't happen!* They'd got no reason – but he didn't know what reason they'd got.

I mustn't think – I must act, he told himself savagely. If you can't fight, run away. If you can't run away – hide!

He whipped his dressing gown from the bed, stuffed

106

the torch from his bedside drawer into his pocket and sprinted down the passage.

She was lying on her side, snoring very softly, one white shoulder picked out by the moonlight. He shook the shoulder urgently.

'Faith! Wake up – and be quiet!' he whispered.

She moaned, and then came to life, startled.

Before she could speak he put the palm of his hand to her mouth.

'We've got visitors,' he hissed as clearly and quietly as he was able. 'Three visitors. We're not going to wait to find out what they want . . . we're going to hide . . . if you understand what I'm saying – nod.'

She nodded, wide-eyed.

'Hide your clothes, smooth down your bed – and I'll meet you outside your room in half a minute!'

She nodded again.

He slipped out of her room and raced down the passage again to his study, blessing the day he had chosen to transfer it to the first floor. Pausing only to grab his brief-case he flew back to his bedroom, hurriedly bundled his clothes into a drawer, and pulled up the bedspread.

Faith was waiting for him, pale in the moonlight and hugging her dressing gown round her. She followed him obediently as he made his way to the deeply-recessed window at the head of the stairs.

Audley handed her the brief-case and the torch. Very gently he released the heavy iron catches which held back the shutters and closed out the moonlight. Then he took the left-hand catch and began to turn it anti-clockwise.

Oh God, he prayed, it's always worked before – let it work now!

He gritted his teeth and pulled. Very slowly, and with the smallest subdued rumble, the whole section of the wall between the window and the carved oak newel post which ran from floor to ceiling began to pivot outwards.

Behind it was a second wall of smooth stone, broken only by a narrow aperture set low down in the outer corner.

'In you go,' he whispered. 'Crawl along for about ten feet and you'll come to some stone stairs. Wait there – and mind your head!'

She stood irresolutely, looking from him to the pitch-black hole.

'Where does it go?' she whispered back urgently.

'For God's sake, don't argue – remember Morrison!'

Reluctantly she bent down and wriggled into the aperture, shining the torch ahead of her. For a moment Audley stood in the darkness, straining his ears. The geese had temporarily run out of abuse, and the silence was thick and heavy. Then from somewhere below him, inside the house, there was a muffled click.

Audley pulled the wall almost shut and eased himself backwards into the hole. Mercifully it was always easier to shut than to open. He reached up and felt for the iron ring on the inner face, and then fumbled for the locking bar. They could turn the iron catch until domesday now.

Awkwardly he crawled backwards along the cold, dusty stone floor until he was able to lift his head and turn round at the foot of the flight of stone steps. Faith was sitting hunched about halfway up.

She shone the torch into his eyes.

'David, I'm not going a step further until you tell me where the hell we are.'

'We're perfectly safe now.'

'I don't care how safe we are. Where are we? What is this – place?'

'It's a priest's hole.'

'A priest's hole?' She shone the torch around her. Cobwebs and dust and rough stone.

'Go on up the stairs. But mind your head until you get to the top. There's a room there.'

At the top of the steps they emerged into a tiny room,

barely big enough for the polythene-covered mattress which was its sole contents, apart from a pickaxe and a battered pewter candlestick with a new candle in it and a box of matches beside it. The room was doorless and windowless, but there was a faint draught of air from two small pigeonholes. It was dry, but cold.

Audley lit the candle and turned off the torch. Then he stripped off the plastic covering from the mattress to reveal an old army blanket.

'Wrap that round yourself,' he said, squatting on the end of the mattress.

She looked at him in the light of the spluttering flame. From her expression he was not sure whether she was going to burst into tears or laughter.

'A priest's hole! I've never seen one before!'

She wasn't going to cry.

'It's not surprising, really. It's an early sixteenth century house, and this was an obstinately Catholic district. Once it was a much bigger house too – we're living in what used to be the servants' quarters, next to the old barn. The rest was burnt down years ago.'

'David – it's romantic! Did the secret pass from father to son, right down to you?'

'Quite the opposite, I'm afraid. My family didn't move here until the Prince Regent's time, and no one told us any secrets. I'm probably the first person to know about this room for centuries. And I only found it by accident.'

'By accident? You opened that crazy door, or whatever it was, by accident?'

'Nobody opens that door by accident, Faith. It's designed not to be found even if you're looking for it.

'No, they built this room by adding a false wall to the end of the barn, where it joins the house. Except for this room and the passage to it, that wall's over ten feet of solid masonry, only the barn's so long you don't notice

109

it until you measure it accurately. And that's how I found it.'

He pulled his dressing gown tightly round him. In the little stone box of a room spring had not yet begun to thaw out winter.

'I had an idea of building a squash court in the barn. It cost too much, but I found out that the outside length didn't match the inside one. I had a feeling that there might be a room here then – no one builds walls ten feet thick. But I couldn't even find an echo. I had to cheat in the end – I broke through the roof, and then through the ceiling.'

He pointed to an irregular patch of new plaster above her.

'So I learnt how the door worked from the inside: the catch turns a diagonal bolt on a ratchet. But you can lock the bolt from the inside – and there were dressed stones ready to pile up in the entrance hole so there wouldn't be any echo there if the priest-hunters started knocking around.

'And the whole wall there is wedge shaped – the false wall – and built on an iron plate. The old owners probably had servants to help swing it out, but I've fixed a little roller at the bottom, underneath. And the whole thing pivots on the newel-post. It's – rather clever.'

She smiled at him in the candlelight. 'There was a good Catholic David Audley in Elizabethan times, obviously! Did you find any relics in here?'

'Relics?' He stared at her. It was hardly the moment to admit that he had actually hoped for long-lost treasure, and had been bitterly disappointed at finding only a few bits of worm-eaten wood and a candlestick. 'No, I'm sorry to say that the hole was very empty.'

'And this mattress? Is that a precaution against . . . visitors?'

'Good God, no! This sort of thing's never happened to

me before. I simply slept in here one night, out of curiosity. I never thought I'd have to take refuge here.'

'Who are they, David – those men outside?'

'I haven't the faintest idea, Faith. This is out of my experience, I'm afraid. But after what happened this afternoon – after what may have happened, I mean – I didn't fancy staying to find out. I know that's not very heroic – but I'm just not heroic . . .'

She put a hand on his arm. 'But very sensible. And far too good-natured to remind me that you had me hanging round your neck anyway!'

She was certainly an understanding wench, thought Audley. And more than that!

'If I'm not heroic, then you make up for it,' he said. 'Not many young women I can think of would sit here as cool as you are with three Russ – ' He stopped too late.

'Russians?' She completed the word for him. 'Is that really what you think they are?'

He shook his head uneasily.

'It doesn't add up, Faith. It just doesn't add up. Morrison – and now this. And all for a heap of museum loot – I don't care how valuable you say it is.'

She sighed. 'You still don't understand, do you, David? If it was some silly plan for some silly rocket, or the details of a secret treaty, you'd believe it at once. But with something that is truly worthwhile you just can't believe your eyes. Well, perhaps your high-up Russian doesn't have such schoolboy values. Perhaps he thinks this is more important – and naturally he doesn't trust *you*!

'But we've been all through that, haven't we! And as for being cool – I'm absolutely frozen! How long do we have to stay in this arctic hole? Your old priests must have been made of stern stuff.'

He stood up stiffly. Another hour might be enough, but in the meantime he ought to try to make her comfortable.

'Here – you stretch out on the mattress, and I'll wrap the blanket around you,' he said.

'What are you going to do?'

He wrapped the loose ends of the rug round her legs. 'You try and snatch some sleep. I'll be quite all right sitting against the wall.'

Actually he was not all right. The unevenness of the wall gouged into his back and the cold stones spread their chill through him. He hunched his shoulders and wrapped his arms tightly across his body.

'David?'

He grunted.

'What's the pick for?'

'The pick?' He tried to think. 'Just insurance. If the door jammed we'd have a job getting out.'

'Couldn't we shout through the air holes?'

'The air holes have got a double-right angle in them. It might be days before anyone heard anything.'

She shivered, and he relapsed into unhappy silence. The door jamming had been his special nightmare in the past. That it had worked at all had always rather surprised him. If it failed now, forcing him to hack his way out – that would be the ultimate humiliation. Was it Murphy's Law or Finagle's Law that recognized the malevolence of inanimate objects towards human beings?

'David?'

He grunted again, miserably – what could the woman want?

'Your teeth are chattering.'

He gritted his teeth. 'Sorry.'

There was a pause.

'You can come in with me if you like, under the blanket.'

Audley sat bolt upright, unable for a moment to believe his ears. But there was no mistaking the invitation: she was holding up the edge of the blanket. The flame of the

112

candle flickered and her shadow danced on the wall behind her.

At length he shook his head.

'I'm cold and I'm tired and I feel a hundred years old, my girl. But I'm still flesh and blood. And when I crawl under a blanket with a woman it'll never be to stop my teeth chattering. You just try and go to sleep.'

She raised herself on one elbow, looking at him.

'I'm cold and tired too, David. And I'm frightened and I've mixed myself up in I don't know what. And I think my father stole something so big it makes me sick just to think of it . . . And – and I'm flesh and blood too.'

She tossed back her pale blonde hair and he saw with surprise that same curiously haughty stare which he remembered from the churchyard. Yet the offer of comfort in exchange for comfort could hardly have been more explicit. Bafflement, rather than any last ditch shred of conscience or caution, held him back.

She wasn't wearing her glasses!

The contradiction which had plagued him since she had knocked on his door the previous night dissolved: it wasn't haughtiness – she simply couldn't see him clearly!

Without stopping to analyse the curious mixture of relief and lust and protective affection, he reached out for her, and she met him halfway, and more than halfway.

'You silly, silly man,' she whispered in his ear.

He pressed her gently backwards, feeling the old, long-lost excitement: the softness and firmness of her small breasts, the length of her, the smell of her hair mingling with the faint perfume he had sensed in her room.

She was shrugging herself out of her dressing gown, out of her nightdress – as it came over her head, loosing the pale hair, he felt the skin move over her ribs, skin that impossibly combined warmth with coolness.

The candle was extinguished suddenly – knocked over, snuffed out, it no longer mattered. And the tiny secret room was no longer cold: it was no longer tiny and no longer a room. It was a velvety nothingness moving in its own time and space, starless and endless, with nothing outside it or beyond it, spiralling into infinity.

And then she was holding him tightly and he felt the rough blanket on his shoulders and the sweat prickle on his chest, and he lay holding her until the darkness stopped revolving around them.

She moved into the crook of his arm and he reached across her to feel for the candle.

The matches spilt as he fumbled for them, one-handed, and he struck one against the stone wall. She lay unmoving beside him with the blanket drawn down, unmoving, strands of hair lying damp across her forehead.

'It can't happen often like that, can it?' she said slowly, without looking at him. 'It can't be so good?'

'I don't know. Never before for me.'

'Nor for me.'

Maybe it was only once in a lifetime, he thought. Maybe only when the need and the desire and the fear are united in exactly those proportions. And the person?

He looked down at her again, and then drew the blanket over that little schoolgirl's bosom, so different from his old imagined ideal.

My God, he thought: what have I done? I've laid John Steerforth's daughter – maybe got him a grandchild!

She turned towards him, with a small, satisfied smile which faded directly into seriousness as she saw his expression.

'Was I a disappointment then?' she said.

'You know very well you weren't! But that doesn't make it – ' he searched for the word ' – right.'

It was the wrong word, and she laughed.

'Dear out-of-date David! If it's like that it *has* to be right. That's what it's all about!'

'It's not right to mix business and pleasure.'

'Business and pleasure ought to be mixed – why on earth shouldn't they be? And it was my fault, anyway. You only did what you had to, in the line of duty.'

She was mocking him, and she was wholly irresistible now. He kissed her softly on the mouth, then on the breast, and took her in his arms again and lay still beside her.

'That wasn't in the line of duty, David,' she said very quietly.

'No, Faith. That was just for me.'

'Then I think I'll go to sleep, David, because nothing nicer can possibly happen to me now . . . and I couldn't possibly be safer anywhere than here, could I?'

She snuggled against him.

'You don't think those old priests would mind, do you? Mind our doing this – here?' she said drowsily after a while.

Audley considered the possibility. They had been men of the world, although they had renounced all the good things for the dangers. They must have understood human fears and needs better than those who had no need of such refuges. This sin, of all sins, they could absolve and forgive: the sin of love.

'They'd understand,' he said soothingly. 'Go to sleep.'

8

In the end he had drifted off into an exhausted sleep, no longer cold but wedged uncomfortably with one shoulder against the wall to ensure her comfort. And when he came slowly back to wakefulness he found that he was neither able to reach the torch – the candle had guttered out – nor see his watch, which was on the wrist of the arm she was using as a pillow.

There were nagging aches in his shoulder, back and legs, and a larger uneasiness in his mind about the day ahead. But with this girl in his arms he could not feel unhappy any more, and he delayed moving until he was sure of the faint reflected glimmer in the pigeonhole in the outer wall – that was as close as the room ever came to daylight.

Even then, when he had woken her, he managed to get her dressing gown over her shoulders and into his own before switching on the torch: no harm in salvaging a little dignity on such a morning after.

When he was sure she was fully awake he explained his plan of action.

She nodded. 'What you're saying is that it comes down to burglary, booby-traps or – what do you call them – bugs?'

'Most probably bugs. At least on the phones. They've invented some extraordinary little devices – and I wouldn't know where to look for them. We shall have to get the experts in to search the place. As soon as I've dressed I'll walk down the road to the phone box and get some help.'

He felt his way gingerly down the narrow stairway and

carefully drew back the long iron bolt. The door-wall swung open easily, with only that same subdued rumble.

The house was perfectly silent, with the morning sunlight streaming in through the windows to dispel the memory of the night's events like a dream. Nothing was disturbed, nothing out of place. He had to tell himself that the three shadows on the lawn had not been imagination. And then the distant raucous screams of the geese reminded him: now he felt an absurd gratitude to those ridiculous, bad-tempered creatures.

There was a reassuring matter-of-factness about the department's duty man, to whom he explained matters ten minutes later. It might have been an everyday occurrence – perhaps it was, for all he knew!

He didn't question Audley's going to earth in his own house, either. Which was just as well: that was one secret he intended to keep, now it had proved its value.

'Forty minutes – we'll have a team with you then, Dr Audley. Er – yours is an old house, isn't it?'

He said it was, wondering how they knew and why it was important.

'No cover story's going to be very convincing on a Sunday morning, but we'll do the best we can. We'll send you a team of woodworm, dry rot and damp-proofing specialists,' said the duty man, answering his unasked questions. 'At least they'll make a nice change from electricians and gas men. They'll be with you on the dot!'

He found Faith hunched over the kitchen table, still in her much-crumpled dressing gown, nursing a mug of tea. She looked somewhat battered, with dark rings under her eyes and hair unbrushed, a far cry from yesterday's cool, self-confident self.

She gave him a bleary version of the now familiar short-sighted-haughty stare, which forced him to smile inwardly.

117

'I took a risk and plugged the kettle in,' she said hoarsely. 'Without a cup of tea I'd have died anyway, so it was a necessary risk.'

Unaccountably Audley felt on top of the world now, better than he had felt for days. But it would be too cruel of him to admit it at that moment.

'I don't feel very sprightly myself, to tell the truth,' he lied.

She raised her eyes from the mug.

'To tell the truth, I feel thoroughly – '

She stopped in mid-sentence, realizing too late the implication of what she was saying, but making things much worse by leaving the sentence in the air.

He couldn't stop himself from laughing as the colour spread across her cheeks. She buried her face in her hands, and for a cold moment he thought she was weeping. Then he realized her shoulders were shaking with laughter, not tears.

Evidently laughter was the therapy she needed, and it was reassuring to discover that she could laugh against herself. It seemed perfectly natural to take her in his arms, without passion or urgency. She melted against him momentarily, and then held him away from her, shaking her head.

'I'm not grumbling!' she said. 'It was a unique experience! But next time I'd prefer a more conventional setting, I think . . .'

She put her hand to her mouth suddenly and glanced about the kitchen. Audley realized he had forgotten the possibility of bugs himself, and beckoned her out into the garden.

'They'll be here in half an hour, then!' she said in panic when he told her his news. 'God – and I must look a sight!'

* * *

And it was, indeed, exactly thirty minutes later that a smart red Bedford van squealed to a halt on the cobbles. KILL-AND-CURE it promised in bold letters emblazoned on a board fastened to its side panel – 'Instant death to wood-borers – relief from rising damp.'

A plump, ginger-haired man in an ill-fitting suit climbed out of the van, accompanied by a younger assistant with trailing hair and a Ringo Starr moustache. They surveyed the house with professional disinterest.

The ginger man rapped sharply on the kitchen door.

'Kill-and-Cure, sir,' he announced loudly. 'About your request for estimates for our woodworm treatment and electro-osmotic damp-courses. I have your letter here, sir – Dr Audley, it is, isn't it – and my authorization to make a Sunday call. "Sunday stipulated" it says here.'

He held open a red folder for Audley to see. It did certainly contain an authorization, complete with identification. But no mention was made in it of Sunday or woodworm or electro-osmosis, whatever that was.

The ginger man inclined his head slightly towards the van, and Audley followed him outside.

'I'm Maitland, Dr Audley. That's Jenkins with all the hair. Three men, you said. And they had plenty of time in the house.'

Audley nodded.

'But you think it possible they may not know that you observed them.'

'It's possible. I can't be sure.'

'Well, we won't spoil their fun, just in case. Mr Roskill's coming to take you to London, but we'll check the cars first just in case you want to use them. And the cars'll tell us just how good they are.'

He nodded to Jenkins and gestured towards the cars in the barn. The hairy young man pulled a bag of tools out of the van and trotted off obediently, whistling tunelessly.

'The cars?'

'No one can resist cars these days, Dr Audley. If they really don't like you they'll have done a little surgery on the steering or the brakes. But that's not very likely – much too chancy. A "Bo Peep", though – so they can follow you at a safe distance – that's as near a certainty as dammit is to swearing.'

Jenkins had disappeared into Faith's Mini.

'He won't be long,' said Maitland happily. 'There aren't many places in a Mini. Not many clever places, anyway.'

They made their way back into the house.

'Now, sir,' said Maitland loudly again, 'if you don't mind giving us the run of the house while you're out we'll measure up for the damp-course, internal walls included, and let you have our estimate within three days. But if you could spare time to show me round once before you go – '

As they toured the house Maitland treated him to a continuous, detailed and persuasive catalogue of Kill-and-Cure's techniques, services and previous triumphs. Only the fact that at the same time he virtually ignored the tell-tale holes in the beams and rising damp stains on the walls spoilt the illusion; instead he gently poked and pried into drapes and under furniture.

At length, he led Audley back outside.

'Well, if you've been bugged it's been done by experts,' he said. 'There's nothing obvious to be seen.'

Audley experienced a sinking feeling. Nothing could be more humiliating than a false alarm – if his visitors turned out to be innocent locals looking for unconsidered trifles. And it would also make a sad comedy of what had passed in the hole . . .

'Maybe Jenkins has struck oil,' continued Maitland.

Audley followed him unwillingly towards the barn. Jenkins had evidently finished with the Mini, which was in itself a bad sign. His legs protruded from beneath the

Cambridge. Beside them a transistor radio blared insanely.

The ginger-haired man casually kicked one of the legs.

'You down there! Any joy?'

Jenkins eased himself from under the car. He had certainly struck oil, which he proceeded to rub off with a filthy rag, without much success.

'That Mini'll never pass its MoT test next time,' he observed cheerfully. 'Shocking state underneath! Never buy an old Mini. Old Minis are like – '

He stopped talking and stared past them.

Audley swung round to find Faith standing in the barn doorway.

But it was a very different Faith from the morning-after one he had last seen – and different, too, from the earlier Faiths, funereal, tweedy and jeaned.

He had asked her to dress for action, and that was exactly what she had done: the sage-green medium mini dress in what looked like suède combined expensive simplicity and provocation. The pale hair was pinned up at the back in a vertical roll – was that what Liz had once described as a French pleat? And the blue-tinted glasses completed the tantalizing don't-touch look.

Certainly the final product had a dynamic effect on Jenkins, who couldn't be expected to know that the line of those breasts now owed more to art than nature.

'And what's wrong with my car?' she inquired sharply, glasses tilted arrogantly.

Jenkins looked questioningly at Audley.

'Miss Jones is aware of the general situation,' said Audley.

Jenkins relaxed. 'Well, in that case,' he said in dulcet public school tones, 'she'd better not go visiting anyone important.'

He held out his open hand to reveal what looked like a dirty Oxo cube with a silver drawing pin stuck in it.

This, presumably, was what a 'Bo Peep' looked like. Maitland lifted it gently out of Jenkins's palm and held it close to his eye.

'Little beauty, isn't it?' Jenkins spoke admiringly. 'Nicest little navigational aid I've seen in months, nestling in its little bed of mud and rust! If it had acquired a bit of genuine mud I just might not have spotted it, not straight away at least. But they had to make do with some home-made mud of their own, which was rather careless of them.'

Maitland cut through his enthusiasm: 'And the Cambridge?'

'I haven't found it yet – but it's there somewhere. They've got more options in a bigger car.'

Maitland turned to Audley. 'That settles it, then. They wouldn't send three men just to fix the cars. One on the cars, one in the house and one to keep watch. You can take it from me they mean business, Dr Audley.'

'Have you taken the – whatever it is out of my car?' said Faith uneasily. 'Is it safe to drive?'

Jenkins grinned. 'Safe, but so dull, Miss Jones! It'd be much better fun to put it back again. I mean, now we know about it we can take them on a tour of Britain any time – it's the only chance some of their chaps get to see the beauties of the countryside. Saving your presence, of course!'

She regarded him disdainfully. 'Do you think you could turn down your radio,' she said coldly. 'It's getting on my nerves.'

His grin widened. 'Sorry, lady,' he replied in his Kill-and-Cure persona's accents. Then he switched back: 'I don't enjoy it any more than you do, actually. But I haven't checked on this barn yet. Pop's marvellous for blotting out conversation in the meantime.'

With his hair cut he would be an uncommonly presentable young man, thought Audley enviously. And more her age.

He moved to cut off the conversation: 'Is the – device – a Russian one?' He couldn't bring himself to use the colloquial term they had used, all too aware that his knowledge of gadgetry was minimal.

Jenkins shook his head. 'Now there you have me. I'd assume it was – it's a first-rate job. You've no reason to think the Americans are interested in you, have you?'

'Why the Americans?' asked Audley, shaking his head in turn.

'Then we'd be in real trouble: the Americans are streets ahead of the Russians. They don't just miniaturize things now – they make them look like something else! I'd have to start unscrewing nuts and bolts to find out if they really were just nuts and bolts.'

Audley remembered that he had initialled a report on the latest developments in such equipment a few days before, without reading it. It had not been in his field then: he wished it wasn't in it now.

But he was saved from further embarrassment by Roskill's appearance at the wheel of a gleaming Triumph which made his own Austin seem depressingly dowdy. Roskill was also more Faith's age, he thought gloomily. And more her style, too. He made Audley feel as shabby as the Austin.

But that was an undignified and unprofitable line of thought. What had happened during the night certainly didn't give him special rights over the girl. Young women set less store on physical relationships these days; it wasn't even as though he had been Faith's first lover. He couldn't even decide whether he was glad or sorry about that, but it was an unarguable fact.

Maitland was talking to him though.

'We'll give the house a thorough going-over, Dr Audley. And when we've finished we'll set someone to keep his eye on the place, and he'll let you have a copy of my report. We'll give you two clear rooms – your study and the kitchen – but we'll leave the rest in place. That may keep them happy for a time. After all – well, these bugs have a limited life span, and they'll know soon enough that we've tumbled to them, likely as not.'

That was to be expected. Even in his own limited sphere Audley knew that advantages were ephemeral. Better to assume the worst quickly.

'And don't trust the telephone any more,' added Maitland. 'I can't guarantee that at all.'

It was the sort of nightmare Audley had never expected to find himself in, but it had to be borne with equanimity. He thanked the man – it was obviously a more high-powered team than he had first thought – and turned to introduce Faith to Roskill.

But he saw at once that he was already too late; they were in deep conversation.

Faith turned to him. 'I took the liberty of introducing myself to Mr Roskill, Dr Audley,' she said with a malicious deadpan formality. 'I told him that I was one of your team now, but I think he still wants a reassurance from you.'

Roskill looked down at his feet, and Audley thought the better of him for it. The use of amateurs in his profession, no matter how attractive, was quite properly anathema to him. It was not that they were stupid, but rather that their ignorance of the basic rules of procedure made them at once dangerous and vulnerable.

'Miss Jones has one unique advantage over us, Hugh,' he explained. 'She's her father's daughter – and that may prove very useful to us. And I'll be with her all the time, in any case.'

Roskill conceded the matter with a graceful nod in Faith's direction. 'Nothing personal, Miss Jones. It's simply that I've also got some concrete information to contribute now, even if I haven't had such an exciting night as you have.'

Audley was glad that she had chosen to wear tinted glasses, only to find that it was he whom Roskill was observing speculatively.

He started guiltily.

'The post-mortem on Morrison?'

'My report's in the car. But I'd rather you read it on the way. We've got quite a way to go, and not a lot of time.'

The inside of the Triumph was like a pilot's cockpit. Evidently Roskill was a car enthusiast – and he was beyond doubt a skilled driver, for no unskilful one could drive so consistently fast and stay alive. Audley tore his eyes from the roadside which was flashing by so terrifyingly, and started to unzip the plastic folder Roskill had handed to him. Then he stopped; it was always better to hear a verbal report if possible – reports could not answer questions. And it would serve to bring home the realities of the situation to Faith, if that was still necessary. It might slow down this hair-raising drive, too!

'Did he fall, or was he pushed?' he inquired.

'Neither,' replied Roskill, slowing down not in the least. 'He was dead when he was slung down those stairs.'

He changed gears with casual skill, and drifted the car coolly round a badly-cambered bend with an ease Audley envied bitterly. How was it that some people could bring machines alive, and then achieve a symbiosis with them?

'But you were right, Dr Audley,' Roskill continued. 'It was an accident, most likely. He actually died of heart failure – he had a heart condition that only needed the right shock to set it off.'

'And that shock was – ?'

'Somebody slappped him around a bit. Not hard, but hard enough. Made his nose bleed. We frightened him,

125

but we weren't in any hurry. Someone else was, apparently.'

'They'd have hit him to make him tell them something?' asked Faith.

'That's right, Miss Jones. He'd just spoken to us, and he knew we were OHMS. He'd know that his next visitors weren't official – but he also knew that we were coming back soon. So he might have tried to stall them and that was very unwise of him.'

'Unwise?'

Roskill was silent for a moment. Then he spoke more seriously: 'Miss Jones, most people think that types like me are just like – the men on the other side. They think we're just tools, like a gun or a fighter; same basic object, just a different make. But it isn't quite true, you know.'

'You're good and they're bad?'

Audley wriggled uncomfortably. The old argument was rearing its head.

But Roskill avoided it.

'I'm bound by laws, very strict laws, and they aren't. In this country, anyway.'

'But you'd stretch those laws.'

'Stretch – maybe. But break – never! With a free press and civil liberties I wouldn't even if I wanted to. Which I don't, oddly enough.'

Audley intervened. 'Hugh means that if Morrison had refused to talk to us there isn't a thing we could have done about it. And there aren't many places in the world where that's the case. That's why you're coming up to Knaresborough with us, as I told you: because I've a feeling that Tierney won't be panicked like Morrison.'

Roskill nodded.

'True – but that isn't really what I meant to say, Miss Jones.

'I meant to say that if ever you *should* be in Morrison's situation, don't try to be brave or clever. Just tell 'em what they want to know. Sing like a canary.'

'I'll remember your advice, Mr Roskill.'

'It was just a thought. And please call me Hugh – everyone else does.'

'Well, then, Hugh – what was it they wanted to find out from that poor man? David didn't seem to think that he had much of value to tell – except that he knew my father brought the treasure in.'

The speed of the Triumph dropped all of three mph, only to rise sharply. Audley remembered from the Dassault interview that Roskill had flown fighters: he drove exactly as one would expect a fighter pilot to drive.

'Treasure?' said Roskill innocently.

Audley told him briefly about the Schliemann Collection, and was exceedingly gratified to find that his information was received with the same caution as he had accorded it. This not only vindicated his attitude, he reflected, despising the jealousy he was unable to stifle; it relegated Hugh to his own level in Faith's eyes.

'All this trouble for a load of museum exhibits!' The prospect seemed to amuse Roskill, and although Audley refrained from turning to look at Faith he could sense her bristling on the back seat.

'All what trouble?' she asked.

Roskill gave Audley a quick sidelong glance.

'That's the thing that's been disturbing me more than somewhat, Dr Audley: the priority service we've been getting. I'm used to being told to get on with it, and mind the expenses. But ever since that JIC fellow set eyes on me it's been all "Ask and ye shall receive" – and I don't like it!'

'The Schliemann treasure – ' began Faith.

'The Schliemann treasure may be the biggest thing since Tutankhamen, Miss Jones. I'm sure it's enough to set all the thieves in Europe drooling – '

Roskill stopped for several seconds, conscious at once

that he had dropped a brick. Then he plunged on.

' – But it isn't the sort of thing that gets me out of bed. And certainly not Dr Audley here. And *never* the other lot – them least of all.'

Faith opened her mouth to speak and then closed it suddenly. She had evidently realized that she had let slip the treasure ahead of schedule, although Audley had given her no instructions about it. But like the admirable young woman she was, she had caught herself in time before mentioning Panin.

She glanced at him and he smiled at her. Not so much out of gratitude at finding a woman who could hold her tongue – it was high time that Hugh was introduced to Panin, anyway – as because she had heightened his regard for her. It was a new thing for him to desire and admire a woman at the same time.

'There's one man who might be interested,' he began. Strictly speaking he ought to get Stocker's clearance before telling Hugh about Panin. But the cat would be out of the bag on Tuesday in any case.

Hugh listened, nodding at intervals.

'Well, that's a bit more like it!' he said at length. 'But I still don't quite understand why he's so worked up about it. Is there a chance he's going to defect?'

That possibility had already passed very fleetingly through Audley's mind, only to be rejected utterly. It was not so much unlikely as plain ridiculous. Defection was for the system's victims – for intellectuals like Kuznetsov and poor devils in the field like Khokhlov and Gouzenko. It wasn't for the men who made the system work, the coming men.

'Not a chance,' he replied flatly.

'I only asked,' said Roskill unrepentantly. 'The word is that with the Czechs and the Rumanians and the Chinese – and the Americans in Space – they're all at sixes and sevens over there. If I was one of 'em, I'd be looking for a cosy billet.'

But not Panin, thought Audley. The Russians were in an unhappy situation not unknown in the West: they had fallen into the hands of a junta of second-raters, all jockeying for power. It might be a mere historical accident, or it might be a basic built-in defect of the one-party system, which admitted another Stalin as the only alternative. Either way the prospect was quietly terrifying.

But Panin was not a second-rater. More like a first-rate Father Joseph looking for his Richelieu. Or maybe a potential Richelieu himself . . .

'But you wanted to know what Morrison knew that might have been valuable, Miss Jones,' said Roskill, sensibly changing the subject. 'They might have wanted to know how far we'd got, of course. But more likely they wanted the addresses of the other crew members – Tierney the second pilot and Maclean the navigator. Right, Dr Audley?'

'Do you think they got them?'

'Probably not, Miss Jones. I think Morrison's heart gave out on them inopportunely – which is perhaps one reason why you had visitors last night!'

Faith digested the sequence of events which had brought her to the priest's hole. Audley could almost hear her mind working, although the dark glasses gave away nothing. He wanted to tell her that it wasn't so; that it was fear and the need for an anodyne, not death, which had thrown them together. But there was nothing he could say.

Finally she spoke: 'Then logically, if they are at all efficient, they should be following us now.'

Audley thought it highly unlikely that anyone was capable of following Hugh Roskill's Triumph.

'That's all taken care of,' said Roskill. 'It isn't likely, but we'll be swopping cars on the M1 in due course. And we've got chaps watching over Tierney and Maclean already – we're efficient too, you know, when no one's pulling the purse-strings tight!'

He whistled contentedly through his teeth.

'You know,' he said conversationally to Faith, 'I used to think that with enough manpower to cover all the contingencies, and someone like Dr Audley to do my thinking for me, this job would be easy. Not *this* job, I mean, but things in general. But now I've got 'em I'm more at sea than ever . . .'

Audley retreated into the plastic folder. He envied Roskill's ability to make easy conversation, interesting yet self-mocking, as much as his driving skill. He knew he was incapable of diverting her with tales of his own modest triumphs and humiliations. He recalled the last bitter session of recriminations with Liz, when she had piled his dullness on top of his seriousness and his inability to talk to her. 'Like a bloody pedantic German professor, with no room for me except in bed and in the kitchen' had been her parting shot, all the more wounding for its element of truth.

He remembered guiltily that he ought to have phoned Theodore now that he knew the answer to the problem which he had set. But it might be better to let him come up with the answer independently. He could be suitably grateful – he could take the old man out to one of those heavy lunches he loved so much, talking the whole afternoon away. Theodore was alone among his contacts in wanting nothing but companionship in return for knowledge.

He blocked out the chatter around him – Faith was laughing at something Roskill had said – and plunged into the report. The man's casualness concealed an incisive efficiency, which was why he had been seduced from a peace-time air force into this work. All too often the service recruits were those who would never have risen in

130

their original professions. That was the bane of peace-time intelligence. But both Roskill and Butler were exceptions to this rule, conditioned to take orders but with their curiosity and initiative unblunted.

Roskill had evidently charmed the police and the police surgeon; they had worked hard and had given him everything they had found. He had set up precautions, had got through to Butler and had planned today's moves with absolute precision, elaborating on Audley's half-formulated instructions at some points and even anticipating them at others. His style was economical, but occasionally enlivened by asides which gave dimension to the bald facts. Audley was used to reading between the lines of such documents, but they seldom gave him such satisfaction.

He zipped up the folder and stared out of the car window at the kaleidoscopic scene. Unlike ordinary roads, which were as much part of any community as the houses and people, motorways were intruders, foreign territory belonging not to the countryside through which they ran, but only to their termini miles away.

He dozed uneasily, conscious that he had lost sleep to make up. And then he remembered how he had lost the sleep, drifting into a delicious half-dream of recollected passion.

It was the change in the steady engine note that roused him in the end. The Triumph was leaving the fast lane, slowing and sliding into a slip road, towards an ugly motel sprawl. It drew up alongside a Rover in the nearly empty parking lot, and Audley recognized Butler's rufous bullet-head.

Butler didn't stir, but his driver was out of the car before the Triumph had stopped.

'We're swopping cars here just in case,' said Roskill, without turning the engine off.

Audley climbed stiffly out and followed Faith and

Roskill into the Rover. The Triumph rolled away from them with its new driver, towards the petrol pumps, and Roskill accelerated past it without a sideways glance. The whole manoeuvre had been accomplished with the suspicious smoothness Audley associated with bank robberies.

He sighed. This was the aspect of his work which he had hitherto managed to avoid – and rightly, for it was as boring and superficially childish as he had always imagined it to be, undignified by the undertone of danger.

Butler passed him a file, the identical twin superficially of that Roskill had passed him earlier.

'Georges Leopold Bloch,' he explained brusquely. 'The *late* Georges Leopold Bloch.'

This time Audley did not begin to open the folder, but merely waited for Butler to elaborate.

'Late and unlamented for the last quarter of a century. Fished out of an Antwerp dock ten days after we chucked him out of England. Knocked about first, then knocked out and dumped over the side. No clues, police not interested. Case closed.'

There was no need to ask why the Belgian police had not been interested. Before he had strayed briefly and fatally into private investigation Bloch had been a policeman, and he had been a little too helpful to the German occupation authorities. Not helpful enough to be prosecuted, but enough to be sacked. There'd be some scores to settle there and his former comrades would not be unduly disturbed that someone had settled them. Bloch would have been an inconvenient memory conveniently erased.

'I talked to his widow,' said Butler. 'Re-married and not pleased to be reminded about him. Stupid little man, she said he was. Backed the wrong horse, and nobody would employ him.'

But somebody had employed him in the end.

'Then one night he got a phone call. Spoke in German and cheered up no end. Told her he'd got friends and things were going to be better. Went to England – came back scared stiff. Four days later, went out and didn't come back. Good riddance – she didn't actually say it, but she said he was a loser, with the mark on him.'

It fitted well enough. The cargo had to be received by someone. If the hi-jackers were German they'd not have been able to get into England very easily just then. A Belgian would do well, particularly a Belgian who had been tied in with them. It might even be that Bloch's helpfulness to the Germans had been more incriminating than his colleagues had suspected. In which case his new employers would have a useful guarantee of his loyalty.

But why had the price of failure been so severe? It certainly hadn't been Bloch's fault that he had failed to make contact. Nor would failure under such circumstances frighten him.

It could only mean that Panin had been back-tracking to catch up with the hi-jackers, and that Bloch had guessed he'd caught a tiger.

Audley shivered. The hands which had slapped Morrison yesterday had been controlled by the same agency, motivated by the same aims, as those which had beaten up Bloch in Antwerp all those years ago. Steerforth had raised the devil again.

9

The chill remained with him as he walked beside Faith through the Sunday morning streets of Knaresborough. If Steerforth had raised the devil, they were also in some sense on the devil's work, with their own load of trouble and mischief.

With a start he realized they were actually passing Tierney's electrical shop. It seemed quite substantial, with one window loaded with television sets garnished with offers of allegedly amazing terms. Tierney had done better in life than Morrison – which wouldn't do at all. Except that the rich were often greedier than the poor . . .

Roskill's man was waiting for them in his hotel room across the street, from which he had been able to keep a comfortable view of the shop.

'Richardson – Miss Jones – Dr Audley, I've been looking forward to meeting you!'

Richardson had a long brown face made longer by a jutting chin, but redeemed by good-humoured dark eyes, and Audley couldn't imagine why he had been looking forward to the encounter.

'I saw you play for the old Saracens, Dr Audley,' explained Richardson.

'That was a long time ago,' said Audley. He felt pleasantly flattered, despite the implication of hoary old age in the young man's memory of him. He searched for something suitable to add. 'You've got the build of a wing three-quarter.'

'Scrum-half, actually. And it wasn't so long ago that

you played either – I was always afraid I might meet you on the receiving end!'

Faith laughed. 'He was brutal, was he?'

'Sheer murder, Miss Jones. It must have been like being run over by a locomotive! Do you know the game?'

'I've got two young step-brothers who are besotted with it.'

They were suddenly like children sharing a joke, and Audley felt he had to call them to order. Their sudden pleasure didn't fit his mood.

'Is Tierney in?' he asked sharply.

'He is,' said Richardson, unabashed. 'By the grace of God he lives in a flat above the shop, with no rear entrance. The flat entrance is just to the left there. So I've had it easy!'

'Give me a rundown on him.'

Richardson flipped open a notebook.

'Arthur Lawrence Tierney, born Leeds 1922 – '

'Not a biography, man. Tell me about him here and now. I know what he was. But what do people think of him here? What's his credit like? Don't read it out. Tell me.'

Richardson looked uncertainly at his notebook.

'There's one thing I should have told you first, sir. They want you to phone the department, extension twenty-eight – as soon as you can. Sorry about not telling you right away.'

Audley sat unmoving. Richardson's jumbled impressions would be all the better if he wasn't given time to rearrange and edit them. The department could wait.

'Tell me about Tierney.'

The young man took a breath, stuffing his memory into his pocket.

'A nasty character, for my money. Tricky, certainly. He's a sharp enough businessman – he's respected for that. Always got an eye on the main chance, and not too finicky about what sort of chance it is too. I talked to a detective sergeant – he didn't say so in so many words, but I think he'd like to get his hands on him, and he thinks he will one of these days.'

'What sort of thing has he been up to?'

'Nothing proved – but otherwise, you name it and he's done it.'

'Name it.'

'Receiving mostly. But the sergeant reckoned he'd squeezed out of a nasty dangerous driving charge. And he's beaten the breathalyser. *And* they think there was something very smelly about his divorce. He's had a convenient fire in small warehouses he rented, too – an electrical fire. I tell you, sir, they don't like him at all.'

Tierney hadn't changed; the 'receiving stolen goods' was a shaft in the gold.

'And his credit?'

'That's rather hard to say. The business seems sound enough. But in a small way, and he's a big spender – runs an "E" registration Jaguar, drinks a fair bit. Girl-friend in Harrogate, and an expensive one, according to rumour. The same source says that's why the business hasn't expanded: never enough loose money in the kitty.'

Audley felt better now, so much so that he began to regret pushing Richardson. Tierney's nerves would be in middling shape, his sense of public responsibility non-existent and his greed unlimited. That had been the original assessment of him, and it was always reassuring to find leopards with all their original spots in place.

He smiled at them both, wondering as he did so what Faith made of her father's choice of a right-hand man.

'That's well done,' he said. 'You must have sunk a few beers to get that lot.'

Richardson grimaced. 'They all drink whisky in Tierney's circles. It was touch and go at the end whether they were going to tell me about him or I was going to tell them about me! And it's cost the nation a fortune . . .'

A few minutes later Audley added to that cost with a reversed call to the department. Mercifully the hotel's public telephone was located in an enclosed sentry box of dark varnished wood, with additional privacy provided by a giant plant which flourished aggressively beside it.

Extension twenty-eight eventually brought him Stocker, as he had expected. For the time being, and perhaps permanently, Fred was no more than a friend at court. And at this time of a Sunday morning he would be only just leaving the church he so dutifully attended.

But Stocker beamed insincerely at him down the phone.

'David!' – So he had ceased to be Audley at some point in the last twenty-four hours – 'I'm glad you were able to get through to me so soon' – was there a reprimand there? – 'I gather you know all about G Tower?'

At least he wasn't prevaricating.

'I do – yes.'

'You must tell me about your private network some time. It appears to have the virtue of efficiency.'

Audley grunted non-committally. That would be the day.

'And I gather you have also heard about the missing Trojan antiquities.'

It was a statement, not a question. Audley gloated briefly over the vision of Sir Kenneth Allen's reaction at being disturbed twice in one evening to answer the same question.

'You consider it likely that that was Steerforth's cargo?'

'I'm reasonably certain it was.'

'You have corroborative evidence? From the daughter?'

Roskill *was* reporting back everything to Stocker, for no one else had known about Faith until that morning. But it was only to be expected. If he was dealing with someone as awkward as himself he would have done no less.

'Yes.'

'Good. And you consider her involvement in the next stage necessary?'

'I think it may be essential.' Fred had become resigned to monosyllabic answers until he was ready with a full report, but it would be too much to expect the same of Stocker, Audley warned himself. He was already forgetting the tactical errors which had got him into this mess in the first place.

'I don't think Roskill and Butler will get anything out of Tierney,' he elaborated. 'Not unless we let them lean on him hard, and probably not even then. So I'm going to try a different approach and Miss Jones will be my – my passport.'

'Proof of your *mala fides*? I see! And is she a chip off the old block?'

Audley found the suggestion that Faith had inherited anything from her father except that physical resemblance oddly distasteful.

'Not in the least. But she's an intelligent young woman, and she wants to help.'

'Very well – I leave her to your discretion. Now about last night's business. Your three visitors.'

'They put – devices in the cars and they may have bugged the house.'

'They did bug the house. I received an interim report half an hour ago. They're still looking.'

Audley loathed asking questions of his nominal superiors. Apart from their reluctance to give straight answers, which provided him only with negative intelligence, it suggested incompetence on his own part. But he had been pitchforked into this puzzle at such short notice that it would be folly to pretend that he understood what he was about.

'I don't understand why they did it,' he admitted. 'I can't see why it's so important. And I can't see why a man like Panin has involved himself personally in it. I take it we've offered him full co-operation?'

'We have – yes.'

'In that case there must be something I don't know about.'

'I give you my word, David – for what it's worth – that we know no more than you do. Probably less, on your past form. Panin is a man with very little past, a big present and an even bigger future. We'd like to know more about him, and this is a great opportunity. We don't want to offend him if we can help it, either!'

Nothing had changed since yesterday.

'I think you should at least admit the possibility, Dr Audley, that he simply wants to recover the Trojan antiquities. He's an archaeologist. He lost them in the first place – and that probably rankles. He's on holiday, too. On his own time, as it were. Taking precautions could be second nature with him. All we can do is to find those boxes for him, show him the sights and send him home happy.'

Audley felt his irritability returning as he retraced his way to Richardson's room. Stocker must know something else, but he wasn't going to divulge it, even in answer to a direct appeal. It must therefore be a matter of high policy, something relating to the official attitude to Panin, rather than to the Steerforth aspect. All he could do was to obey orders without fully understanding them – which might suit the field operatives, but didn't suit him at all.

Roskill's large feet propped on the end of Richardson's bed were the first thing he saw. Richardson himself was still stationed by the window; Faith sat on the only comfortable chair and Butler was perched on a stool next to the washstand. The overall effect almost restored his spirits: crammed suspiciously into this little room they generated an atmosphere of conspiracy strong enough to set all the bank alarms in sleepy Knaresborough ringing.

He caught Roskill's eye and saw disconcertingly that his thoughts were being read and shared. And there was a slow smile spreading across Faith's face. In another second this council of war would slip into farce while he was still searching for the right words to bring it to order.

Butler saved him: 'You were right about Tierney, Dr Audley. You said we'd get nothing from him, and nothing is exactly what we got.'

Roskill swung upright on the bed.

'Master Tierney's memory is very poor. He remembers exactly what's in his little blue log book – which he still has, incidentally. No more, no less. Twenty-four years is a great healer for him. All his harrowing experiences have faded into nothing. He wishes he could help us, but he can't.'

'I prodded him on Steerforth.' Butler took up the narrative again. 'Said we had reason to believe that he was bringing in contraband goods and warned him about certain non-existent regulations. He didn't quite laugh at me, but he obviously knows we can't touch him.'

'Major Butler put on his sergeant-major act,' said Roskill. 'Then he went to get the car and I told Tierney what a rude bastard Butler was, and how nasty he could get, and how I could smooth things over if he'd just give us a little help. He didn't laugh at me either – but he wanted to.'

'I expect he recognized the technique,' said Richardson. 'He's been through the mill more than once up here. He's a Fifth Amendment man.'

'I don't think I'd buy my TV set from him, certainly,' said Roskill. 'He's not a man who inspires my confidence.'

Butler snorted. 'The set would be all right. It would be the small print of the maintenance agreement you'd have to read carefully.'

Somewhere in the hotel a clock began to chime. It was midday and Audley was abominably hungry already as a result of a sketchy breakfast and a barbarously early start to the day. But there was still work to be done and he nerved himself to organize everyone.

'What does Tierney do for his Sunday lunch?' he asked Richardson.

'Drinks it at a flashy pub down the road.'

'Right. Miss Jones and I will approach him there. Then we'll take Maclean.' He glanced down at the list from Roskill's file. 'I see there are only two of the ground crew short-listed. Where are the other two?'

'One died in '54 – natural causes. The other emigrated in '50 – Australia.'

'You and Butler can split the others then. I'll see you both tomorrow at 9. I'll be at the Bull, Newton Chester.'

'And the Pole, Wojek?'

'Monday evening for him – if we have time. I'd like to see Wojek myself. One of you can phone him and make an appointment – say I'm writing a history of Polish aircrew in the RAF.'

Richardson broke in suddenly, beckoning him to the window.

'He's coming out.'

Audley moved beside him, following his gaze. Time had accentuated that distinctive ferrety face. The slope of the forehead and the receding chin had not been so apparent in the photograph; buck teeth for gnawing, long nose for sniffing, separated by the same slightly ridiculous toothbrush moustache. The nose was sniffing now as Tierney stood in his doorway quartering the view nervously with the abrupt little movements of the head of an animal in a hostile environment.

It would be awkward if Tierney didn't follow his Sunday routine now. But for all his coolness with Roskill and

Butler he'd probably need the reassurance of the pub more than usual.

'Come on, Faith,' he said quickly. 'Time for us now!'

In a final flurry of decision-making he took the Rover's keys and location from Butler and adjured Richardson to continue covering Tierney. By taking the car he was leaving them a transport problem, but that was their headache.

By the time they reached the street Tierney was a small figure in the distance. But the need for speed was all to the good: Faith had not shown the least sign of nerves so far. She had evidently repaired her make-up while he had been phoning Stocker, and still presented a cool, almost cold, front to the world – the tinted glasses lent her face something of the haughtiness it had without them. The less time she had to think, the less chance there was that the mask would slip.

Tierney's pub was a perfect example of the tarted-up olde worlde style beloved of the breweries, all beams and padded red plastic and bar ablaze with light. The Sunday morning rush had not yet started and Tierney was alone at one end of the bar drinking whisky greedily.

Audley ordered gin for Faith, filled up his own small whisky to the top with water and instructed the barman to fill up Tierney's glass.

Tierney looked up sharply as the barman muttered to him. He had looked them over as they had entered, dismissing Audley but lingering over Faith. But now he was trying to place them both.

He hesitated for a moment, sipping the drink as though to establish its genuineness. Then he sauntered over to their corner.

'I don't think I've had the pleasure?'

His eyes shifted from Faith to Audley, and back to Faith as he spoke. Neither of them replied, but Faith

142

carefully removed her glasses and stared up at him for a long moment.

'Are you quite sure of that?' she said.

A lot depended on Tierney's memory for faces, and it would still require a remarkable leap of the mind, even after this morning's reminder of things long past. But to Audley, knowing the answer, the resemblance was plainer than ever: she had somehow caught the tilt of the head which had been characteristic of her father's pictures.

It was enough to shake Tierney, but he still failed to make the connection.

'Steerforth is my name. Faith Steerforth. You haven't forgotten John Steerforth, have you?'

'My God!' said Tierney.

'Sit down, Mr Tierney,' said Audley. 'My name's Audley. We'd like to talk to you about old times.'

Tierney tore his glance away from Faith. 'Old times?' He sat down, raised his glass to his lips and then abruptly set it down untasted. His alarm bells were ringing loud and clear.

'Johnnie Steerforth's daughter! Damn me, but I can see it now. Margery Steerforth's baby!'

'Margaret,' said Faith levelly.

'Margaret – of course! How well I remember her!'

Faith took a photograph from her handbag.

'Then you'll recognize her now. And of course you will recognize me with her, won't you!'

Tierney studied the photograph.

'That's good enough then,' cut in Audley. 'We can get on to those old times.'

Tierney looked at him innocently. 'Funny you should be so keen on the old times. I had a couple of chaps asking me about them only this morning.'

Audley leaned forward. 'Don't mess around with me, Tierney,' he said conversationally. 'I'm not Special Branch and I'm not playing old comrades in this crummy little town for fun. I'm here on business and if you're very lucky you'll be able to help me.'

'I don't know what you're talking about.' Tierney picked up his drink and started to get up.

Audley reached forward and put his hand casually on the man's leg just above the knee, squeezing powerfully with his thumb and forefinger. Tierney gave a little snort of pain and sat down again as the leg gave way, slopping some of his drink on the table.

Tierney looked from one to the other in a mixture of surprise and outrage. Possibly no one had ever done anything like that to him before, certainly not in a public place. Faith had put her glasses on again, and her face was closed behind them.

Audley turned the relaxing squeeze into a gentle pat. Now he had to turn the outrage into fear.

'That's better,' he said quietly. 'I wouldn't wish you to misunderstand me, like your little friend Morrison.'

'Morrison?'

'Sergeant Morrison that was. Your look-out man. He didn't help us at all. So now he's not going to help anybody.'

'Who the bloody hell are you?'

It was not such an anguished cry as Morrison's had been. There was still a hint of fight about it. But this man lacked poor Morrison's years of blameless citizenship: he had no one to turn to.

'I've told you my name. You don't know who I am, but I know very well who you are. You brought it here, but your share in it has lapsed. Miss Steerforth has her father's share and I have the rest. And I might throw you a bone or two.'

Tierney drained his glass slowly, trying to charge his confidence at same time. There was a sly look about him now, a compound of caution and greed brought to the surface by the prospect of profit.

'I don't even know what it is – or was.'

That could quite easily be true, thought Audley. Morrison hadn't known either. There was no real evidence that Steerforth intended to double-cross his own associates, but whether he did or nor it would be a sensible precaution to keep them in the dark about the nature of the cargo.

'We don't need you to tell us that. And if you did know it wouldn't matter. You haven't got the form to dispose of it, not in a million years.'

Tierney smiled obsequiously and gestured to the glasses on the table. It was dawning on him that he might actually be in a bargaining position, and that thought was giving him confidence.

'My round, I think!'

Audley put the palm of his hand over Tierney's empty glass. Now was the precise time to demolish Tierney.

'Nobody's round. I see that I still haven't made myself plain. Morrison's *dead*, Tierney. He stuck out his silly neck and it got broken. He was the victim of a tragic accident – I believe he fell down a flight of stairs. I wouldn't like to think that you were accident-prone too.'

Tierney sat very still, his slyness wiped from his face and his confidence draining away, leaving only a thick sediment of fear. If he knew anything about the jungle in which he was a petty scavenger, then he would also know that there were fiercer predators in it, man-eaters some of them.

'Who was your contact over here – the man you were going to cheat?'

'My contact – our contact?' Tierney stared at him. 'I – I don't remember. And that was Johnnie's job.'

In Steerforth's place Audley would have used Tierney to make the contact, first to report that the cargo lift had been delayed and second to report that it had been lost at sea. Dirty work for Tierney.

'His name was Bloch, wasn't it?'

145

'It might have been. I don't remember – honestly. It was the hell of a long time ago.'

'It was Bloch, Tierney. And he was a poor swimmer.'

Tierney frowned, uneasily perplexed.

'Which is a pity,' continued Audley, 'because he's been for a long swim. That was a little test for you – and you failed it miserably. You ought to remember Morrison and Bloch. They were both stupid, and they're both dead.'

Two mini-skirted girls settled noisily at the table next to them, but Tierney was oblivious to the disturbance. Audley felt a warm sense of power; with Morrison he had been repelled by his own success, but with this hollow man it was different. He was almost enjoying himself. In fact he *was* enjoying himself.

'Let's try again. How did you unload it at Newton Chester?'

The ferrety man breathed out, as though relieved that he had a simple answer to give.

'We used the Hump.'

'Tell me about the Hump.'

'It's on the runway, when you're taxiing in. It isn't a hump really – it's a sort of dip in the land. But it looks like a hump when you're taxiing in. You can't see the control tower when you're in it, it's down the far end, quite near the perimeter.'

He licked his lips anxiously.

'Johnnie spotted it. I mean, if you can't see the control tower from there, they can't see *you*. We used to just slow down an' drop things there, an' then go on in bold as brass.'

'And what happened to the things then?'

'One of the ground crew was there to pick 'em up. There's a little hut just not far from the runway. There's a firing range further on, just near the old castle – we didn't use it, but when it was a bomber field they kept the range ammunition there I think.'

'In the hut?'

146

'Yes. It was empty and locked up. Johnnie broke the lock off an' put one of his own on it just like it. He called it his safe deposit – no one worries about a hut if it's properly locked up. And then he came by and picked the things up later – he had some excuse for walking up that way.'

'And that's what you did the last time.'

Tierney nodded. 'We had to stop so Morrison an' me could lower the boxes out – Mac wouldn't help. He wouldn't have anything to do with it.'

Maclean was the odd man out in the crew, the honest one. Morrison was probably basically honest too, but willing and scared – too scared to admit that he had even handled the cargo years afterwards.

'It was a two-man job?'

'It was a two-man job to lower the boxes out of the Dak – some of those boxes were bloody heavy. But Ellis'd got a little trolley from somewhere.'

Audley warmed to the memory of John Steerforth. The minor smuggling was nothing, the artificial crime created by avaricious governments and economics beyond the grasp of ordinary men. The major crime was equally forgivable – a plundering of the plunderers doubly absolved by daring, ingenious last-minute improvisation and attention to detail. Faith's father had deserved his good luck, not his misfortune.

And for him Ellis was a bonus: he was one of the accessible survivors of the ground crew whose address had been traced.

But Tierney was still talking.

'. . . five minutes, but it seemed like hours. We'd never brought anything so big in before. Johnnie said it was worth it because it was the last time.'

The last time. It had been that all right; the very last time.

'So Ellis put it in the safe deposit. And when did you go and check up on it?'

'Check up on it?' A shadow crossed the man's face, as the resurrected memory of wealth won and lost took hold of him. 'I never did – at least not till much later. Johnnie said it was put away safely, an' we'd have to wait and be careful for a long while.' He stopped and gave Faith an oddly pathetic glance. Like Jones, he'd never quite believed in the death of the clever, indestructible John Steerforth. 'And I trusted him,' he said simply.

'I told that man – the Frenchman – that we couldn't bring it in the first time, and Johnnie was like a cat with two tails.'

'When was it that he told you it was put away safely?'

'It was next day – at the afternoon briefing, just before I went to see the Frenchman. At the Bull I saw him.'

'And you finally checked the hut – how long after?'

'Three weeks – more – I don't remember. I broke my sodding ankle baling out. There was a thunderstorm and we'd lost a lot of height – we were too low.' Tierney was no longer looking at Audley; he was looking through him and far away, back into the thunderstorm.

'Far too low. I thought we were going to come down in the sea. But Johnnie nursed her along – he said the old bitch knew what he wanted, she just hadn't understood her orders properly and he wasn't going to let her spoil everything.'

There was a squeal of laughter from the next table. One of the youths who had joined the mini-skirts had spilt beer down his shirt. Tierney's eyes focused on Audley again.

'But the old bitch got him, didn't she! She bloody well got him! I never thought I'd see her picture again!'

'And how much of this did you tell Bloch and his colleagues?'

'Colleagues? I never saw any colleagues. Only Bloch. He got into the hospital a couple of days after I was taken there. I didn't even know Johnnie was missing – they didn't tell me. So I told him what we'd agreed on: that Johnnie wouldn't dare crashland with the stuff on board and we'd lost the lot.'

'Did Johnnie have a car?'

'A car – no. He didn't even have a licence. I remember he said it was silly, being able to fly a plane and not being trusted with a car.'

That was another bonus, and a wholly unexpected one. The possibility of handy transport, even in those austerity days, had been the one insuperable danger. It had never remotely occurred to him that Steerforth could not drive. Rather, he'd taken it for granted that he could.

'It's still there, isn't it!' Tierney was looking at him with a look of total incredulity. 'Of course it's still there. It has to be still there, and it was staring me in the face . . .'

Tierney had really been remarkably slow to follow the drift of the questions. Or slow at least to recover after being shocked into co-operating. Either way he would give nothing more which could be relied on. Audley took out his wallet and extracted five £10 notes from it.

'Fifty?' Tierney's assessment of his value was inflating rapidly with the birth of understanding. 'What I've given you's worth more than fifty!'

Audley was tempted to put the money back in his pocket. But it was more a gift to the blind goddess than to Tierney.

'What you've given me is worth nothing,' he said brutally. 'Nothing to you, anyway. You had your chance long ago, but because you were stupid – and because you didn't trust John Steerforth enough in the end – you missed it.'

'I could still queer your pitch – I could go to the authorities. I could report you! Both of you – '

The threat was empty and Audley was weary of the charade anyway. He reached into his pocket for his identification folder.

'We are the authorities, Tierney. You've been had, I'm afraid.'

Tierney squinted at the folder, then at Audley and finally at Faith. And longest at Faith.

'I could have sworn – ' he began.

'Johnnie's daughter?' It was the first time she had spoken since showing him the photograph. 'You weren't had there, Mr Tierney. I'm Johnnie's daughter. But you'd have done better not to have trusted *me*.' She spoke sadly.

'And Morrison – and the other man?' Now Tierney was really empty, with not even fear left.

'You weren't altogether had there either,' said Audley. The least he could do was warn the man off – and make Richardson's job simpler. 'You're just lucky that we reached you first. There are other people around who wouldn't bluff you. You'd best take yourself and your fifty pounds on holiday – a week would do.'

Tierney reached forward and scooped the five notes off the table, where they lay in a little puddle of spilt whisky.

Audley got up.

'A short holiday, Tierney – and we'll be keeping an eye on you, for your sake more than ours. And don't try to be clever. Don't go poking around Newton Chester trying to make up for lost time. I might see you there, and then I'd have you out of the way before your feet touched the ground again. Is that clear?'

He bent down, close to Tierney's ear.

'And go today, Tierney – go this afternoon.'

10

Richardson was just across the street outside the pub, peering morosely into the window of an antique shop.

'Tierney's going for a trip somewhere,' Audley told him. 'Just see him on his way. If he isn't off by four, go and remind him. Are you still mobile?'

The long face split into a grin.

'Hugh Roskill didn't fancy my old heap – he whistled up that souped-up racing car of his.'

'Phone Newton Chester and book us a couple of rooms at the Bull. We'll meet you there with the others tomorrow morning.'

'Make that a double room,' said Faith casually.

'Yes, ma'am.' Richardson's eyes flicked between them. He was no longer grinning; it occurred to Audley that he was not only not grinning, but had apparently been struck by some facial paralysis which had stranded his features in between emotions. Certainly no one could accuse him of grinning.

Audley wasn't sure that he approved the way she was setting the pace of their relationship, even if it was one of the logical outcomes of emancipation. But he knew equally well that with a pace maker one either keeps up or drops out of the race altogether.

'With a double bed,' he added in what he hoped sounded an equally casual tone. If Richardson too was required to report back on his progress, then he might as well have something to enliven his report.

It wasn't until they were settled into the Rover that Faith spoke again.

'I suppose I was out of line there?' she said, with a

151

suggestion of truculence rather than apology in the question. 'Not in front of the help? You didn't like it much?'

Audley could think of no suitable reply, short of admitting that he was old-fashioned, but she didn't wait for one anyway.

'Well, I didn't like what happened in that bar very much either,' she continued. 'I didn't like *you* very much. I didn't even like myself.'

He tried to concentrate on his driving; the Rover's transmission was automatic and his unoccupied left foot seemed unnaturally large.

'Actually I thought you were hamming it a bit at first. I expected him to laugh in your face any minute. Or sock you, even though you were twice as big. But then you started to gloat – and it wasn't funny then. It was nasty!'

Audley's left foot shrank back to its normal size as he saw the truth of it, and the chasm. He was not suited to this kind of work; not because he was too soft-hearted, as he had cretinously believed, but because with a little practice he could grow to like it too much. He'd been lucky with Morrison and Tierney – forgetting Jones and the police inspector. But when he'd learnt more he wouldn't need such luck . . .

'I just don't know what sort of man you are! I've seen a gentle side – Mrs Clark's side. And a diffident side. And Daddy said you were very clever. And that nice man Roskill thinks the world of you – and so does Richardson, and he'd never even met you! But I think there could be a dark side I wouldn't like.'

Damn her, thought Audley. She was fogging the issue when there were things, other things, he ought to be worrying about. Except that in the long run they might be less important things.

'You still asked for a double room,' he said cruelly.

She shook her head.

'That wasn't just for you, David. It was for the Bull.'

'For the Bull?'

'That's not quite fair on you – it's only a hotel to you. You can't know about it.'

'You've been there?'

'Been there?' She sighed. 'No, I've never been there, not in the flesh. But it's part of my family history – I've heard them all talk of it. Grandmother used to tell me how they all met there. It was the squadron pub – "See you at the Bull" was their good luck saying! It was his special place – Johnnie Steerforth's pub. He met Mother there before I was born; I think he met her there the very first time. And Daddy met her there afterwards, my stepfather, I mean. It was the only place . . .'

She left the sentence unfinished and Audley writhed inwardly. He couldn't have known, and she was honest and had conceded it. But he could hardly have been more ham-handed in his egotistical misconstruction. Among all those ghosts of the living and the dead she didn't wish to be alone. Again it had been the need rather than the man, he told himself sadly.

'I'm sorry. I've been rather thick, haven't I!' he confessed heavily. 'We can go somewhere else. Or you can. In fact you could easily go home – you've done your part better than I deserve.'

'Do you want me to go home?'

'It's not for me to say. You've earned the right to decide that for yourself, I think.'

She laughed. 'I'm not just a camp-follower any more then?'

'Faith, you know damn well you were never just a camp-follower.' Audley nerved himself to abase his pride. 'If you want me to say whether I want you to go to the Bull to share a double bed with me in a double room, the answer is "yes", as you know very well. For me it would be a pleasure – and a privilege.

'And as to that dark side of mine – the answer is "yes"

153

to that too. I think there's a KGB man inside me trying to get out. And maybe that's another reason why you should stick around: we can both try to keep him in check now we've spotted him. At least until I can get back to my old job where he doesn't have any chances!'

She put her hand softly on his arm.

'Poor David! Things are complicated enough for you without a KGB girl of your own to watch your KGB man! I haven't even been straight with you, either. I do want to go to the Bull with you very much. I think I'd like to get the Bull out of my system and you into it. And I want to find Schliemann's treasure!'

'Steerforth's treasure now. It'll always be his treasure as well now, whether we find it or not.'

'But David – do you really think you can find it?'

He shrugged. 'The Russians think we can, Faith. And we're the first people to look for it, after all. So given time maybe we can. Tierney's given us a good start, anyway – better than I expected.'

'He has? Honestly, I couldn't quite see what you were driving at. I mean, it doesn't matter where it was put at first. It's where it ended up, and that could be – just anywhere.'

'Oh, no, it couldn't. Your daddy was an extremely resourceful character, but he wasn't a miracle worker.'

'I still don't see –'

'Time, love! Time and trust and opportunity. I haven't been trying to find the treasure so far – I've been trying to find what the limiting factors were.

'He didn't trust Tierney, and if he didn't trust Tierney he didn't trust anyone. So he shifted the treasure from the safe deposit hut by himself. And he did it that same night – he told Tierney it was put away safely next day. But he couldn't drive, so there's a physical limit to where he could manhandle it.'

'There was the trolley.'

'Even with the trolley it can't be very far away from the hut. There has to be a *place* of some sort – he'd never leave it just lying about.'

'He'd get the place ready in advance then.'

Audley shook his head.

'I'm betting he didn't know in advance he was going to hi-jack the cargo. So it had to be a ready-made hiding place, and at the same time somewhere it could stay safely for a long time – twenty-four years, in fact.'

Faith frowned. 'I think you're assuming a lot, David. He could have had a place ready for what's-his-name, the Belgian, to collect the stuff – a hole in the ground would do perfectly.'

'Fortunately holes in the ground are the one thing we don't have to worry about. If I thought it was under the ground I wouldn't bother to look – we'd need a regiment of Royal Engineers, mine detectors and God knows what else before we could think of tackling holes in the ground!'

'Well, it's the traditional place for buried treasure, and I still think it's the most obvious place,' said Faith, somewhat nettled. 'I don't see why you're so sure of yourself.'

Audley checked himself from another scornful reply, aware suddenly that he was close to selling the lion's skin before he had killed it.

'It's traditional, Faith,' he conceded seriously. 'But England isn't a desert island. People have an inconvenient habit of noticing large, convenient holes dug in the ground, as quite a few murderers have discovered to their cost. They notice them after they've been filled in, too. In fact there's only one place where a hole isn't suspicious, and that's in a churchyard!'

She turned towards him eagerly, but he cut her off with a shake of the head.

'Unfortunately Newton Chester churchyard is all of three miles from the airfield, on the other side of the village. Too far away to trundle a trolley two or three times without being seen or heard. And frankly I can't see your father settling down with pick and shovel either, not to that extent: it would have to be a big, deep hole, a grave-sized one. And that takes quite a lot of digging, even if he had time – which I still don't think he had.'

Faith nodded thoughtfully. 'You've made your point, David. But if it's not under ground, it's above ground. And that seems even more unlikely – unless it's in that castle Tierney mentioned.'

'That's a possibility, certainly. But I don't think there's much point in discussing possibilities until we see the place. As I said, I've been after the limiting factors. In any case, we've got one more job before Newton Chester. We've still got to see Maclean.'

'Maclean? He was – the navigator, wasn't he?'

'He was the navigator, yes.'

'But we're not going to do another tough act for him, I hope – I don't think I've got the stamina!'

Audley smiled. 'I don't think it would be very wise to attempt that act on a respectable citizen like Mr Maclean.'

Faith sighed with relief. 'Thank Christ there was one respectable member of the crew! I was beginning to get a jaundiced view of the air force. But then I suppose if anyone has to be steady and reliable it would be the navigator. Sort of father figure, like Captain Cook!'

Like most women she was prone to subjective judgements, reflected Audley: her step-father had been a navigator. But it was reassuring to find such a mundane flaw in her character; in some other respects she was formidable enough to be Jones's true daughter.

'I don't think your father's crew was very unusual – or unusually bad, come to that, Faith. Morrison was the weakling and Tierney was a potential crook, but they did their jobs perfectly well. They helped to win the war so people like me could come and hound them in peace years afterwards. Their generation did something big – which is more than mine has done.'

'And my father?'

'Same thing, love – only more so! Don't go drooping through life thinking he was just a villain. In some ways he was quite a man. He won his DFC fair and square.'

'Don't I know it! It was Grandmother's favourite bed-time story. So he was a war-hero. It's just that now I don't think he would have been a peace-hero . . .'

'Maybe not. But there were plenty like him –

> "A daring pilot in extremity . . .
> But for a calm unfit."

You shouldn't be sad, then. You've been damned lucky!'

'Lucky?' Faith sounded bitter.

'Every one of you! You got a good step-father out of the deal. And your mother has a good husband.'

'And my father and his crew – were they lucky?'

'They were luckier still. Your father went out quickly just when he thought he was home and dry – and the others saved their skins.'

'And lost their treasure!'

'But that was the luckiest thing of all – for them. You don't think they'd really have got away with it, do you? More likely it would have been their death sentence.'

'But you said – you've implied, anyway – that it was a marvellous plan?'

'So it was. But it had one terrible flaw they didn't know about – the flaw you've forgotten about and I still don't understand. They'd got Panin after them!'

'Panin – ugh!' Faith shivered. 'Every time you mention him it gives me the shakes – is he some kind of bogeyman?'

Audley shrugged. 'I wish I knew. But I know the Russians never gave up looking for that Dakota, so the odds are they'd have been on your father the moment he tried to dispose of his loot. And judging by what they did to Bloch they wouldn't have been gentle.'

She stared down at her feet miserably, and Audley cursed his runaway tongue, so proud of itself. He had set out to cheer her up and he had only reminded her of the real reason for this ridiculous treasure hunt. For a time he had almost forgotten it himself.

It was his turn to put a reassuring hand on her arm now.

'Never mind, Faith love. You don't have to meet the bogeyman on Tuesday. And you should get on splendidly with Maclean.'

She turned to him in surprise. 'Panin's coming here – to England?'

'You don't have to meet him.'

'Don't have to? I want to! The only way to deal with nightmares is to get them out into daylight – and I don't believe he can really be so awful, not if he thinks the treasure's worth his precious time.'

She was an innocent really, as so many of her kind were innocents. Always trying to transpose their safe, cosy world with that other, very different one: brave old Uncle Joe, puffing his pipe; cuddly Mr Khrushchev, dandling his grandchildren on his knee; mild, worried-looking Mr Kosygin, playing the dove to Brezhnev's hawk. But he had to accept her jibe – it would only frighten her to point out that the worst nightmares were those which refused to dissolve in the morning sun.

'Besides, if he's such a big wheel it would be an experience to meet him. I've never met anyone really important!'

Audley felt another surge of affection for her: she was quite a girl. And it could do no harm, provided she held her tongue. It might even be an advantage, for equally

158

Nikolai Andrievich Panin would probably never have met anyone like her. She might put him off his stroke, if only just a little.

'Very well, then, Faith. You shall meet him. But I still think you'll find Maclean more congenial.'

'Just because he's honest? I don't even see why you're interested in him. Tierney said he had no part in anything.'

'That doesn't mean he was blind or deaf. He was still one of the crew, and because he wasn't interested in making his fortune that way, your father just might have been more talkative with him. Besides, he was with him for one whole day between the trips – he went to London with him and Wojek on the Thursday. That was the day your book on Troy was bought, I've no doubt.'

'How on earth do you know so much about what they did?'

'It's all in the original investigation file. Our people were trying to find out what your father had done that made his plane so interesting to the Russians. They didn't find out, of course, but they managed a pretty detailed breakdown of his movements. And some shrewd character assessments, too.'

Butler had originally described the file as an assembly of non-information. And so it was, to the extent that it had failed to provide any conclusive answers. But like an old but painstaking geological survey it contained a wealth of information which became useful in the light of further knowledge.

'And as for Maclean being up your street – does Wadham Hill Comprehensive School mean anything to you?'

Faith raised her eyebrows. 'Wadham Hill? Isn't that the one that got the spectacular Oxbridge results?'

Audley nodded. 'I thought it might ring a bell with you. There was an article on it in one of the colour supplements, and it made the popular press too. One in the eye for the grammar schools. And all thanks to James W. Maclean – or "Big Jim" as he's known to his pupils. The papers liked that fine!'

'And that's *our* Maclean?'

'The same. Headmaster of Wadham Hill and sometime Flying Officer of 3112 Squadron. If we're nice to him perhaps he'll offer you a job sometime.'

'To Steerforth's daughter? I should doubt that – unless he's got a special remedial class for budding criminal scientists! I think I'll be plain Miss Jones to him.'

'You'll never be plain Miss Jones. But never mind – it's his memories we're after, not his professional approval. Always supposing he's available; it occurs to me that it may be his half-term too.'

11

But James Maclean was available. He received them readily and courteously in the immaculate study of his home which overlooked the equally immaculate glass and concrete campus of Wadham Hill. It had been his boast, Audley remembered now, that as a headmaster he was ready to meet anybody at any time – the colour supplement had made much of that.

But the 'Big Jim' nickname was puzzling. Clearly it didn't stem from size, either literally or by schoolboy inversion; Maclean was a neat, compact, average-looking man. Or perhaps it *was* a case of inversion, with the rough-hewn name contrasting with the man's intellectual precision – a compliment to the personality lurking beneath the neutral surface. There must certainly have been a measure of respect between him and Steerforth for him to have stood aloof from the hi-jacking without arousing ill-will.

Maclean came round his desk to meet them.

'Dr Audley – Miss Jones – your card says "Ministry of Defence", and I must admit that I'm curious to learn what your Ministry wants with me on a Sunday. I thought at first it might concern the Combined Cadet Force, but neither of you has the Cadet look!'

Maclean smiled as his eyes came to rest on Faith, but when she failed to return the smile the twinkle of good humour was replaced by a more speculative look.

'It's good of you to spare the time, headmaster,' said Audley, reaching into his pocket for his identification. Maclean studied the little folder carefully, nodded and returned it without comment.

'We're hoping you may be able to help us with information about something which happened rather a long time ago. It concerns Flight Lieutenant John Steerforth – you were his navigator during the war.'

Maclean stared at Audley steadily, with a slight crease of surprise wrinkling his forehead.

'John Steerforth!' he said, repeating the name and savouring it as though it had a special taste. 'It's a very long time since I've heard that name. But I remember him, of course. As you say, I was his navigator. What do you want to know about him? He's been dead twenty years or more – he was killed just after the war. We had engine failure flying back from Berlin. We baled out, but Steerforth stayed with the plane until too late – that was the presumption, anyway.'

'You remember him well?'

'Do I remember him well? I knew him very well once, certainly. John Steerforth! It wasn't John, actually – it was always Johnnie – Johnnie Steerforth! As a matter of fact I've been reminded of him off and on down the years a number of times.'

'How was that?'

'By boys who were like him. Not the same – no one's the same. But the same type, the Steerforth type. And oddly enough I don't mean the Johnnie Steerforth type, either; I mean the original "J. Steerforth" – David Copperfield's Steerforth. It's a curious coincidence. The Steerforths of this world can be useful in the right settings and dangerous in the wrong ones. Good in war, because they enjoy taking risks. The trouble starts when there aren't any risks to be taken.'

'"A daring pilot in extremity",' murmured Faith.

Maclean regarded her with interest.

'I see you know your Dryden, Miss Jones. Very apposite – it sums up Steerforth very well, that whole passage.'

He turned back to Audley. 'As I remember now there were a lot of questions about that last flight of ours at the

162

time. They never found the plane, or Johnnie for that matter. I never understood why they made such a mystery of it; it was just pure bad luck.'

Maclean had evidently missed the newspaper reports of the Dakota's reappearance. And naturally he hadn't been privy to the ditching plan.

'We're not interested in that last flight, headmaster. We're only interested in the previous one from Berlin to Newton Chester.'

'The previous one?' Maclean frowned. 'But that was just – ' His voice tailed off slightly, then rallied unconvincingly ' – just routine.'

Maclean remembered well enough, or at least had just remembered well enough. But Audley judged that with him frankness might pay a bigger dividend.

'Headmaster, we know all about Steerforth's cargo. We know what it was, where it came from and how it was taken off the plane. We also know that you had nothing to do with it. We're not trying to cause trouble for anyone. All we want to do is to find out where Steerforth put it.'

Maclean looked at him incredulously, and then on through him back into the past.

'Do you mean to say that Johnnie's precious boxes are still where he put them – after all this time?' he said at length.

'Do you know where he put them?'

'Good heavens – no! You'd do better to ask his second pilot – his name was Tierney. Or Morrison, the radio operator. I'm afraid I'm the person least likely to know.'

'But do you remember the boxes?'

'I remember the circumstances,' Maclean admitted ruefully. 'Now that you've reminded me I remember them all too well.'

He paused. 'I really didn't want to be involved. I wanted to finish my service with a clear conscience – I even used to congratulate myself with the thought that we hadn't actually killed anyone – except accidentally, when we hit them with canisters of supplies: Johnnie had the instincts of a bomber pilot, you know. It sounds rather naïve, and quite false from a moral standpoint. But it kept me out of Johnnie's little rackets.'

'The boxes?' Audley tried to prod him gently.

'He was always offering to cut me in. To save me having to spend the rest of my life teaching Shakespeare to small boys! But I remember that on that penultimate flight he varied the offer: he said if I'd set my heart on teaching I could buy a school of my own with my share.'

'And what did you say to that?'

'I don't remember what I *said*. But I recall that it scared me considerably. I thought that if one share in Johnnie's boxes was sufficient to buy a school – you don't make that scale of profit from American cigarettes and nylons! I was afraid desire might have outrun performance with Johnnie. And evidently I was right!'

The man's casualness had to be a sham, though not a guilty sham: no intelligent person could fail to be consumed with curiosity about the boxes' contents, least of all someone who had been involved with Steerforth, however innocently. Unless, of course, he already knew; but that didn't ring true of him, Audley judged.

'I'm sure I can rely on your discretion, headmaster, if I tell you that those boxes contained priceless objects from a German museum. You were very wise to avoid the temptation.'

'Johnnie looted a museum?'

'Not quite. Say rather he looted the looters.'

Maclean smiled. 'That sounds more like him. In fact it would rather have appealed to him.'

He hadn't approved of Steerforth, or helped him, but he still had a soft spot for him – much as David Copperfield had for the other Steerforth. It vaguely irritated Audley that he had failed to see the Dickens analogy, even though it was as irrelevant as it now was obvious.

'The point is we suspect the boxes are still somewhere on or near the old airfield at Newton Chester, sir. Do you have any suggestions as to where they might be, even if only in a general sense?'

Maclean pursed his lips thoughtfully, and then shook his head. 'I don't think I have, really. It's a very long time ago, after all – half a lifetime. My memories are rather fragmentary. I wouldn't know where to begin to look: Newton Chester wasn't a big station, as I recall it, but it covered quite a large area. There were – let me see – about half a dozen boxes, and fair-sized boxes too – but it would still be like looking for a needle in a haystack. What makes you think they're still there?'

'Steerforth didn't have the time or opportunity to move them far. We've covered his movements between the flights fairly well. He was duty officer on the Wednesday and he went to London with you and Flight Lieutenant Wojek on Thursday. Did he say anything about them then?'

Maclean was staring at Faith, who was absent-mindedly polishing her glasses. He turned slowly back towards Audley.

'I beg your pardon? We went to London? If we did I can't think why! It was a beastly journey there, and even worse coming back. A day trip was hardly worth it.'

He spoke absently, and Audley could sense his interest slipping. Or rather, not slipping, but shifting to Faith.

'Miss – Jones – I can accept irrational coincidences, but I have a good memory for faces, and I don't see how you can be a coincidence.'

Faith started to put on her glasses, and then stopped, returning Maclean's curiosity coldly.

'Steerforth had a baby daughter,' continued Maclean. 'She'd be just about your age now . . . You have your father's eyes and forehead, Miss Jones, and some of his disdain too, I think. A stronger chin and mouth, but the resemblance is quite striking nevertheless.'

'It's been remarked on before – your memory is very accurate.'

Maclean gave her a satisfied nod, smiling at her.

'I was at your christening, Miss Jones – Miss Steerforth. As a matter of fact I was a proxy godfather. I remember the occasion quite well.'

'It's a pity you can't remember what my father did with his stolen treasure,' said Faith icily. 'It's a pity you weren't able to keep him on the narrow path with you in the first place. It would have saved a great deal of heartache.'

Maclean's face clouded. 'You think I was the Pharisee who passed by on the other side? That's not quite fair, my dear. You ought to know that young people don't interfere with their friends' private affairs – only the old and the middle-aged do that. And I *was* worried about your father; I said to him . . .'

He stopped, and then swung to Audley again, nodding in delayed agreement.

'You're quite right: we did go to London. My sister had tickets for a Myra Hess concert. Johnnie and Jan Wojek were going up on their own, and I just tagged along for the journey. We met up again to get the last train from King's Cross.'

He tailed off, but Audley didn't dare to prompt him for fear of breaking the chain of remembrance.

'I'd been sitting there thinking about your father, Miss Steerforth, and thinking about his boxes. And when he got in I asked him if he'd got rid of them all right.'

He paused. 'He said, "Forget you ever saw those boxes of mine, old boy. You've had your chance" – or something like that. And he laughed and said that the German would be turning in his grave. I said, "What German? You haven't been fraternizing, have you?" – because we weren't supposed to have anything to do with the Ger-

mans then. He nearly fell off his seat laughing at that –
and he said his private German had been dead for ages.
"The joke is it would take someone like him to find it
now", he said.'

He gazed at them both rather sadly. 'Perhaps that
means more to you than it does to me. It was a private
joke to him, but that's more or less what he said. And
whatever you may think, Miss Steerforth, I *did* care. But
your father went his own way – we even had some more
of his boxes on that last flight, as a matter of fact.'

'He was with Wojek when he came to join you on the
train, was he?'

'He was, yes – but I doubt that Jan Wojek will
remember anything. They'd both had rather a lot to
drink, but Jan was in the worse condition . . .'

In the end Maclean had become rather fed up with his
inebriated comrades, the Englishman full of excitement
and misplaced elation, the Pole full of sadness, still
fighting the well-founded suspicion that he had won his
war and lost his country. So Maclean had settled back in
his corner seat listening to his sensible conscience, which
told him it was high time to stop flying and start his real
career. To him, unlike the other two, the war had never
been the great adventure, and now it was over anyway.

Audley crunched away down the well-tended drive beside
Faith, once more in a gloomy world of his own. He was
aware that they had been less than gracious to Maclean at
the conclusion of the interview. Faith had rebuffed the
man's conventional questions about her mother with short
answers; his own equally conventional gratitude had been
short and insincere. And each was merely projecting
personal feelings.

With typically feminine unfairness, Faith obviously
blamed Maclean for everything. He could have been the
cohesive force in the crew, tipping the balance against

temptation. Instead he had left well alone, saving his strength for himself, so it must seem to her. But human relations were never as simple as that in reality.

His own disappointment was better founded, for that feat of memory which Faith's disapproval had stirred had thrown the whole question of the boxes' whereabouts into confusion again. If that private joke of Steerforth's had been recalled with any accuracy the boxes were below ground again, where Schliemann had found their contents in the first place. And that would make their rediscovery appallingly difficult, even impossible.

He was tempted to throw in his hand – to insist that the whole idea of tracking down long-lost treasure was a nonsense for which he had neither the aptitude nor the experience. His bouts of confidence seemed in retrospect as misplaced as Stocker's confidence in him – if Stocker ever really had such confidence.

But even if Stocker's confidence was assumed, there was still the reality of Panin. The Russian's coming was the one sure proof that the treasure existed and could be found. Yet it made no sense – or it meant that he'd been approaching the problem from entirely the wrong direction. In that case what was needed was – what was it the Arabs called it? – a *tafsir il aam*: the calculated throwing away of the old rule book which stopped one winning the game.

But to do that would mean returning to London, and then to an unwelcoming home full of electronic eavesdroppers. And it would also lose him the chance of getting into a real bed with Faith.

That was the one worthwhile product of the whole operation, and he wasn't going to ruin it now. As he climbed into the car he could see that she looked as gloomy as he felt, but that smartly-pinned hair would look better spread on a pillow. So the idea of quitting and the *tafsir il aam* could both damn well wait, and he would go on as planned.

They drove off in silence. The last sight he had of Maclean was of the compact man still standing where they had said goodbye to him, deep in his memories. Audley hoped the life-jacket of his clear conscience would keep him afloat. Then a gleaming wing of Wadham Hill cut him off from view.

They continued without speaking, and for once he concentrated on his driving; Butler's Rover was a car which rewarded effort, very different from his undemanding Austin. But in the end he had to break the silence.

'You didn't enjoy that either?'

'Enjoy it? In a way it was worse than Tierney. You should have been nicer to Tierney and nastier to him – my proxy godfather!'

'And then I would have got nothing out of either of them. But he wasn't so bad; you've just got a prejudice against headmasters.'

'Against that one, anyway. He could have stopped my father dead in his tracks if he'd really wanted to. And I think he knew it, too, whatever he said, the sanctimonious bastard.'

She sighed. 'But then my dear father would have got up to some other murky little scheme, I suppose – gun-running, or something like that. You're right, of course: this way's no worse than any other – and at least I've met you this way, David!'

She reached over and put a slender hand on his, and then leant across and planted a light kiss on his cheek.

'"Meet you at the Bull",' she whispered in his ear. 'This way I'm following the family tradition as well!'

12

If there had ever been any ghosts in the Bull, old ghosts or shadows in RAF blue, they were gone now, thought Audley. The central heating would have been too much for them.

He sat on his luxurious bed and watched Faith double up on hers in helpless laughter. There might be a suggestion of hysterics in it, but it seemed genuine enough even if he was not disposed to share it: the Bull had proved a more daunting experience than he had expected. Worse still, the management evidently took them for honeymooners, if not elopers, and this was its special bridal suite.

It might have been the way Richardson had booked them in. It might even have been the awkward way Audley had claimed their room. It might very well have been their arrival without a single item of luggage, an oversight which had struck him much too late.

But he suspected that it had been their actual reaction to the Bull itself which had finally convinced the staff of their romantic status. No hardened adulterers or casual fornicators would have behaved so eccentrically.

Faith had spent the last half-hour of the journey describing the decaying establishment which had been the rendezvous for the Newton Chester air crews, their families and hangers-on.

Not that the old Bull had been prepared for its sudden wartime prosperity. It had in fact been left high and dry by time until Hitler's rise and renewed friendship with France had caused the migration of the RAF bomber squadrons from their old haunts in the south midlands to a new generation of bases spread across East Anglia, Lincolnshire and Yorkshire. Newton Chester had been the last and the least of these airfields, a temporary intruder which had never managed to attract the biggest bombers.

But if the creaking beds and antique plumbing of the old pub had been strained to the uttermost, so too had the stamina of the wives and girl-friends who had descended on it. Its draughtiness and arctic conditions beyond the two cheerless bars had been a byword; it was a folk legend that the rear upper gunner of a Hampden, who should certainly have been inured to cold, had frozen to death during the winter of 1940 in one of the bedrooms. Circumstantial evidence for this was that his girl had forsaken him for a pilot in the next room – one of the advantages of the place was that it encouraged passionate night-long embraces simply as a means of keeping warm.

It was famous also – or infamous – for running out of beer, for the landlord's habit of despatching patrons to borrow fresh supplies from a pub in the neighbouring village and for his unblushing overcharging of the samaritans who had helped him. And his whisky, on the rare occasions when it was available, was so heavily watered that flies falling into it were able to swim to safety and take off at once, cold sober.

The meals were more reliable; except so far as Jewish aircrew were concerned, for the menu was always a Hobson's choice based on illicit pigs which the landlord fattened on the choicest scraps bribed out of the sergeants' mess at the airfield . . .

One way or another, from the reminiscences of her grandmother, mother and step-father, Faith knew the Bull inside out, from the decrepit creaking floorboards at the head of the stairs to the notice in the unlockable upstairs lavatory appealing to the users not to pull the chain after midnight because of the noises which then racked the water pipes. She was an expert in every legend, tradition and horror which 3112 Squadron had inherited from its long-suffering predecessors.

The Bull she raised in Audley's imagination was built of nostalgic wartime gaiety and stark discomfort – 'The Way to the Stars' staged in Dotheboys Hall. But as the discomfort was more likely to have survived than the gaiety he began to have the gravest doubts about the night ahead of them. It promised to be even less comfortable than the previous one.

His doubts were strengthened by the rambling pub's unchanged appearance. It was as beautifully Old English as she had said: what had survived by luck, accident and sheer lack of prosperity since Jacobean times was now its greatest attraction. The lattice of timbers, the uneven plaster and the tiny, irregular leaded windows would be preserved as long as chemicals and crafty restoration could hold them together.

But 3112 Squadron's Bull vanished like a dream in warm air, expensive continental cooking smells and deep carpeting the moment they stooped through the low oak doorway. Before Audley had got his bearings, while he was still looking for one of Faith's landmarks, a darkly handsome waiter in a white coat and tight maroon trousers materialized at his elbow.

Audley unwillingly admitted that he was the Dr Audley who had booked a double room.

The waiter was joined by an even smoother and swarthier grey-suited manager who expressed his gladness at their arrival and his desolation at their lack of a double bed. Faith, at his other elbow, gave an odd, muffled snort.

Nevertheless, the manager assured him, there could be no doubt about their comfort, as the beds in every room were of the latest American design, identical with those supplied to the London Hilton. The measurements of these beds –

Audley hastened to assure him back that what was good enough for the Hilton was good enough for him.

And the luggage? Well, there had been a silly misunderstanding about their luggage. It had been left behind and a friend was bringing it down later in the evening. Understanding smiles spread from face to face like treacle. A tragedy – but all would be well, assuredly. If Mrs Audley was inconvenienced in any way, the hotel would spring to her assistance.

They followed the white coat up the staircase – not the narrow alpine climb on which the drunken wing commander had broken a leg in the winter of '44, but a gentle, generous stairway which neither sagged nor creaked – and along the soft-carpeted, well-lit passage.

Was there anything else the Doctor required?

The Doctor had already had more than enough. Except for one thing: 'Which way from here to the airfield?' Audley inquired.

The man looked at him, mystified. Then he grinned like a small boy who has come up with the answer to an unfair adult question.

'Nottingham,' he said happily.

Audley shook his head. 'The old airfield here – at Newton Chester.'

The black curls shook back at him. There was no airfield here. The airfield was near Nottingham.

As the door closed on the man Faith flopped back on her Hilton-standard bed.

'Mrs Audley is inconvenienced,' she murmured. 'No double bed, no toothbrush – no Bull.' She began to laugh. 'And no airfield!'

Audley watched her slowly give in to the laughter. What spoilt the joke for him was that she could well have added 'no treasure'. But stretched out on the bed – and a generous bed it was – she did take his mind off that unhopeful prospect. She herself was, after all, the only attainable treasure of the operation now. He eyed her long legs speculatively; and an end attainable there and then, for the asking.

But the compulsion to see the airfield while the light held was still stronger than sex, rather to his regret. He told himself savagely that it was common sense rather than incipient middle age which took business before pleasure.

'Come on, wench,' he said hoarsely. 'Put on a new face! We've got one more call to make.'

Faith groaned. 'You're a slave-driver, David! God, there's no romance about your job, is there?'

'Doesn't staying in a strange hotel with a strange man count as romance?'

'Camp-followers' duty – I'm just following the family calling. That's not romantic, only patriotic. And which grotty bit of my family history are you about to dredge up this time?'

'This is merely a courtesy call. RAF Newton Chester is plain Castle Farm now. We're going to call on Farmer Warren to ask him to let us look round.'

'Is he expecting us?'

'If the First Class mail can be relied on he won't be too surprised by my appearance. What he'll make of you I shudder to think!'

She had loosened the French pleat, and to attempt to pass her off as a Ministry of Defence secretary on Sunday overtime would seriously impair the public image of Civil Service morals.

She tossed back the pale mane of hair. 'What the devil am I supposed to be, then?'

'I think you'd better go on being the first Mrs Audley – keeping an eye on her hard-working husband. I doubt if Farmer Warren will believe it, but it will just have to do.'

She smoothed down the mini-dress over her hips. 'And what exactly is my hard-working husband doing?'

'He's leading a survey team examining the condition of abandoned air strips. And don't laugh, my girl, because your taxes have been spent on far less likely things than that. We're just the advance guard, and you've come along for the ride.'

Faith wrinkled her nose. 'Old Farmer Warren'll have to be a turnip to swallow that. He'll put me down as a shameless hussy – but since that's just about what I am, I suppose I'll have to bear his displeasure.'

But if Farmer Warren did not swallow the story, equally he did not view Faith with displeasure: Farmer Warren was in his thirties, or mid-thirties, and if he wasn't exactly handsome he was engagingly good-humoured, with white teeth flashing like a toothpaste advertisement in his weather-browned face.

'Got your letter, sure enough – and it rather put the fear of God up me. You're not thinking of moving back here, by any chance, are you? My family moved off once, and fair enough with the Germans over there. But I don't reckon to be shifted again,' he said frankly, with the hint of steel in his smile.

Audley reassured him. 'The runways would never do for jets anyway, Mr Warren,' he lied comfortingly. He hadn't the faintest idea what sort of runways were suitable for jets. 'We just want to see how the temporary wartime strips have weathered in different parts of the country. We won't do any harm.'

'They've weathered too darn well, if you ask me – wasted a lot of good land. But help yourself. Just don't frighten my silly sheep too much and don't tramp down too much of my rye grass. We're taking the first cut for silage next week. Come and go as you please – you'll have to come through this side because the old airfield entrance is all wired up. There's not much left there anyway.'

Audley was about to thank him when a diminutive,

pretty auburn-haired girl in a mini-skirt far briefer than Faith's joined them.

'Don't be boorish, Keith! Take them round yourself. You can show them your wonderful Longwools at the same time!'

'They don't want to see my Longwools,' Warren growled back at her proudly. 'Even if they are worth seeing – better than dead concrete and tarmac. But of course I'll show you round – I should've thought of that. At least show you the lie of the land, that's the least I can do.'

He swept aside Audley's protests. 'We'll take the Land-Rover – first bit's too bumpy for that nice car of yours. It's your coming on Sunday that's put me off. Never expected a Civil Servant to work on Sunday like me . . .'

He prattled on gaily as they shuddered down a rutted track through a belt of young trees. The hedges on either side were thick and overgrown, brushing against the side of the vehicle.

'I ought to cut 'em back,' shouted Warren. 'Pull 'em out. That's the way with hedges now. But where'd the birds and such like go? And you'll see in a moment why I like a bit of undergrowth.'

Magically the bumping ceased and the Land-Rover shot forward on a smooth road surface which began without warning.

'Perimeter!' shouted Warren, and they roared out of the enclosing hedgerows into the open. 'Airfield!'

A prairie was what it was: an immense unnatural meadow, treeless into the distance where the first blue haze of evening was gathering.

But it was a prairie with aimless highways on it, highways on to which the grass overlapped and pushed from every crack and cranny.

'No sheep this end,' said Warren, bringing the Land-Rover in a great careless sweep leftwards, totally disorientating Audley. 'This is one of the main runways. You can really let her go here – just the place for those go-karts. We'll have a couple when my son grows up.'

Ahead Audley saw a black water tower, with two ugly Nissen huts nearby. Beyond them a series of grassy banks rose unnaturally – blast pens? Sheep pens now, though, with their entrances blocked by straw bales and hurdles.

Warren brought the Land-Rover to a standstill, but without turning the engine off.

'This was where the main buildings were. Nissen huts mostly. Wooden control tower. Only the concrete bases left now, except for a couple I use as food stores. When the bombers were here they kept the bombs over the other side.' He pointed vaguely across the prairie.

'You lived round here then?'

'Born and bred here. Father farmed what was left during the war. I was only little, but I remember them – Hampdens, Beauforts, Bostons and Dakotas. Bostons were my favourites.'

Audley climbed awkwardly out of the cabin and walked a few paces across the tarmac. A slight breeze had risen – or perhaps there was always a breath of wind across this open land; it stirred the young spring grass, rippling over it in waves. He could smell sheep, and everywhere the runway was marked with their droppings. There was a pervasive loneliness about the place. Not the loneliness of the open downland, which had never been truly disturbed. Men had been very busy here once amid the roar of engines, with all the purposefulness of war. Where the downlands were eerie, this was only sad, as though time had not yet been able to wash away the human emotions which had been expended here. The airfield was not quite dead yet, not quite one with all the other debris of old wars.

He got back into the Land-Rover.

'Queer old place, isn't it!' said Warren. 'I've sat here of

an evening, and I could almost hear the planes. And I've waited for one of 'em to come up from nowhere on the runway down there, like they used to do!'

Audley exchanged a quick glance with Faith. Her face had a curiously frozen look, as though talking of the past could conjure it up again.

'That would be down there, towards the old castle?'

'That's right.'

'Can we go down that way?'

Warren nodded, and started the engine. 'Nothing easier!'

'Do you mind if we get off the runway, though. There should be a taxiing lane to the left somewhere. I'd like to see what that's like.'

Warren slowed down and turned on to a narrower roadway which curved away from the junction of the runways. As far as Audley could see, the airfield stretched ahead of him, dead level. He twisted himself in his seat to look backwards: the control tower had gone and he would have to use the water tower as his point of reference.

'If you want to see the old castle, you're going to be disappointed,' shouted Warren. ''Tisn't a castle at all. It's just a few hillocks on the ground – a Roman camp it was. Not a proper one, either. The archaeologists said it was what they call a practice camp probably. You wouldn't know what it was just to look at it.'

Audley listened with one ear, both eyes on the receding water tower. The Nissen huts dwindled as the taxiing lane unrolled smoothly behind them.

Then slowly the tower began to sink from view. He looked round at the featureless meadow. Sure enough there was a gradual, almost imperceptible slope to it now, a gentle undulation. The Hump!

Steerforth's safe deposit hut must now be somewhere to the left, what was left of it. To the right was the line of the runway, and there'd be no buildings on that side. He looked backwards: the water tower had disappeared completely. On either side the empty airfield stretched, with not a thing in sight.

'Slow down a bit,' he commanded Warren. 'I seem to remember there were one or two odd huts down here, weren't there?'

'Nothing much down here. The old shooting range's over to the left, ahead, near the Roman camp. There was a hut hereabouts, and another down the bottom there for the flare path gear, I think.'

'Where was the hut here?'

Warren braked and coasted to a stop. 'Just over there. There's a bit of concrete still in the grass – it's a damn nuisance every time we're haymaking. I've never got round to grubbing it up – some of those concrete bases are a foot thick and more.'

Audley could just distinguish a break in the waving grass. So there it was: the last known resting place of the golden treasures of Troy. A few square yards of wartime concrete, annoying an English sheep-farmer! And that was where the real search had to begin tomorrow. It would be easy enough to find the spot again, anyway.

'Hey! Come to think of it, there's an old map of my father's which had the old buildings and the runways marked on it – at least, I seem to remember them marked on it,' said Warren with a flash of inspiration. 'I'm sure it's in the attic somewhere with his papers. I could look it out for you if you're interested.'

'That would be very civil of you – it would be a great help,' replied Audley. Actually, wherever the boxes were, they were certainly not going to turn up on the site of any demolished airfield structure. But an accurate map of the area was essential: it had been the one thing which had not been included in the Steerforth File among either the old or the newer papers, understandably, since the airfield itself had been of no significance.

Warren let in the clutch. 'Right, then! We'll be getting back, if you don't mind. I won't be able to find your map straight away – wife's uncle'll be here any moment. I'm making silage for him this year – but when he's gone I'll get up into the attic and have a look round. Are you staying round here?'

'We're at the Bull.'

'Phew! Then you'd better have your cheque book at the ready. Won't let you bend down to pick up your handkerchief at the Bull now, but they don't forget to charge you for it afterwards! Food's good, too – if you can afford it. But it's only the taxpayer's money you're spending, isn't it?'

Warren's combination of self-confidence and casual familiarity grated on Audley's nerves. But the man's grin took the sting out of the jibe. He was being perfectly natural, treating them as he probably treated everybody, and it was impossible to be stuffy with such open good humour. And not just impossible – ridiculous too.

Audley suddenly felt tired and very sorry for himself. Somewhere along the way over the last few years he seemed to have lost both his sense of proportion and his sense of humour. Their arrival at the Bull had been a case in point: Faith had seen the joke and he hadn't. And now this.

Then there had been Fred's original warning about the sheltered existence which had divorced him from reality: it had been a delusion of intellectual grandeur which had got him into this business.

Except that Fred wasn't reality either. Nor was Panin. Warren and Faith and Mrs Clark were reality.

Or perhaps he was simply in the eye of the hurricane, in a moment of sanity surrounded by trouble. Tomorrow, certainly, he would have to face up to the fact that he didn't really know where to begin to look for the treasure, or even why he was looking for it. But in the meantime he could enjoy himself.

13

The atmosphere of sanity created by Keith Warren saw Audley a long way.

It saw him back to the heated comfort of the Bull – Faith even remembered to borrow two suitcases from a sympathetic Mrs Warren. What explanation she gave he never knew, but he suspected it was more for his sake than her own that she added this touch of respectability.

It saw him through dinner, which was not quite as good as Warren had forecast, but good enough to cancel out the sly looks presumably reserved for newly-married guests.

But it didn't quite see him to bed.

Audley sat in his shirtsleeves watching Faith strip down to an absurdly inadequate matching set of multi-coloured underclothes, reflecting that schoolmistresses had never been like that in the old days. Or maybe they had. But she was not so much shameless as quite without shame, and his mingled lust and embarrassment was outweighed by a tenderness which confused him. He had never felt like this about Liz, who had been so much more spectacular.

He shook his head. 'What am I going to do with you?' he said, half to himself.

'I should have thought that was obvious.'

'I don't mean *now*, you over-sexed wench! What are we going to do with each other when this is over . . . This isn't what I do normally.'

'I should hope not!'

'Be serious, Faith – just for a moment. You know what I mean. What you call a game – I shall go on playing it if they'll let me. I think it's important and I'm not going to give it up. But you hate it, don't you?'

She frowned, and then came over and knelt in front of him, taking his hands in hers.

'Dear David, you're not a very masterful lover, are you? You want to be approved of as well as loved, and the two don't necessarily go together these days, you know!'

'Then I'm old-fashioned. And that's because I'm too old for you. So it wouldn't work, would it!'

'It's up to us to make it work. And that's a lot of balls about your being too old. I'm not a schoolgirl exactly, you know. It's no good telling me I'm too young – and I'm the one who decides whether you're too old. And I think you're just pretending to be old: it's a bad habit of yours I'm going to have to break when we're married.'

She was so matter-of-fact that he almost didn't believe what he'd heard.

'I know you haven't even asked me yet – I know! But if you're really so old-fashioned you'll have to get round to it sooner or later. It's called "making an honest woman of me". And I shall accept because I can't possibly have you glowering around the way you did when we arrived here!'

Audley groped for the right thing to say. He had known her for three days and he had never known anyone like her. He had argued with her and lost his temper with her. He had used her as a pawn in his game and he had used her body as much to comfort his fears as to alleviate hers. He could not begin to explain to himself why she had somehow become dear to him; she was not in the least his type of girl. Yet the thought of losing her now was not to be borne.

Yet she was Steerforth's daughter.

Slowly she withdrew her hands from his.

'Me and my big mouth!' she said lightly. 'It's all a joke

really, David – forget it. Don't let it spoil the fun we can have tonight, anyway.'

She began to fumble with the hooks behind her back.

'Here! Do you really think it's fair to describe me as "flat-chested" – those hulking step-brothers of mine used to, you know!'

Audley reached forward and grabbed her arms clumsily, pulling them forward and sliding his hands down to imprison hers. But somehow he became entangled in a strap, and only succeeded in helping her prove that she would never be a rival to Raquel Welch.

'For God's sake, Faith!' he said thickly.

It wasn't the idea he shied away from, but the sheer indignity of the situation. A man simply didn't propose clad only in his shirtsleeves to a half-naked girl in an over-heated hotel room in the middle of an incomprehensible job. Not a man like himself, at least, who liked to calculate the odds and hated to be wrong-footed.

Not a man like himself!

What a pompous, stupid bastard I've become, thought Audley in a flash of clarity which completed the earlier moment in the Land-Rover. Dignity and reputation were like the Emperor's Clothes – a mere self-confidence trick. If he surrendered to this delightful beanpole of a girl he would never be able to wear them again, but in any case they would never again fit him comfortably if he let her escape. He needed her much more than she needed him.

'My dearest Faith – if you and Mrs Clark both agree, who am I to question your decision? Will you make an honest man of *me*?'

She nodded, wide-eyed. 'David – '

'The job still goes with the man, remember.'

'The job still goes with the man.'

He raised her hands to his lips. It was a marvellous thing for once to have no reservations about a decisive decision.

184

'And the man, my dear, is going forthwith to his Hilton-standard bed. We've got a lot to do tomorrow.'

He started to raise his hand to forestall what he guessed she was going to say, only to find that his thumb was still entangled by the strap of the ridiculous rainbow brassière.

'I know – I know! We've got a lot to do tonight, too! Come on, then, Mrs Audley . . .'

It was only much later, on the threshold of sleep and lulled by that soft snore to which he must henceforth accustom himself, that he thought again of Steerforth.

Somewhere out in the darkness, under the grass and the sheep not far away, lay the treasures of Troy. Priam's gold, Schliemann's gold and Steerforth's gold. And if, by some unlikely miracle, it came to the light again, it would be Nikolai Panin's gold.

And there was the unresolved puzzle, plaguing him still. The motives of the owner, the discoverer and the plunderer were crystal, but Panin's were opaque –

> The Gold I gather
> A King covets
> For an ill use.

That was among the runes on Welland's sword –

> It is not given
> For goods or gear
> But for The Thing.

As a child he had never grasped what Kipling had meant by 'The Thing', and now another Thing eluded him . . .

There was an insistent buzzing in his ear which he couldn't place. It refused to stop, and Faith's hair was tickling his face and Faith herself was stirring in his arms.

185

It was morning and the buzzing came from beyond Faith, from the pale green space age telephone beside the bed. As he reached over her she wound her arms round him sleepily. He knocked the receiver off its stand, fumbled for it and dragged it towards him by its coiled cable.

He groaned into it.

'Dr Audley – London call for you – putting you through now!'

Audley squinted at his watch. Seven-thirty and trouble: only trouble telephoned before nine o'clock.

'David? Are you there, Dr Audley?'

Audley admitted that he was, unwillingly.

'Stocker here, David. Sorry to rouse you early again. Have you got any closer to those boxes?'

Whatever made Stocker telephone him it wasn't to inquire after the progress of the treasure hunt. Not this early, anyway. He rubbed his chin, reminding himself unhappily that he'd have to get a razor from somewhere.

'To hell with the boxes! What's happened?'

Stocker laughed. His ability to exude good humour at this time of the morning was irritating. In fact there was a lot about Stocker that was potentially irritating, most of all that he probably knew better than Audley what was going on, and not least that he had probably never really expected the boxes to turn up.

'You're not even close to them, are you?'

'Not within a mile.'

'Well, you'd better pack things in and come on back to London. Our friend Panin has put his schedule forward a day – he's flying in this morning instead of tomorrow.'

Somehow it didn't come as a surprise. He had been driven by events from the start and every time he started to settle down to work Panin had popped up inconveniently to put him off balance. He had stopped his dig in Colchis to begin the whole mystery. Then he'd appeared in East Berlin. Then he'd announced his intention to come to England. And now he'd set them all by the ears by putting forward his arrival. If he'd deliberately set out to dislocate things he couldn't have phased his movements better.

Audley lowered the phone on to his chest in a moment of perfect stillness, blotting out the insistent voice at the other end. What a donkey he'd been! What a complete donkey – hobbled and blinkered, led and driven, with an occasional carrot to keep him happy and the odd smack across the rump to keep him moving!

If Panin had deliberately set out to dislocate things, he couldn't have phased his movements better! The plain fact was that they'd known too much about Panin from the start, not too little.

He looked down at the angry phone in his hand, fresh and untested implications crowding into his mind.

Time now for *tafsir il aam*. Time now to spoil the pattern, to cut the puppet's strings, to set the cat among the pigeons!

He lifted up the phone again: 'I can't possibly come to London today.'

'What? Where have you been?'

'I was disturbed. I said I can't posssibly come to London today.'

'You're due to meet Panin at London Airport at 11. You've got to come!'

'You meet him. Send him on down here – he knows the way.'

'And what exactly will you be doing?'

'Well, for one thing I'll be busy finding Schliemann's treasure. That's the whole object of this operation, after all, isn't it?'

'But you said you weren't even close to it.' Stocker sounded a little testy now.

'Not within a mile of it – but maybe within two miles.

Maybe only a mile and a half! Don't worry, Stocker. I'll find your boxes. It's just a matter of a little time and trouble now.'

Stocker didn't answer this time.

'And for another thing – ' Audley looked down at Faith, who was now wide awake and regarding him with proprietorial satisfaction ' – I've just got engaged to be married, and I've got a bit of private life to attend to.'

There was another short silence. Richardson hadn't reported the double bed, obviously.

'Well – congratulations, David.' Stocker finally rallied gamely. 'That does rather alter the situation. But I'm afraid your fiancée will have to take herself off when Panin arrives in Newton Chester – I'm sure he'll want to come and watch operations.'

'Oh, I don't think it will be necessary for her to disappear,' said Audley casually. This was the rabbit punch. 'The whole thing's going to be a family affair: it's Miss Steerforth I'm going to marry.'

He grinned down at Faith and savoured the renewed silence at the other end of the line.

'You're a bit of a dark horse, aren't you, David!' Stocker took his punishment like a man in the end. 'But no one can grumble if you deliver the goods, I suppose. I take it you'll need some help to conjure up the treasure?'

'I can lay that on – I take it I've still special priority?'

Stocker reassured him with a better grace than he expected. It could be that he'd made another important enemy in the last five minutes. But the hell with it – he'd been kicked around enough.

He put down the receiver and turned to Faith.

'"Sock it to 'em",' she murmured. 'You certainly socked it to him, whoever he was! Was that the effect of a good night's sleep – or me?'

He swung his bare legs out of bed.

'Come on, now,' persisted Faith. 'One minute you were

188

on the ropes, and the next minute you were beating the daylights out of him! And – my God – you talked as though you could just about put your finger on my father's loot! Do you really know where it is?'

'My dear Faith, I haven't the faintest notion where it is, and I don't know where to begin to look. But I do know one thing now, and that is that I've been humbugged.'

'Humbugged?'

Audley pulled on his trousers and sat on the unoccupied bed.

'There are a lot of things I've missed because I've been too busy hunting your father's treasure and sleeping with his daughter. Now I think I was meant to miss them.'

'Such as?'

'Such as how we learnt so quickly that Panin was still interested in your father.'

'Couldn't that just be a piece of luck?'

'We've never been lucky before with Panin. Every bit of information on him has been out of date by the time it reached us. But ever since your father's Dakota turned up we've been fed with information about him.'

'Maybe someone was efficient.'

'That's just it! But it's Panin who is the efficient one.'

'So what does that prove, David? I'm sorry to be a devil's advocate, but Panin wants his treasure and he doesn't trust you. You've known that all along.'

'All along I've been stupid – I know *that*. My sin's pride: everyone behaved as though I could find what was lost, so I really took it for granted that I could. But now I don't think anyone expected me to find it – not Stocker, and not Panin. And I clean forgot what every half-wit knows – that treasure-hunters never find treasure, not once in a thousand times. The only way treasure turns up is by pure accident!'

'But the treasure does exist?'

'I'm damn certain it exists – that's the one thing we have established. And I'm sure Panin knows it, too. But I don't think it really matters to him any more. What matters is that I should be kept busy looking, with the minimum chance of success.'

'But, David, for heaven's sake – why?'

Audley recalled Jake Shapiro's reference to 'that goddamned Byzantine set-up', and shook his head sadly.

'That's where I'm stuck. It could be so many things. If it wasn't for what happened to Morrison – and what happened to us – I'd think the whole thing was a cover for something quite different. But all I know is that it doesn't smell right.'

'Well, what are you going to do? You practically promised to find the treasure!'

Audley brightened. If there was no comfort in the long-term prospects, there was short-term enjoyment to be had from mischief-making.

He rubbed his hands. 'Everyone's been pushing me about. Now I'm going to do the pushing. And the only way I can think of doing that is – '

'Is to make them think you're just about to do the impossible!'

Faith sat up sharply in bed.

'Just so. And I'd like to see Panin's face when poor old Stocker gives him the good news at London Airport. If I'm right he'll be down here like lightning.'

'But what will that achieve, David?'

'I shall enjoy it, for one thing. And it may baffle Panin somewhat. He's not infallible, after all. In fact he's already lost us for a whole day, thanks to the incompetence of his agents – he doesn't know what we've been up to, and that may put him off a bit. Come to that, it may be the reason why he's arriving today instead of tomorrow.'

'So that was what the phone call was about! We're staying here to meet him?'

'That we aren't! We're going to London.'

Faith looked at him in surprise. 'But you said – '

'That was for Stocker's benefit. We're going to London because I've got some checking to do. I can leave instructions for Roskill and Butler to reconnoitre the area outside the airfield for suspicious bumps and so on – that'll keep them happy.'

He moved over to their rumpled bed and stared down at her.

'And you, young woman, have got a trousseau to buy – and a toothbrush. Then we'll have lunch at Feyzi's and a quiet drive back to the Bull for a reunion dinner. Panin should be nicely on the boil by then!'

But Faith was frowning at him.

'David, I think I'm having a bad effect on you. You're acting out of character – you're sticking your neck out. And they'll chop it off for sure, and I'll have an unemployed husband. Don't you think you ought to stay to meet Panin?'

It was a new experience for Audley to have someone actually worrying about him, a rather confusing experience. He looked at her tenderly. She was without doubt rather flat-chested, and with her hair in confusion and her glasses perched on her shiny nose she no longer looked the sort of girl to drive a man to reckless action.

He smiled affectionately. 'If you are having an effect, it's long overdue, Faith love. For years I've been sitting in my tower thinking what an important person I was just because they treated me politely. But actually I think I was just a sort of cheap computer substitute – as soon as I started giving inconvenient answers they booted me into the first vacant job somewhere else. So just this once I'm going to programme myself, and if they don't like it –

191

well, we'll see if they do like it first. Maybe they'll promote me!'

Before she could reply – he could see she was still unconvinced – he jerked the covers back.

'Hey!' she cried, scrabbling for the sheets.

'Too late for modesty now, love. And too late for inquests too – I'm like old Sir Jacob Astley before Edgehill.'

'Sir Jacob who?'

'"O Lord! Thou knowest how busy I must be this day",' he quoted at her. Damn them all: she was the one who really mattered. '"If I forget thee, do not thou forget me"!'

14

Jake Shapiro set his beer down carefully on the mat on the faded plush tablecloth, wiped his moustache carefully and grinned a broad, gold-filled smile at Audley.

'Surprise, surprise! I didn't expect to see you again so soon. Comrade Professor Panin running you ragged?'

'For me not a surprise, but a pleasure, Colonel Shapiro.'

Audley looked curiously round the publican's snug, which was furnished as though time had frozen it in late Edwardian times. The only concessions to modernity, a garish TV set and a glossy telephone, were banished to a dark alcove in one corner.

'Cosy, eh? And the best beer south of the river, take my word for it, David, old friend. Have some with me.'

'I've got a long haul ahead of me, Jake. It's too early for me to go on the beer.'

'Your loss. But I do understand your predicament. "Vodka and beer – no fear." You must keep a clear head for the Professor.'

The word was out, with a vengeance, evidently.

'You know about Panin, then?'

'There's been a lot of talk, certainly,' admitted Jake generously. 'Mystery Man's got a public relations man all of a sudden. I don't know what effect it has on you, but it'd scare the life out of me.'

'That's the point, Jake. What I want to know is – '

Shapiro raised a large hand.

'Me first, David.' He drank deeply, set the glass down carefully again and wiped his moustache once more. 'My turn, after all. The Portland trials of the Nord Aviation

AS15 – much better than the AS12, I hear. But I'm sure you heard better.'

Jake was presenting his bill, and Audley thought not for the first time that Jake's grapevine must be very good indeed. If the AS12 was the answer to Egypt's Russian missile boats, the AS15 was the answer with knobs on.

'Much better.'

'Range?'

'Five miles.'

'Cost?'

'Since devaluation? Maybe £2,400 a time.'

'Cheap at the price. But the bastards are still overcharging us. What about that Swedish one?'

'Let the other side buy that.'

'I thought so. And I thought you'd be in the know. Now, just one more thing.'

Audley scowled at him. 'No more things, Jake. I've given you classified information. All you've given me is what's common knowledge in the bazaar, it seems.'

Jake guffawed. 'That's nothing more than the truth, my friend. I have to admit it: I've done you down.'

Then he stopped quite suddenly, and became almost serious. He wagged his finger at Audley.

'But you knew it was common knowledge and you still paid up, you perfidious Englishman. You knew I'd have to make amends.'

He waved his hands and squinted down his nose. This was his special Jewish character role, which hadn't changed since he'd hammed Shylock in a monstrous college production years before.

'I acknowledge the debt. Take your pound of flesh!'

'Stop fooling, Jake. How do you know it's common knowledge?'

'Joe Bamm called me from Berlin. He hadn't got me anything more, but his thumbs were twitching. He said he'd just got that little G Tower story from another source of his. He said that once could be luck, but twice was more than coincidence. Then he came back with Panin's Tuesday booking to London. I tried to phone you then, but you were off on some dirty weekend with your secretary.'

Audley winced. So the G Tower story was planted too. He remembered now how Stocker had spoken about G Tower as though he had heard about it independently of Audley's source. They'd all been so pleased about it they hadn't bothered to question it. A lovely, succulent carrot for the donkeys!

'The trouble is that's the lot, David. I haven't got one damn thing to add to your little store of knowledge. I haven't got a clue about what dear old Panin's up to, not a clue.'

'Is there anything cooking in Russia at the moment?'

'Search me! Except that there's always something cooking there. Hawks and doves, old Marxist-Leninists and new thugs, Red Army and the KGB, Stalinists, Maoists – not many of them now – slavophiles, liberals, peasants. Davey boy, they can play their little games in more ways than I can make love. And they call it the Soviet Union! I tell you, Barry Goldwater's got more in common with Sammy Davis than some of those characters have with each other.'

He paused for breath. 'Why don't you ask your own Kremlinologists? Latimer's a sharp lad, they tell me. Or are you off on a do-it-yourself spree?'

Audley felt his early morning courage slipping. It all came down to a matter of time, and time was what he hadn't got. Panin had seen to that.

'Tell you what I'll do, David, seeing that I owe you something. There's a real nice American I know – Howard Morris – do you know him?'

Audley nodded. Howard was a refugee from Nixon's America, a bright hope in the days of the much-maligned

Lyndon Johnson who now held a nebulous post at Grosvenor Square.

'Of course you do! I forgot you were persona gratissima there since the Seven Days. Well, Howard owes me a fat favour and I'm sure he won't mind me passing it on to you. He probably trusts you more than he trusts me, anyway. You're both part of the world-wide Anglo-Saxon conspiracy against the lesser breeds like me and Nasser.'

Shapiro consulted a little dog-eared address book, and then dialled a number on the shiny telephone.

He put his hand over the mouthpiece.

'You know Howard's only real claim to fame? Hullo there – could I have a word with Howard Morris . . . ? He isn't? No matter. I'll try again later.'

He replaced the receiver, consulted the little address book again and dialled another number.

'When he was in Korea he was one of the select band of brothers who accidentally bombed the main Russian base outside Vladivostok. Hullo! Is Howard Morris being overcharged at your bar . . . ? Yes, it's me . . . He is? Well tell him I've come to collect on my last loan. Thanks . . . Where was I? Yes, they bombed the living daylights out of it – thought they were still over North Korea. And the Russkis never said a word. They thought is was deliberate.'

Jake's thesaurus of cautionary scandal was unsurpassed on either side of the Atlantic.

'And the moral of the story – or one of the morals – is that the burglar is in a poor position to complain about burglary. I commend that thought to you, David – Hullo, Howard, old friend . . . You are . . . ? So am I! Look, Howard, I have our mutual friend, David Audley, with me. I know you're busy Kremlin-watching these days. I'd count it a favour if you'd lend an ear to him for a minute or two – a real favour . . . You will – splendid!'

He passed the beery receiver to Audley. 'He's all yours. Make the most of him.'

'Hullo, Howard.' Audley was uneasily conscious that he was too ignorant even to ask the right questions, never mind understand the answers.

'Hi, David. I know your job forces you to consort with that horse-thief Shapiro, but don't tell me you're both moving into my territory.'

'Just me, Howard. And only temporarily, I hope. But I need someone to fill me in on the current situation over there. Is there a big row on, or anything like that?'

'What's wrong with your boys Latimer and Ridley? No, those were the Oxford Martyrs, weren't they! That's a Freudian slip if ever there was one. Latimer and Rogers?'

'You come well recommended.'

Jake grinned hugely, making a circle with his thumb and forefinger with one hand while giving the thumbs-up sign with the other. The effect was obscene.

'I do?' There was a mixture of resignation and uneasiness in the American's voice, and Audley knew exactly how he felt. Jake always took twenty shillings in the pound.

'Well, there's nothing special – except Round Sixteen in the Conservatives–Progressive fight. At the moment the Progressives are on the canvas, because that bastard Shelepin's got the Army on his side as well as the Young Communist League. And of course the KGB is playing its own game. But the Army's been acting up ever since Czechoslovakia showed how efficient they were – they don't think they're getting the appropriation they need. Or the respect they deserve. And they'd like to bomb the hell out of China, too.'

He paused for a moment. 'European liberals get worried about our generals. If they had one good look at some of the Soviet top brass they'd head for the hills, I reckon! You stick to the Middle East, David: you'll sleep sounder than I do.'

'Which corner is Nikolai Panin behind?'

Howard did not reply, even interrogatively. If Jake knew about Panin's visit, then it was certain that the American did. And Panin would be very much his concern, which meant that Audley himself might soon have something of potential value to contribute to the Anglo-Saxon conspiracy.

'I might be able to help you concerning Panin, Howard – always providing you can help me.'

Howard took a deep breath. 'Panin's behind all four corners as far as I can see. He's the sort of character who has subscriptions to *Ogonyek* and *Novy Mir*, and leaves 'em both lying around for everyone to see. The day you tell me which side he's on I'll get you a Congressional reception. What in the name of heaven and hell is he coming to England for, David?'

'You tell me, Howard. You've got a nice fat file on him, I've no doubt.'

'You must be joking. I've just been reading it; we've got a few pages of hearsay and Kremlin scuttlebut, but we've hardly got one solid thing on him since '45.'

'Nineteen-forty-five?' Gently now. 'He was just a line captain in '45.'

'He was a major when we met him. We'd picked up some Forschungsamt files – Research Office stuff – in an AA Barracks in Stefanskirchen. Perfectly innocent stuff. But he wanted to see it and we let him have a look. We didn't get another make on him until after Stalin's death. I tell you, David, if you want a line on Panin I'm not your man, and I don't know who is. I wish I did!'

Audley wondered what the Forschungsamt was. He had never heard of it, so it could be highly secret or, more probably, highly unimportant. Jake's Berlin man, Bamm, would certainly know, but that would mean more favours, and Jake was too interested already. Besides, there wasn't time.

But Theodore Freisler would know, of course – it was exactly the sort of thing he would know. He had been meaning to phone the old man for twenty-four hours without taking the trouble to do it. Now he had an adequate selfish reason for doing the right thing.

He thanked Howard Morris as sincerely as he was able to with the grinning Shapiro at his elbow, carefully deprecating his association with the Israeli. Apart from being a pleasant fellow, the American would be a useful contact in the future; the sort of man with whom the nuances between the lines of indigestible Soviet journals could be enjoyably discussed. He thought nostalgically of his old, quiet life, which had ended a thousand years before, just last Thursday.

Sincerity was not required for his farewell to Jake. That was the one real virtue of their relationship – it was founded on naked and unashamed self-interest on both sides, needing no false protestations of friendship. He was going to miss Jake.

He was tempted to phone Theodore from the first call box as he had done before, but his guilt drove him to search out the grimy house behind the vast complex of the British Museum and to climb the interminable and even grimier stairs.

The huge, brutal face at once creased into a happy smile which hinted at the nature concealed behind it. One of the things that kept Audley from visiting more often was the undeserved welcome he always received. Theodore would stop whatever he was doing, no matter how important, and give him hours of his time.

'David, you arrive most opportunely! I have just made myself some of this excellent new tinned coffee. A big tin of it I bought at a specially reduced price last Friday, and already I have nearly finished it! And you and Professsor Tolkien are to blame.'

'Professor Tolkien, Theodore? Who's he?'

Theodore heaped spoonfuls of evil-looking brown powder into a large mug and stirred it vigorously.

'He is the author of *The Lord of the Rings* and I'm most surprised you haven't heard of him.' Theodore tapped three substantial volumes with a heavy finger. 'A writer of fairy stories for grown-ups. My friends have been telling me to read him for years, and I was too stupid to take their advice. Now I have done nothing but read him for three whole days – except to wrestle with your puzzle.'

'I have heard of him, actually, Theodore. But fairy stories really aren't my line.'

'Your puzzle is a fairy story, my dear David. I have thought and I have telephoned friends of mine in Berlin, and I tell you there is nothing, nothing, that fits your puzzle. Time cancels out the value of things: what would be valuable to a thief then would not be valuable to *them* now. Not worth their trouble.'

'We had a tip that it might be the Schliemann Collection from the Staatliche Museum.'

'The Trojan treasures? No, David, the psychology is wrong. Worth stealing – yes. After all, the Russians stole it and it was stolen from them, I know the story. But it was not theirs in the first place, so they would not pursue it. If it had been the amber from the Winter Palace, that would be different. That was *theirs*. But that was never brought beyond East Prussia.'

'Never mind, Theodore. It was good of you to take time from Tolkien to try.'

Audley sipped his coffee. It was surprisingly drinkable.

The old man was shaking his head. 'No, I have failed you. But even if your thief had catholic tastes and took a thing here and a thing there I find it hard to imagine a collection of objects which would tempt them now.'

'Tell me about the Forschungsamt instead, then.'

The great bullet-head stopped shaking. 'What do you wish to know about the Forschungsamt, Dr Audley?'

'Anything, Theodore. I don't know the first thing about it.'

Freisler pondered the question for a time.

'The most interesting thing, of course, is that it illustrates the relationship of the old German bureaucracy to the Nazi Party. If you have time to read the relevant chapter in my book on the Civil Service between the wars I think that will become apparent to you.'

Before he could get up Audley managed to restrain him.

'I haven't really got the time. Just tell me what it was.'

Freisler looked at him pityingly. 'What it was? Why, it was the office that grew out of the old Chiffre und Horchleitstelle, Cypher and Monitoring. What I believe you would call "passive intelligence". I knew a number of people who worked in it – good Germans, too, not Nazis. That was the remarkable thing about the Research Office: the Nazis were always trying to take it over, but they never really managed to do so.'

He smiled. 'I think it was partly because they all wanted it that they failed. Goering was nominally in charge, but all he knew was that he wasn't going to give it up. Let me see – Himmler tried, and Kaltenbrunner tried. And Diels.' He counted them off on his fingers. 'The only one who got close was Heydrich. He managed to move some of his prewar Sicherheitsdienst files into its headquarters on the Schillerstrasse. But then he was killed by the Czechs in '42, and the office was bombed out by your air force in '43. After that nobody really knew what was happening. The records were spread all over the place, and many of them were destroyed in the end to stop the Russians getting them.'

He looked up at Audley. 'But your clever thief wouldn't

have wanted any of them. They had no great value then, and they'd have less than none today, except to the historians. As I recollect, the Forschungsamt officials were considered so innocent that they weren't even called to the de-nazification trials!'

He rose and picked his way between piles of journals and manuscripts to his bookcase.

Audley rose too, but in alarm. Once Theodore gave him the book he would be honour bound to wade through it, or he would never be able to face the old German again.

'Theodore, I really ought to be going.' He looked at his watch. 'I'm lunching with my fiancée and I mustn't be late.'

But Theodore was already thumbing through a thick volume, as unstoppable and incapable of changing direction as a rhinoceros.

'Schimpf – Schimpf was the first director. He committed suicide. Then came Prince Christophe of Hesse. He was killed on the Italian front. Then Schnapper, I think . . . Ah! Here we have it! The office went to Klettersdorf after the 1943 air raid. Then back to Berlin when the Russians were approaching. And then to the four winds!'

He tapped the book with his finger, staring owlishly at Audley, who had reached the door.

'Some of the documents I saw in England in 1957, at Whaddon Hall. But there was nothing of interest to you in them. They would have been from the section captured at, let me think now – at Glucksberg, of course . . .'

Audley made his way slowly down the staircase. Once Theodore had mentioned passive intelligence he had known that any further research into the Forschungsamt was likely to be a journey up a blind alley. It had been a wasted trip. But as he reached the street doorway he heard Theodore bellowing unintelligibly from above. He stopped guiltily and waited impatiently as the heavy footsteps thumped after him from landing to landing.

The old German was breathing heavily when he finally appeared. 'David, forgive me! My mind was not listening to you properly. A fiancée, you said – and for a fiancée there must be a gift!'

Audley's heart sank as he saw the square, untidy parcel, a battered carrier bag lashed down with scotch tape. The famous two-decker history of the German civil service, through all the convulsions of the Empire, the Weimar Republic and the Third Reich, had cornered him at last.

'Theodore, it isn't necessary . . .'

The great hands thrust the parcel into his and waved his protest aside. It was necessary. It was a small token of deep esteem. It humbly marked a great occasion.

It was also coals of fire on Audley's head, coals which glowed as Theodore beamed and shook his hand and became increasingly guttural, as he always did on the rare occasions when his emotions outran his vocabulary. Audley had fled in cavalier fashion from an unselfish and undemanding friend. His punishment was just and appropriate.

As he drove away to meet Faith he resolved to invite Theodore down into the country for a week. Faith would approve of Theodore; not only because of his grave courtesy, but also because they could meet on the common ground of their own high sense of moral responsibility.

15

But in the event Audley did not so easily extinguish the coals of fire. They glowed again even more brightly some hours later when Faith was excitedly unpacking her mountain of shopping in the bridal suite at the Bull.

'David, what on earth is this extraordinary parcel?'

She held up the carrier bag.

'It's our first present, from a very good and honourable man, my love.' He hoped desperately that she wouldn't laugh at it, and he couldn't bear to watch her undo it.

She ripped away the covering.

'How lovely! But I've read it, of course. Still, it's something you can read again and again.'

Audley looked in the mirror at his astonished face, half of it covered with shaving soap.

'It has written in it *"Ein Märchen aus alten Zeiten, Das kommt mir nicht aus dem Sinn* – but may you never be sad." What does that mean?'

It would be from Heine, Theodore's idol. He turned round: Faith was sitting with the three volumes of Tolkien's *The Lord of the Rings* on her lap – Theodore's own copies.

But before he could reply there was a light tap at the door.

Hugh Roskill entered gingerly, as though his feet hurt. Possibly his feet *did* hurt, if he had spent the whole day exploring the environs of the old airfield. But Audley somehow felt that it was because he had half expected to find some sort of orgy in progress. He seemed quite relieved to see Faith clothed and Audley engaged in the unexceptionable act of shaving.

But then poor Roskill had had rather a trying day, it transpired. It had been windy and cold, a return to the weather of Friday's funeral – odd, that, for it had seemed pleasant, if not exactly sunny, to Audley.

They had passed a tiring morning marking pimples and pock-marks on a large-scale Ordnance Survey map which Butler had brought with him. Roskill had given himself a shock on one of Farmer Warren's electric sheep fences and Butler had slipped into a ditch which was no longer wet, but still muddy.

In the afternoon Richardson returned from his assignment in Cambridge with the latest equipment for detecting buried metallic objects, the archaeological department's newest toy.

'DECCO,' explained Roskill, 'which Richardson claims is short for Decay of Eddy Currents in Conductive Objects. But it just looked like a souped-up mine detector to me.'

Unfortunately, either Richardson had failed to master DECCO's intricacies or DECCO had developed some minor fault. Having lugged the device two miles or more across country to the most promising pimple they had had to carry it all the way back unused. Richardson had returned with it to Cambridge and neither had been seen since.

Shortly after he had retired from the field Stocker had arrived with Panin, and Stocker had not been noticeably pleased to find that Audley was not present (though it could be simply indigestion, since the timing of his arrival suggested that he had not been able to linger over his lunch).

'I rather got the impression,' said Roskill, 'that he expected to find us at work with pick and shovel, with you standing over us with a rope's end. I'm afraid Butler was a bit short with him. We told him you'd been on the job continuously . . .' He paused fractionally as the other implications of that statement flashed through his mind, but recovered splendidly '. . . since Friday. I said you were probably chasing the Pole, anyway, and he cooled down a bit.'

It must have been a trying day for Stocker as well. After the early morning Panin call, the hitherto subservient Audley had turned awkward. Then Panin had rushed him out of London at uncomfortable speed, only to find two disgruntled but unintimidated operatives doing nothing in particular.

'Not to worry, though,' Roskill reassured him, mistaking his silence. 'Butler showed him his map, all covered with meaningless red and blue crosses and lines and circles – Jack could snow the recording angel if he set his mind to it. He went back to London happy enough, I think.'

'What about Panin?'

'Our Russian colleague?' Roskill cocked his head. 'The Professor – that's how Stocker refers to him, by the way – is still very much with us. As a matter of fact he's sinking beer with Butler in the bar at this moment. But I don't think Butler snowed *him*. I've got a feeling he's a downier bird altogether. He doesn't say much, but Butler's talking cricket to him at the moment, so he hasn't had much opportunity yet anyway – when I left them Jack was just launching into his favourite story, about the time Bill Farrimond played for England and Lancashire Second.'

'Is he alone?'

'Oddly enough he is. Or he appears to be. But Butler and I are going to have a scout round after dinner. If he's alone then he's top brass, isn't he?'

'Panin's top brass, Hugh. No doubt about that. But tell me how you got on yesterday.'

'Wash-out, I'm afraid, sir.' Roskill shook his head sadly. 'We couldn't track one of 'em at all. And the other one shut up tighter than a clam.'

Then he smiled. 'Actually, I rather liked the old boy

Ellis. He was regular RAF. Joined as a boy when there were still Bristol Fighters around and his last station was supersonic. He'd seen it all!'

'He wouldn't talk about Steerforth?'

'Oh, he talked. But he didn't give anything away. I think Ellis knew every racket that'd ever been thought of. But he liked Steerforth – said he was a gentleman, which means that Steerforth always paid the rate for the job in advance. And he practically told me I *wasn't* a gentleman for checking on another pilot!

'Then Butler appealed to his patriotism and he just laughed at us.' Roskill's eyes flashed. 'He said that he knew his pilots, and patriotism was one thing and a bit of smuggling on the side was another. He said he's been on an air-sea rescue station where the Warwicks ran a regular service from Iceland with the lifeboats under their bellies full of nylons and whisky and ham. That'd stopped when they had to drop a boat to a ditched crew, and the chaps were picked up roaring drunk, but if Steerforth had put one over on us, so much the better. He was a splendid old boy!'

So there was no help there. Panin was waiting and his bluff was in danger of being called. When Roskill had gone he stood silent, staring at the dried shaving soap on his face.

Faith put her hand on his shoulder. 'No good, David?'

He shrugged. 'We're simply running out of time, Faith love. We never had much in the beginning. But instead of playing for it I've just speeded it up. I'm rather wondering now if it was the right thing to do.'

Faith held up Theodore's gift. 'Well, don't give up yet. The Fellowship of the Ring did just the same in *The Lord of the Rings* – they forced the Dark Lord to attack before he was ready, and he came unstuck. Maybe Panin will come unstuck too.'

Audley smiled at her. Woman-like, she had committed

herself with her affections. Panin was the enemy now, the Dark Lord, whoever he was. And the least he could do in return for such loyalty was to play the game out.

He watched her in the mirror as he shaved, and Panin faded into immateriality. Not just Panin either – Stocker, Fred and all the rest as well. At some stage since Saturday night they had all changed places in importance with this girl. The longer he was with her, the closer he came to reality. And whatever happened, the real world was Faith struggling with her zip-fastener.

She turned towards him at last.

'Will I do, then?'

The long white dress, slashed in front from the ankle to the knee, was classically severe, but the heavy golden earrings and elaborate necklace were barbaric – no, not so much barbaric as pre-Hellenic.

'Take your glassess off.'

'But David, I don't see so well without them. Don't you like me in glasses?'

'I like you better in them. But not tonight.'

She slipped them off and stared vaguely at him: Steerforth's daughter to the life now, almost as her father might have dressed her. Except that the costume jewellery was from Bond Street, not Troy.

'Now you'll do very well. Very well indeed!'

'I hope so! But I've got butterflies in the tummy, David. Don't ask me to play the *femme fatale* ever again – this is positively the last time.'

Audley shared the same stomach-turning mixture of excitement and fear as he followed her down the passage. He had nothing with which to face Panin except pure bluff. Yet Panin didn't know it was bluff. And this was the home ground, for all its soft carpets and heated air: 3112 Squadron's home ground, where the Russian had been beaten once before. The ghosts were on Audley's side here.

A subdued murmur led them towards the bar. The swarthy waiter smiled unselfconscious admiration at Faith and honest envy at Audley before sweeping open the door for them.

They had their entrance, anyway.

For Nikolai Andrievich Panin.

But he had his back to them, engrossed in watching Butler cut an imaginary cricket ball down past gully and third slip for four easy runs. Roskill stood politely at his elbow in the act of raising a tankard to his lips.

Then the tankard stopped, the imaginary bat was lowered and Panin slowly turned towards them.

Audley had known what to expect; that face was in a dozen pictures in the file. Yet it was a sickening anticlimax nevertheless: Faith's Dark Lord was a very ordinary little man, totally without any aura of power or menace. The sheep-face with its bent nose was greyish and deeply-lined like an eroded desert landscape. It was the file brought to life, giving away nothing – not even a raised eyebrow for Steerforth's Trojan daughter.

Audley put out his hand.

'Professor Panin.'

'Dr Audley.'

There was hardly a trace of an accent. Indeed, the foreignness of the voice lay in its complete neutrality.

'This is Miss Steerforth.'

Panin regarded Faith without curiosity.

'Miss Steerforth,' he repeated unemotionally.

Faith took the smooth, dry hand he offered her. 'Professor Panin, I'm afraid my father once caused you a great deal of trouble,' she said in a voice equally devoid of emotion. 'But I think it's rather late for an apology.'

The Russian considered her for a moment.

'Miss Steerforth, we are not responsible for our fathers. Mine was a sergeant in the Semenovsky Guards – the Tsar's guards, Miss Steerforth. And after that in the

White army. But that was not my business, for I was a babe in arms. So you have nothing for which to apologize.'

He turned back to Audley.

'Major Butler has been instructing me in the finer points of cricket. I know the theory of the game, but the fascination of a game lies in the finer points, would you not agree?'

'For the spectator, certainly. For the player it's winning that counts.'

'But you played rugby, I believe – and that is a game of brute force played by gentlemen. At least, so I have heard it described.'

'Whoever described it for you obviously never played in Wales, Professor Panin. I might just as well describe yours as a dirty hobby for scholars.'

'A dirty hobby?' A note of puzzlement crept into the voice. He hadn't expected to be insulted.

'Archaeology, Professor.' It was comical to see Butler relax. 'Archaeologists at work are indistinguishable from navvies.'

'But an innocent hobby, Dr Audley. Archaeologists are safely sealed off from modern history. Historians are too often tempted to stray from their chosen field, are they not?'

Parry.

'Very true. And also there's always the danger that they'll make inconvenient discoveries.'

Thrust.

Panin nodded. 'And then they discover that the truth is not as indivisible as they thought. Not a clear glass, but a mirror sometimes.'

It was time to stop playing, thought Audley. 'But we're not concerned with history or archaeology, are we! Only indirectly, anyway. I take it as confirmed that you want me to find the Schliemann Collection for you?'

210

Panin inclined his head. 'I gathered from Brigadier Stocker that our small secret was out. Yes, Dr Audley, my government would be most grateful if you could do that. Then we will jointly restore it to the German Democratic Republic.'

Just like that, as though it was a mislaid umbrella!

'Well, I think we have a fair chance of finding it tomorrow, given a little luck.'

Try that for size, Professor.

Panin was unmoved. 'So soon? But I am gratified to hear it. I had feared that it might prove a needle in a hay stack.'

'It certainly might have been easier if you had confided in us from the start – and I mean from the very start.'

The lines deepened around Panin's mouth.

'There was a certain . . . embarrassment about the loss of the collection in the first place, Dr Audley.'

Sir Kenneth Allen had hinted as much. To abstract the collection from G Tower had been the prerogative of the conquerors; to have lost it then so quickly reduced the conquerors to bungling plunderers.

'And then we formed the opinion that it was irretrievably lost,' Panin continued. 'We believed that there was nothing anyone could do. It was only when I heard of the recovery of the aircraft that I revised my opinion.'

There was a great deal left unsaid there: the whole Russian obsession down the years with ditched Dakotas. A little honest curiosity would not be out of order.

'Professor Panin, we all know of your reputation as an archaeologist,' said Audley slowly, 'but I must admit I find your interest in the collection – and your government's interest – a little curious. Couldn't you have left it to the East Germans? After all, it's not a political matter.'

'There you have put your finger on the truth, Dr Audley. It is *not* a political matter. For me it is a very personal matter. It was I who lost the Schliemann Collection. I lost it in Berlin, and I lost it again here in England.'

He stared lugubriously at the many-stranded necklace which rested on the false swell of Faith's chest.

'There is a German scholar,' he went on, 'a Dr Berve, who argues that there was never a siege of Troy – that Homer's Troy was a village overthrown by an earthquake. But I have handled Schliemann's treasures, and I have never forgotten them. In fact, as I have grown older I have thought of them more often.'

There was neither conviction nor passion in his voice. He was simply stating facts for Audley to accept or dismiss as he chose. Sir Kenneth might have used the same words. Faith had said it outright and Stocker had suggested it.

And now even Audley found himself wanting to believe it too. Treasure – above all, treasure of gold – had always driven men to irrational acts. Cortés and Pizarro and all the victims of the search for the Seven Cities and the Gilded Man. Schliemann's treasure had been enough to tempt Steerforth to risk five lives and lose his own. It had killed Bloch quickly and Morrison after half a lifetime.

But was it enough to haunt a man like Panin?

He realized with a start that he was staring directly at Roskill, and staring that young man out of countenance. And there was something else –

It was the hotel manager, standing at his elbow, now beautifully dinner-jacketed and still sleekly out of place against the dark oak beams.

'Excuse me, Dr Audley.'

And marvellously out of place in Newton Chester too, thought Audley. The sleepy place could have seen nothing so Mediterranean since the Roman legion from Lincoln had come marching by to build its practice camp down the road.

'Excuse me for interrupting you, Dr Audley, but Mistaire Warren, of Castle Farm – he was looking for you

212

this afternoon here. He left a package for you which I have.'

The man took each aspirate like a show-jumper on a tricky course of fences, landing triumphantly on the final full stop for a clear round.

Butler already had an airfield map, but Audley suddenly wanted to get away from them all – to consider Panin for a moment by himself and to collect his thoughts again. This was a sufficient excuse.

He followed the manager out into the hall, where the fellow darted into his office and reappeared flourishing a large envelope so exuberantly that Audley thought for a second that he was going to spin it across the hallway.

But the flourish was converted into an elegant little bow, and Audley felt honour-bound to open it there and then as though it was a document of the highest importance.

There was a note pinned to the folded map, biro-scrawled in a childishly copperplate hand.

'Dear Dr Audley – I enclose my father's map, as promised. I'm sorry it isn't quite what I thought. The runways are marked in pencil though, but none of the buildings. My father was very interested in – '

The next word stopped Audley dead in mid-sentence.

Carefully he unfolded the creased section of the large-scale Ordnance Survey map. It wasn't luck really, he told himself. He would have come to it himself in the end, sooner or later. Indeed, he could see the signposts pointing to it along the way, which he had left behind only half-read.

And there it was, of course: Steerforth's treasure neatly and precisely marked for him. Marked as exactly as if it had been Steerforth, and not Keith Warren's father, who had recorded it.

As for luck, though – if any man had had good luck, and then equally undeserved and final bad luck, it had been John Steerforth.

16

For the second time Audley watched the water tower sink slowly into the tarmac skyline behind him.

He did up another button on his raincoat. Roskill was driving with his window down, and the Land-Rover was draughty; it was another unseasonable morning, clear enough, but grey and unfriendly. One of those mornings when spring hadn't even tried to break through, even falsely. Morning had purged the old airfield altogether of the atmosphere it had possessed on Sunday evening: it was no longer melancholy and forlorn, but merely bleak.

But it was a good morning for digging – that had been Butler's only comment as he dumped the spades in the back. And Butler, in navy-blue donkey-jacket and baggy gardening trousers, had undeniably come prepared to dig.

Roskill's confidence was not so complete; or perhaps it was simply that his equally ancient tweeds still retained a lingering elegance. As he had explained unapologetically the night before, he had no garden of his own, and consequently no gardening clothes.

Audley superimposed the ribbon of runway and the waving sea of grass on the map which was now etched on his memory. At about this point, on the left, there should be the break in the grass which marked the concrete base of the safe deposit hut.

'Stop here for a moment.'

He climbed out of the cabin and took in the whole circuit of the surrounding landscape. Ahead of him the taxiing strip stretched away, narrowing until it merged with the trees in the distance. Behind him the slow incline of the Hump obscured the old built-up area of the field.

On each side the prairie lay wide and open. It was still a lonely and naked place, with only the distant racket of a tractor out of sight to the right: Farmer Warren was busy cutting his Italian rye grass for his wife's uncle's silage.

Audley climbed back into the cabin, pointing out to Roskill the low irregular line of hillocks ahead and off the tarmac strip to the left, insignificant in themselves, but perfectly discernible in their level surroundings.

His confidence was almost absolute, and he recognized it as that same inner security which he had known sometimes before examinations, when he was sure that he could translate preparation into action. It was attended by the same uncontrollable physical symptoms, too – the dry mouth, the tight chest and the fast pulse.

He signalled Roskill to stop as they approached the nearest mound, little more than 300 yards from the edge of the taxiing strip, and walked to the top of it while the others unloaded the equipment. From the runway it had seemed to be no more than one of a haphazard group, but now he could see clearly that it marked the exact corner of the old Roman Practice Camp, the meeting point of two lines of hillocks and low banks now related to one another as the time-eroded remains of the earth ramparts.

He turned back to speak to the men behind him and saw with surprise that the water tower was once more in view. The changes in the land were extraordinarily deceptive, its rise and fall so gentle here that they tricked the eye. Yet it was perfectly logical: no Roman military engineer would ever have marked out a camp in a hollow, not even a practice camp, but would have used the rising ground to advantage. And it even added a touch of perfection to Steerforth's opportunism.

He stepped down to where Roskill and Butler stood amid a small pile of equipment.

'Where to now?' The resignation in Roskill's voice

suggested that although DECCO was a far cry from the old mine detectors it was heavier than it looked.

Right or wrong, Audley knew this was his moment and he couldn't resist underplaying it.

'Where you're standing, near enough.'

Butler looked around him disbelievingly.

'Here? But, damn it – we're still well inside the perimeter! Why, you can see this patch from miles away. No one could dig a hole here without its being spotted, not when the airfield was in use!'

'Let's try here all the same,' said Audley patiently. 'Let's see what the machine has to say.'

Roskill began to fiddle with DECCO, and with a shrug Butler emptied half a dozen reels of white tape from a canvas haversack.

'We'll lay down the start lines first, then. How long do you want for the base line, Dr Audley?'

'Ten yards, say.'

'*Ten yards?*' the scorn was stronger now than the disbelief in Butler's voice. 'I've got a hundred yards in each of these reels! You must be joking!'

'Jesus Christ!' whispered Roskill. 'I've got a reading!'

Butler swung round towards him.

'I've got a reading,' said Roskill. 'It's right here under my feet!'

Butler set the tape down and strode over to him, peering over his shoulder.

'It's a strong one, too. Left a bit . . . a bit more . . . steady – that's it!'

They both looked up at Audley.

'Well, there's something down there right enough, and it's fairly substantial,' said Roskill. 'Richardson said this thing was so sensitive it would pick up the studs in an old boot. But we've got a lot more than an old boot here.'

Butler looked accusingly at Audley.

'And that wasn't luck, Dr Audley. You knew damn well it was there – you knew to the inch!'

Roskill set DECCO down carefully to one side.

'After what we went through yesterday,' he said gently, 'I do think you owe us some explanation for this sudden fit of – what's the word – serendipity . . . Just tell us, Dr Audley – is this the real thing?'

Audley breathed out heavily, conscious suddenly that he had been holding his breath.

'I rather think it must be,' he managed to say. 'But I give you my word I didn't know until last night. I hadn't a clue up to then. Or rather, I couldn't make sense of the clues we had.'

'Never mind the clues,' cut in Butler. 'Just tell us how the hell Steerforth dug a hole in full view of everyone for miles around without anyone noticing.'

'The answer is that he didn't dig it, Major Butler. It was already dug for him. You see, there was an archaeological dig going on here all that summer, off and on. They filled the trench up just at this point on 28 August, and that's the day after he landed his boxes in the hollow just down there.'

Roskill whistled to himself softly.

'They'd known about this Roman camp for ages, of course. But it wasn't a very promising site, and it was only because the farmer who owned the land was interested in archaeology that they decided to excavate it. That was in 1938, actually. But then the RAF got in first and they had to wait until 1945 – and then they only obtained permission on condition that they dug one trench at a time and filled it in before they started on the next one.

'It's all neatly marked on a map the farmer's son lent me, and when I saw the date on this trench I was pretty sure that it was here if it was anywhere. It fitted in with something the navigator told me.'

'And Steerforth was bound to know about it,' Roskill

murmured, looking back towards the airfield. 'He must have taxied past here often enough.'

'That's just it, Hugh – only he knew better than most, because he used to walk down this way to collect things he'd had dumped in a hut just down there. Tierney said he had an excuse for coming. I think that just might have been an innocent interest in archaeology.'

'By God, but he was damned lucky with his timing,' grunted Butler. 'The loot – and then the hole just at the right moment!'

But which really came first? Audley wondered. Was the idea of hiding the treasure in the trench the sudden flash of inspiration he had originally imagined? Or was the existence of that trench the fatal knowledge which tempted Steerforth into doing what would otherwise have been impossible?

'Lucky?' Roskill shook his head in admiration. 'Maybe he had serendipity too. But I think he was a very smart operator. Whichever way you look at it, it was a bloody marvellous bit of improvisation – no wonder old Ellis thought the world of him!'

Like Audley, Roskill was halfway towards giving in to John Steerforth, though perhaps for a different reason. Where Roskill was drawn to the man's audacity, possibly as a kindred spirit, Audley warmed to the knowledge that Steerforth had enjoyed the irony of it: the greatest archaeological loot in history, twice plundered already, planted in another archaeologist's hole in the ground! He need never be ashamed of his future father-in-law . . .

'He was a clever blighter, no doubt about that,' conceded Butler. 'But he'd have done better to have left well alone in the end. He just made work for us.'

He peeled off his donkey-jacket. 'And we're just giving it all back to the Russians, more's the pity.'

'. . . Who are even now coming to collect,' Roskill added, staring past Audley.

Audley swung round to follow his gaze. Panin had said that his official car would be down early, and here it was, creeping directly across the airfield like a black beetle, the sound of its engine drowned by the more distant, but noisier tractor. He hadn't wasted much time.

Butler bent down and picked up one of the spades.

'Come on, then, Hugh,' he said grimly. 'Let's not keep our masters waiting.'

The black car halted alongside the Land-Rover and a stocky man who had been sitting beside the driver got out and hurried deferentially to open the rear door. Panin eased himself out and to Audley's consternation Faith followed him. *That* had not been in the plan, but there was no helping it now.

'Good morning, Dr Audley.' Panin's voice was as flat and featureless as the airfield. 'I am sorry to have missed you earlier; I did not know that you were going to start so early. This is Mr Sheremetev from our embassy.'

The chunky man, who must have been dragged from his bed even earlier than Audley, nodded his head sharply and twisted his lips in a brief diplomatic smile.

'And I took the liberty of bringing Miss Steerforth with me.'

'I'm sorry, David,' Faith broke in. 'I know you said that there probably wouldn't be any action until this afternoon, but I couldn't bear to hang around the hotel by myself. And Professor Panin was coming up here.'

There was a muffled thump as Butler drove his spade into a square of grass which Roskill had roughly shaved with a small sickle. He lifted a segment of turf and placed it neatly to one side.

'And it seems that we were both wise not to delay, Miss Steerforth,' observed Panin. 'Is this the place, Dr Audley?'

'Our detecting device has picked up something just here, Professor. We were lucky to pick it up so quickly.'

Sheremetev gestured around him. 'Is it not rather a – a public space for such a purpose?'

'There were archaeologists excavating here at the time, Mr Sheremetev. They were just filling in a trench at this place.'

He met Panin's stare, only to be disconcerted by its lack of expression. Or was it unvarying intensity about those eyes which was disconcerting? His first impression had been one of anti-climax the night before. But the man's personality wasn't negative – it was simply shuttered.

And now Panin was nodding in agreement with him.

'Public, but not obvious – that is good reasoning, Dr Audley. And it was good reasoning in the first instance, too: the classic doctrine of the hiding place.' He considered Faith reflectively. 'Young airmen in my experience were not so devious, but this man we underrated.'

He walked over to where Roskill and Butler were digging behind a small rampart of turves. Neither of them took any notice of him, and he eventually continued past them up the slope of the nearest mound. Sheremetev followed obediently, as though linked to him by some invisible towline.

'I think he's rather a sweetie, really,' whispered Faith. 'He's got beautiful manners and he was charming last evening.'

After that awkward moment of encounter, the man had been courteous enough in a solemn way. The charm, however, was an illusion created by her own nervousness and a mixture of gin and claret drunk too quickly.

'As a matter of fact he's rather like you, David.' Faith grinned wickedly at the discomposure he wasn't quick enough to hide.

He shut his face against her innocence.

'You would do well to remember the fate of the young

lady of Riga, my girl,' he said, watching Panin quarter the landscape as he had done ten minutes earlier.

'The one who had an affair with a tiger?'

'That's the dirty version. In the nursery version she merely went for a ride with him –

>   "They returned from the ride
>   With the lady inside,
>   And a smile on the face of the tiger".'

'You've got a suspicious nature, David.'

He was only half listening to her now.

'Suspicious? I'm afraid it's an occupational disease, suspicion. But it's rarely fatal. Credulity is the disease that kills more often.'

After a time Panin came down off the mound, and again stood for a while silently watching the diggers.

'A Roman camp, you say?'

Audley nodded. 'The theory is that it was a practice camp built by new recruits from Lincoln. The latest coins they found were of Nero, nothing after that. Apparently they were rather hoping it might have been refortified in the fourth century, but it wasn't. They found very little, as a matter of fact.'

'That period interests you?'

'The Roman occupation? Not really – I'm more of a mediaevalist.'

'That I know. I have read your essays on the Latin Kingdom of Jerusalem, Dr Audley. They are most interesting.'

It wasn't really a surprise. Panin was a man who did his homework quickly. He had known about Jake Shapiro's interest in Masada in just the same way.

'You don't think Israel will go the same way as the Crusaders. Dr Audley? In the end?'

'The comparison's false, Professor. Israel is a Middle Eastern nation – or would be eventually if your country learnt to mind its own business,' replied Audley mildly. It comforted him to hope that Panin might be nervous enough to make conversation. 'Not that I don't appreciate how necessary it may be to stop the rot at home by asserting oneself abroad.'

'It is fortunate for the world, then, that your country is too weak to try that remedy!'

'I couldn't agree more. It's fortunate for us, too, you know. Your people just don't seem to have grasped that the returns aren't worth the effort in the Middle East – and I'm sure ours wouldn't either if they had the power to make any difference.'

Panin shrugged. 'You must find your work a frustrating occupation then, Dr Audley.'

There was a grating sound of metal on metal, followed by an exasperated grunt.

Roskill, waist deep now in the trench, shook his wrist in pain.

'Jarred my bloody wrist,' he explained. Then he bent down and fumbled in the loose earth at his feet.

'Here's what gave us our reading, anyway,' he said. 'Genuine Roman wheels – or maybe Trojan!'

He wrenched a pair of rusty wheels, still joined together on their axle, from the bottom of the trench, gazed at them ruefully, and then threw them out on to the grass.

Everyone stared wordlessly at the wheels. They were even joined by Panin's driver, a wizened gnome who had been pacing up and down beside the car as though he was afraid someone planned to steal it.

Then Audley realized that they were all looking at him. There was sympathy in Faith's eyes, disappointment in Butler's gaze and amusement in Sheremetev's. Only Panin retained his inscrutability.

Or perhaps only Panin understood that the rusty wheels represented not failure, but final success.

'Don't just stand there, Hugh – get digging!' said

Audley. 'The trolley went into the trench after the last box, no point in leaving it around. You're nearly there now.'

It seemed to Audley then that the world shrank to the circle round the trench. Even the distant noise of the tractor seemed to fade, as though their collective eagerness filtered out everything except the thud and scrape of the spades in the earth.

Neither the diggers nor the watchers uttered a word as the first of John Steerforth's boxes came to the light again and was raised from the earth.

They all stood looking at it for a long minute: a very ordinary box, damp-darkened, with its lid already splintered where the first fierce spade stroke which had discovered it had smashed into the wood.

Then Sheremetev knelt beside it and levered up a splintered segment of the lid with the edge of a spade. Beneath the broken wood was the top of what seemed to be another box, made of metal.

Sheremetev looked up at Panin, and nodded.

'This is the box,' he said.

Panin touched Audley's arm gently.

'If I might have a minute in private with you, Dr Audley,' he said courteously.

They drew aside from the group, to the foot of the corner mound of the old camp.

'I know that your instructions are quite clear, Dr Audley. I am to have what you find – Brigadier Stocker has made that plain, and there can be no misunderstanding about it. You have done brilliantly, and my government will not be ungrateful.'

Audley listened to the sound of the tractor, which now came loud and clear across the airfield.

'The Schliemann Collection is here, Dr Audley,' Panin continued, 'and we shall restore it to its owners as promised. But this first box I will have now – I will take it now, Dr Audley. Without fuss, without argument. It is necessary that I do this.'

So Steerforth's loot had truly been a Trojan cargo – what it seemed, but also more than it seemed. That had been the only logical explanation.

'I'm not sure that I can agree to that, Professor,' said Audley slowly. 'My instructions cover the Schliemann Collection. But I'm also bound by the Defence of the Realm Act, which gives me a wider obligation.'

Panin nodded. 'I understand this. But this is a matter which does not concern your country, Dr Audley. It is an internal matter concerning my country alone. If there is any . . . irregularity in my position it arises simply from a crime committed many years ago by one of your officers. But I do not wish to make an issue of that. And it would only bring pain and discredit on innocent people now – people like the young woman back there.'

Audley faced the Russian. 'You know as well as I do, Professor Panin, that I can't simply take your word in this matter, any more than you would take mine. Miss Steerforth must take her chance, I'm afraid. And we must be the judges of what concerns us.'

'I think you are exceeding your instructions, Dr Audley,' Panin sighed. 'But fortunately it is of no real consequence. We will take the box now, and without further argument. That is how it must be.'

He turned on his heel with an uncharacteristically quick movement.

'Guriev!'

The gnome-like driver did not look round, but with a smooth, unhurried movement produced an automatic pistol from inside his coat.

'All hands in view, please,' he said in a surprising bass voice. 'No sudden movements, I beg you.'

'Sheremetev!'

The embassy man, with his inevitable return to Russia

as a *persona non grata* written mournfully on his face, began to check Butler and Roskill for any hidden weapons.

'We are not armed, Professor Panin.' Audley spoke with deliberate bitterness. 'We aren't gangsters.'

Sheremetev folded the donkey-jacket neatly on top of the tweed jacket and shook his head.

'I regret this action most sincerely,' said Panin. 'We are not gangsters either, Dr Audley. But we have wider obligations, too, as you have. You have my assurance that your country's security is not involved. And now you have my apology.'

He gestured to Roskill and Butler. 'If you two gentlemen will be so good as to place the box in the boot of the car . . .'

'No!' Guriev's deep voice cut off the end of Panin's words.

The pistol remained unmoving in his hand, pointing at nobody in particular. But now it pointed at everyone.

'The box remains here,' said Guriev. 'Sheremetev – you will empty the contents from it on the grass there. Then you will take a match from a box which I shall give you, and you will burn them. Then you will grind the ashes under your heel.'

His eyes flicked to Panin. 'And then, Comrade Panin, if you wish to recover the Schliemann Collection, I have no objection.'

Panin's face was stony, with the lines in it cut like canyons. He spoke quickly and quietly in Russian to Guriev, his voice deep and urgent with authority. Audley strained his ears, but could not catch the sense of it, beyond the words 'Central Committee' and the familiar initials of the KGB, coming over as 'Kah Gay Beh' in the vernacular.

Guriev cut him off short again.

'Nyet,' he said with harsh finality. Then in English:

'Everyone stays still. Open the box, Sheremetev!'

Sheremetev gave Panin an agonized look.

'A hole can be a grave, Sheremetev,' Guriev growled. 'If you wish it to be. There is no help for you – we are all alone here.'

'Actually, you're just going to have visitors,' said Roskill conversationally. 'So be a good fellow and don't do anything hasty.'

He pointed across the airfield.

The noise of the tractor engines was much louder already. In fact there were two of them, one towing a grass cutter with an extraordinary raised chute like the head of some prehistoric monster, from the mouth of which wisps of grass were falling; and the other a trailer with tall netting sides bulging with fresh-cut grass. They were coming obliquely across the field, almost exactly in the tracks of Panin's car, straight towards the Roman camp.

'Everyone still,' said Guriev, moving sideways so that the Land-Rover masked him from the tractors. 'There is only one pistol here, and I shall shortly put it inside my coat. Comrade Panin and Dr Audley will join Sheremetev beside the box. You will talk to each other and you will let the farm workers pass you without trying to speak to them . . . Tell them that I mean what I say, Comrade Panin!'

'Dr Audley,' Panin said coldly, 'this traitor is prepared to commit suicide, so I must warn you that he is unlikely to stop short of murder. It would be better if you left him to me.'

'Move, then – but slowly,' ordered Guriev. 'And do not mask one another.'

Audley followed Panin to stand on one side of the box, watching the deafening approach of the tractors.

Panin spoke to him above the noise: 'Please do not do anything brave, Dr Audley – and don't let your associates do anything. The man there is all the more dangerous for being alone. I don't wish to add bloodshed to my own stupidity.'

'Don't worry, Professor,' Audley shouted back. 'We're not heroes.'

The ungainly cavalcade was very close now. Audley could see Keith Warren sitting easily in the seat of the leading tractor, a battered deerstalker jammed hard down on his head. Warren swung the wheel of the tractor to bring it parallel with the line of mounds, waved gaily to Audley, and accelerated away in a cloud of diesel fumes and flying grass.

Behind him the second tractor thundered up, halting with a shudder just abreast of the group. The driver shouted unintelligibly against the roar of his own engine and pointed to the hole.

Audley shook his head and spread his hands.

The tractor driver turned off his engine and reached down out of sight, mumbling to himself. Then he straightened up and the Sterling sub-machine gun in his hands was pointed directly at Guriev.

Richardson rose from the pile of grass in the trailer, also cradling a Sterling.

'Easy there, everybody,' he said loudly. 'These things are bloody dangerous. Once you pull the trigger you can't stop 'em.'

Jenkins, the long-haired woodworm hunter, carefully got down from the tractor. He jerked his Sterling at Guriev, who stood frozen with his hands open and his fingers slightly crooked, like an old-time gunfighter.

'Hands behind your neck, comrade – slow and easy like the man said. If you'd take his gun, Major Butler, I'd feel much happier. Richardson's quite right. These Sterlings are nasty things.'

He paused beside DECCO. 'You can relax now, Maitland,' he told the machine. 'All the silage is gathered in safely.'

Panin looked from DECCO to Audley.

Audley nodded 'They've been listening in, Professor Panin. Like you, I had to be ready if the worst came to the worst. And like you, I rather thought it must.'

Panin shook his head. 'I am too old for this sort of thing – too rusty. Perhaps I should have known better.'

'Major Butler. You and Hugh open that box and have a look at what's inside.'

'Dr Audley,' Panin began, 'I must – '

'Dr Audley,' Guriev broke in, 'you will – '

Audley turned his back on Guriev. Panin might not be the sweetie Faith thought him, but he had the better manners. Besides, he had no orders covering Guriev.

Faith! He had almost forgotten her. She stood at the edge of the group, white-faced: the young lady of Riga!

There was only time to smile at her, and he tried not to make it a tigerish smile. Then he took Panin's arm, much as the Russian had taken his a few minutes earlier, and walked him back towards the corner mound.

Delicately, he must put it delicately.

'Professor Panin, if I can satisfy you I will. But you must satisfy me first.'

Panin had regained his composure. Or rather, he had reassumed his mask of indifference. He nodded.

'You've been leaking information to us from the start, Professor – about G Tower, for instance. Just for our benefit. But why?'

The mask slipped and a look of incredulity passed across the man's face. Then it faded and for the first time Panin actually smiled.

'For your benefit?' The smile was bitter. 'No, not for your benefit, Dr Audley.'

Audley felt a sinking feeling in his stomach.

'Not for your benefit,' Panin repeated.

'For whose, then?'

'Guriev's masters.'

Guriev's *masters*? It flashed across Audley's mind with horrible certainty that he had been too clever by half, yet not half clever enough. Panin hadn't been playing to him at all, but to someone else. Which meant – which meant he'd been right about Steerforth, but for utterly false reasons. And wrong about Panin . . .

Panin looked at him. 'You did well, Dr Audley,' he said, almost soothingly. 'In fact you did too well. It is ironical, is it not, that when I wanted the boxes to be found I could not find them. But when I did not need them, you found them at once.'

'You didn't need them?'

'I never believed they could be found. I wasn't even sure they'd reached England. It was enough that Guriev's people should believe I had found them, and I made all the preparations for that.' Panin paused. 'It seems that I prepared for everything except what actually happened.'

All for Guriev's people! So Panin also had been too clever: it had not occurred to him that Audley would act on the same stimulus. Irony indeed! Whatever this elaborate scheme of Panin's was, it had failed because there was a self-destructive factor built into it – he had convinced Audley that the boxes existed and could be found.

So Audley had found them, by following his own incorrect reasoning.

There was a sharp crackling of wood behind them. Butler was methodically splintering open the metal box's outer wooden cocoon.

Panin watched Butler sombrely for a moment, and then turned towards Audley again.

'How long have you known that there was an extra box, Dr Audley? When all the others just accepted it as part of the collection?'

'You were hunting Forschungsamt files back in '45, and

I never could quite convince myself that Schliemann was enough to bring you all this way today. The – the psychology was wrong.' Thank you for that, Theodore Freisler; for tipping the balance. 'So there had to be more to it. There had to be something else.'

'But you never knew what it was?'

It would never do to admit just how much he'd been in the dark, and no use denying how much in the dark he still was. But there was still something to play for.

'I never knew, no. But that doesn't matter now.'

Panin shrugged.

'You're missing the point, Professor Panin,' Audley said gently. 'I'm sure all the answers aren't in the box, but you can put that right.'

The Russian regarded him woodenly.

'To threaten me, Dr Audley, is mere stupidity. What can you do to me? You cannot hold me. You are not big enough. You can merely inconvenience me by withholding the box from me for a short time.'

'I wouldn't threaten you, Professor – I'd leave that to Guriev.' Audley smiled. 'I think I'm just big enough to hold you for an hour or two. And small enough to let Guriev loose right now. Then it would be no business of mine what mischief he could organize in a couple of hours. On the other hand, if I knew what I was doing I could very easily sit on Guriev for a day or two and obey my instructions to the letter.'

It was a crude bluff, but it was the best Audley could manage. Its strength lay in the fact that Panin had not dealt with the British for years and might still believe in their traditional perfidy. Or if there was an element of doubt there, at least, there could be no doubt about the ruthlessness of Guriev's masters, whoever they were.

'Tukhachevsky,' said Panin. 'Marshal Tukhachevsky.'

Marshal Tukhachevsky?

'I would have thought that name would not be unknown

to you,' Panin continued. 'But possibly not – it was before your time, and there are many of your generation even in Russia who have never heard of him.'

That made it a matter of honour, and Audley flogged his memory. Marshal Tukhachevsky: *the trial of Marshal Tukhachevsky*.

'The Great Purge of the thirties – the "Yezhovshchina".'

Panin nodded. '"The Yezhovshchina", that is right.'

Millions had been exiled or imprisoned, and untold thousands had died, among them nearly all the Bolsheviks – Zinoviev, Kamenev, Bukharin, Rykov. And the great Marshal Tukhachevsky, the hero of 1920. Russia had seen nothing like it since the days of Ivan the Terrible.

'The Army trials,' said Audley. 'He was one of the marshals Stalin liquidated. Yezhov framed him for spying for the Germans. And it was the Nazis who actually supplied the forged evidence.'

'Very good, Dr Audley – a very fair summary. Except that Tukhachevsky was not merely one of the marshals – he was the greatest Russian soldier of his time. And he didn't die alone, either: he took four hundred senior officers with him, the cream of the Red Army. One cannot blame the Nazis for helping to frame them; they were winning their first battle against us without firing a shot. But tell me, Dr Audley – why would Stalin want his best soldiers branded as traitors?'

'Tukhachevsky was too popular, I suppose. He was just another rival. It used to be pretty standard Soviet practice, didn't it? From Trotsky onwards.'

Panin should know that well enough.

'Discredit, then eliminate.' Panin spoke as though he hadn't heard Audley.

The forgeries. Heydrich would have been the Nazi boss to organize them, and Heydrich had mixed some of his old Sicherheitsdienst files among the Forschungsamt records – that brought Tukhachevsky and Panin together.

But if that was in the box the old objection still held: even back in '45 the full details of this scandal would have been a mere embarrassment to Stalin. And today they were utterly valueless. Stalin was dead and discredited; the Party itself could not err; and the ancestors of the KGB had neither honour nor credit to lose.

'But the Tukhachevsky forgeries don't matter now, Professor. They're just dirty water down the drain.'

'And the truth behind the forgeries?'

'The truth?'

'Stalin was a butcher, but he was not a stupid butcher, as the West likes to think. He knew the risk when he ruined his own army.'

'Professor, you can't tell me that Tukhachevsky and four hundred generals and colonels were all in league with Hitler. It won't wash.'

'Not in league with Hitler. *But in league against Stalin and the Party, Dr Audley*.'

Panin gestured abruptly as though tired of arguing and being forced to explain simple facts – and tired above all of pretending that the real Panin was a grey nonentity on a derelict English airfield.

'In 1937 there really was an army plot against the Party. Tukhachevsky had no direct part in it – he was like Rommel in 1944. But it was a genuine plot and a very dangerous one. The soldiers planned to reverse the whole collectivization policy – the Party's cornerstone.'

He spoke harshly.

'Stalin had a nose for such things – it is a talent some Georgians have – and he moved first. He knew it was so, but we never uncovered the proof, the full details. It didn't matter *then*, for it was better that they should be destroyed as traitors than mere party enemies.

'And then it was discovered that the details did exist.

232

One of the plotters escaped to East Prussia – an air force colonel. He took with him a list of names and details of the takeover plans. The Nazis sent him back, and they sent back some of the details. But they kept the documents.'

The Russian faced Audley squarely.

'That's what is in the extra box, Dr Audley: the details of the 1937 Army Plot which everyone believes was just a figment of Stalin's suspicious mind. Everyone except those in the Party and the Army who know the truth beneath the legend. You see, I wasn't the only one looking for those documents back in 1945 – which is why I sent them to Moscow with the Schliemann Collection. There were generals then who knew what that box could do – to the Army. It can still do as much, and I've made sure that there are generals who know about it.'

The Army! *Discredit, then eliminate!*

So that was what was at the centre of Panin's labyrinth: the means to discredit the over-mighty Red Army as a political ally. Elimination then wouldn't even be necessary.

It didn't matter that it was ancient history. An army which could turn against the Party once could do so again: even the breath of such a scandal would open a credibility gap a mile wide between the politicians and the generals in the delicate balance of Kremlin politics. Not even the most ambitious civilians would dare to cross that gap.

'You'd discredit your own army?'

'Discredit?' Panin shook his head. 'It would never have come to that. The generals would have taken the hint, just as they took the bait. This way there would have been retirements, but no disgrace. And no more nonsense about preventive wars in the east.'

It was true. No general could afford to allow the glorious Red Army's loyalty to the Party to be publicly tarnished. The Tukhachevsky documents were quite simply an incomparable piece of blackmail, and the Army knew it. Guriev's presence was proof of that.

God! The Army had taken the bait! And so it had been the Army – the GRU – which had followed him to Morrison, and had raided his home, not Panin. For Panin hadn't been in the least interested in what Audley was doing. He had been far too busy creating an illusion and laying a false trail for the GRU to follow. The overtures to the British had simply been part of the illusion – and Audley himself had been irrelevant. A bit player in a farce with far more important actors in it.

Except that the farce had got out of Panin's hands because of the bit player's stupidity.

He could almost feel sorry for the GRU, whose trail had been much colder and harder than his own. Indeed, all they had to work with were the clues Panin had carefully doled out to them and Audley's own movements.

Not for them the luxury of names and addresses. The best they could do was to pick him up at Asham churchyard, follow him and try to overtake him at Guildford. But they had been baulked there by Morrison's weak heart and then betrayed by Mrs Clark's geese, which left them only Panin to follow.

They had taken all the bad luck, and even so they had nearly pulled it off at the last. Whereas he had had all the undeserved good luck . . .

Audley groped for something to offset his feeling of humiliation.

'But supposing your bluff had been called?'

'But it was no bluff, Dr Audley. There is no one left alive now except me who saw those documents. Until you discovered that aircraft, they were no more than a memory. Recreating them was no problem – we have far better forgers now than the Nazis ever had.

'The problem was to create confidence in them. To create confidence in their – what is the word? – their provenance. As a historian you should understand that.'

'But there's only one way you could really prove that.' Audley grasped at the inconsistency. 'You had to have the Schliemann Collection – and you couldn't forge that!'

The Russian nodded. 'Of course I needed the collection. But you are forgetting how I lost it and to whom I lost it. A gang of petty black marketeers, Dr Audley – German riffraff and Ukrainian deserters dressed in Russian uniforms! And what does the world think they did with it, eh? What *ought* they to have done with it, tell me that?'

He didn't wait for an answer. 'They ought to have melted it down into crude bars of gold and silver, not to have had the wit to smuggle it out as it was. I tell you, Dr Audley, my fiction was far more believable than your truth!'

It was damnable, thought Audley – but it was logical: a few bars of gold for the East Germans, and deep regrets for a tragic case of vandalism. That had been Sir Kenneth Allen's guess exactly.

And all so damnably simple from Panin's point of view, too. In laying a trail of false information and recreating the lost cargo he was independent of events; the more the GRU and the British did, the more they would build up the illusion and baffle each other.

It was perfect except for that one reasonable but fatal miscalculation . . .

And now the consequences of that error had to be faced by both of them.

'But the collection is of no importance.' Panin calmly relegated Schliemann and Troy to the dustbin of history. 'It is enough that it exists. In fact, if you want it for your British Museum that can be arranged – one museum is the same as another. It is only the documents which concern me. And I do not think your superiors will withhold them from me either, Dr Audley. There are pressures which can be brought to bear, believe me.'

Again, just like that! First, the carrot – a golden carrot belonging to someone else, casually offered. Then, the stick – and Audley didn't doubt that it was a real stick. It was the matter-of-fact assumption of authority that took his breath away. The man was brutally sure of himself even now.

Audley walked slowly back towards the others, leaving Panin beside the line of mounds. In a way this was what he always dreamed of having: the power to shift a political balance decisively one way or the other. But he had never imagined that balance would be in the Kremlin. Nor had he expected it to be the reward of false reasoning. Perhaps he'd be able to see the funny side of that one day. But in the meantime he intended to keep the joke to himself.

The group around the box had split up. Butler and Roskill sat on the grass beside it, each engrossed in a buff-coloured file. Beyond them Sheremetev stood alone and miserable – though not as miserable as Guriev, quarantined by Richardson's Sterling.

Predictably, the long-haired Jenkins was chatting up Faith, demonstrating his own addition to DECCO.

Audley paused beside her apologetically.

'I'm sorry for the theatricals, Faith. I really didn't intend you should be mixed up in them.'

She smiled. 'It's all right, David. Mr Jenkins has been explaining how he was ready to come to our rescue. But he hasn't told me how you knew there was going to be trouble.'

It was hardly the time to tell her that he hadn't really known and that he'd been mortally afraid that nothing would happen at all. Or that what had actually happened had utterly crushed his self-esteem.

He shrugged modestly. 'If there was going to be trouble I wanted to have it here in the open. They all thought they were safe here. They didn't know DECCO was bugged.'

'"Jenkins' Ear" we call it,' said Jenkins. 'It transmits a whisper over a mile as clear as a bell.'

'The only difficulty was bringing the rescue team in without any fuss,' Audley explained. 'And Warren was very helpful there.'

Keith Warren had been only too pleased to help. He hadn't believed a word of Sunday's cover story, but found the bizarre truth instantly acceptable.

Jenkins and Faith both regarded him with evident admiration. Like everyone else – everyone but Panin – they would always believe that he had stage-managed events perfectly. And as the Russians would never talk, no one need ever know just how imperfect the stage-management had been.

'What happens now?' asked Faith.

Audley smiled falsely. 'We divide up the loot, love. That's what happens.'

He made his way past the new excavation to where Butler and Roskill were sitting.

Butler got up stiffly.

'Not much here, Dr Audley. Unmarked metal box – we forced the lock. Just two packets wrapped in oilskins, and the rest packing.'

'And the packets?'

'I've got what appears to be a blueprint for a military takeover of Moscow,' said Butler, 'planned to coincide with simultaneous moves in Leningrad, Minsk, Kiev and one or two other places. I've only skimmed it so far, though. There are some letters from military district commanders and a lot of coded material. It's dated 1937, so I can't place any of the names.'

'I expect the names are all placed in my half,' said Roskill. 'Mine's a sort of who's who of the Soviet army in '37 – brigade commander and above. Six or seven hundred names, I'd say – and more than half have been joyfully stamped "deceased" in German. The mortality of the

Russian peacetime establishment appears to have been remarkable.'

Audley nodded.

'Major Butler – I'd like you to take the Land-Rover and go and phone Stocker. Tell him what you've told me. Tell him that Panin's a hard-line KGB undercover man from way back. Back to NKVD days.'

The KGB had sleepers in most countries, men who had nothing to do but to climb to positions of power and wait for their moment of usefulness. And naturally they had sleepers in the homeland too.

'Now the cover's off because the KGB needs to put the Army in its place, and these files are the skeleton in the Army's closet. It's a straight blackmail job, tell him that.'

He looked back at Panin. The cover was off, but there'd be no holding the man now. A success like this would put him into the Secretariat and eventually even into the Presidium, maybe. To have done a Presidium member a good turn would be something to tell Steerforth's grandchildren.

'Tell Stocker that I'm fulfilling his orders to the letter. In exactly one hour I shall give Panin what he wants. If Stocker doesn't like it he can come down and explain to Panin himself – stay by the phone for his answer.'

KGB, GRU – they were all bastards. And in the last analysis Nikolai Panin was probably the biggest bastard of them all. But at least he was an imaginative one, not a crude second-rater like so many at the top of the Soviet pyramid. And if there was any hope for Russia it would start at the top, not from the voiceless, unprotesting masses.

Either way it was Stocker's headache now.

And yet there was one more thing! A small thing to Panin, but no small thing all the same.

'And tell Stocker that all Panin cares about are the two files.'

He looked down at the other boxes peeping out of the loose earth in the bottom of the trench. Inevitably it would go back to the East Germans. Or maybe the West Germans would dispute its ownership. There was precedent enough, in all conscience: a citizen of the world had stolen it from the Turks, who never really owned it, long before the Russians, the Germans and an Englishman had got their thieving hands on it. It had been hidden and lost and stolen so many times that it belonged to everyone now, like the legend of Troy itself.

'Tell him he's got the Schliemann Collection on his hands, poor devil.'

Stocker could do what he liked with Steerforth's loot. Audley would settle for Steerforth's daughter.

STEERFORTH. John Adair Steerforth, Flt Lieut, DFC, RAFVR, killed in a flying accident, September 1945. On this, his birthday – Mother.